SAVING PIPER MOONLIGHT

PINEY FALLS MYSTERIES

JOANN KEDER

Saving Piper Moonlight

Edited by: Sara Williams

Cover Design by Molly Burton with Cozy Cover Designs

Publisher: Purpleflower Press

ISBN: 978-1-7336639-5-3

❀ Created with Vellum

For my family far and wide

OTHER BOOKS BY JOANN KEDER:

<u>Piney Falls Mysteries</u>

Welcome to Piney Falls

Saving Piper Moonlight

Tales of Naybor Manor

Lavender's Tangled Tree

The Twisted Stitch Society

Chaos and Cranberries

Kinnundrum

<u>Charming Mysteries</u>

Oceanberry Blues

Tangerine Troubles

Perilously Pink

A Lime in Time

<u>Emory Bing Mysteries</u>

The Case of the Half-Baked Bing

The Case of the Rootbeer Bungle

The Case of the Fudged Features

The Case of the Chunky, Funky Monkey

The Case of the Clairvoyant Carrot

The Case of the Vegan Vixen

The Case of the Cream Cheese Caper

<u>Cont'd</u>

ACKNOWLEDGMENTS

Thank you to Doug Keder for your endless support and patience. I couldn't accomplish half of what I do without you by my side. DeeAnna Bryson and Dayle Wallien, thank you for answering ridiculous and sometimes repetitive questions. Thank you to the Keder Readers for their time and energy in reading each and every piece of fiction I release. As always, love and appreciation for so many wonderful family members.

"Before I can become an expert on anything, I must first become an expert on me."
— Charles F. Glassman

1

REDONDO BEACH, CALIFORNIA

The Killer

"Are you sure about this?" The Victim moves to the balcony, rubbing his balding head. For the first time in more years than he can accept, he's not afraid.

"The plan has never changed. Not once. You had no problems with it in the beginning."

He stares at the shadow: a twisted soul still entangled in the seaweed. It's ironic to him that through the darkness he can see clearer now than at any other point in his adult life. "I feel sorry for you. There were so many opportunities to leave, so many times things could have changed..."

There is a disembodied snicker. "Only one path. The right one. How did you lose sight of the most important thing to all of us?"

The Victim looks over the balcony railing for a moment. There are people in the pool. Normal, functional people. They are laughing and talking about the trivial, pointless things making up their day, adjusting their sunglasses, drinking cocktails. Their children splash frivolously beside them, unaware of the sacrifices others had to make. How many have ever experienced a universe of near perfection, only to have it pulled away? They are truly the lucky ones. They have no idea what they've missed.

"I only lost the need to hurt others," he whispers. "He told us what to do. He taught us to take the skills we had and make this world better for everyone. Somehow, somewhere, we lost our way."

"You've killed. Hurting people has never bothered you before. It's now, when your own life has reached its conclusion, that you've developed an affection for others." His killer flops down on the bed. He can hear the springs squeak in protest. "Things are still on track. In five years, everything with be in place. At one time, you would have been excited to see how it came together."

"What did I do right?" The Victim asks, stalling for time.

"That's where we are?" There is a long sigh. "We didn't allow anyone else to draw out their ending. Well, let's see... you were a good support, especially when we had to give up the thing most precious to us both–" The Killer chokes up with emotion, just for a moment. "But that was a lifetime ago. And you lied to me from the very beginning. Don't forget that."

"I apologized. A million times. Don't you think we should talk about what we did now? Before I'm gone?"

There is a grunt from the darkness. "Everyone believes in a cause as long as their bellies are full and their bodies are warm. When it comes down to discomfort, or to fighting even though it's the last thing you want to do, the weak drop away. We made the ultimate sacrifice. That's what you did right and the world will be a better place because of it."

"Can I ask–did you ever love me?"

There is laughter from the other room and a chill runs down his spine.

"I assumed we'd already discussed the uselessness of emotions. They get in the way. Imagine if I let that interfere at any time during the last two decades. We wouldn't be where we are, on schedule for the metamorphosis."

"YOU wouldn't be on schedule. The rest of us–well, me– would be fine. You don't remember those times we were gardening at Fallen Branch, talking about the future? You said then you couldn't picture anyone else by your side."

"I couldn't. That didn't mean I loved you, though. You were the perfect partner...for a time. As you've said: you didn't have control of your emotions and I could direct you easily. I gave you a list, you accomplished every bullet point." The Killer stalks closer. "Is there anything you want them to know? I'm giving you this gift that we never gave the others. A thank you for your service. Let's call it my 'emotion' for today."

"Tell them I'm sorry. I wasn't strong enough to continue by your side and I wasn't smart enough to survive on my own."

"That's not at all what I thought you would say."

"What did you expect? A lengthy speech? I've always left those to you."

"I thought you might want them to know you were a brave solider in our war. Kind of make them proud, at least."

He throws his hands in the air. "I give up. You'll make it your own story no matter what. I learned long ago that it's impossible to please you. They'll learn that soon enough."

"I hope not."

"Tell them...I tried. Just get on with it now. I can't bear to think about it anymore."

His killer hands him a cup. "Cheers, my friend. It was a good ride while it lasted."

His hand brushes his killer's and without looking up, he lifts it to his lips.

2

———

PRESENT DAY

Piney Falls, Oregon

"Just set my latte on the table," I call from the antique side of Cosmo's Cakery and Antiques. Recently, I've discovered the unbelievable amount of treasures in this little shop, selling for a quarter of what I would pay for them in my former hometown of Chicago. "I'm picking out decorative tea cups for the new shelves Cosmo is building for my kitchen."

"Cosmo'll be late today. He's fixing the toilet at his sister's place." Doris' voice drifts to my side of the building.

I can hear the rain pounding on the roof. In the rainy season, it can come with such force it shakes the building and you'd think one of the four horsemen of the apocalypse just showed up. I'll be leaving that out of the new brochures we print for visitors.

My mind drifts to the scene last night, how we steamed up the windows in my car like two experimental teens instead of forty-something almost-lovers. I stopped our tryst when he wanted more, even though the thought of him pushes an electrical current through my body. I haven't yet told him my darkest secrets, even though we've been together for almost a year. Engaged, in fact, thanks to his impromptu proposal after we'd solved a hundred-year-old mystery.

"Thanks, Doris. He told me he'd be late. I'm meeting Vem today."

Nobody has less sense of time than my neighbor and best friend, monochromatically dressed November Bean. Today it will work to my advantage. She's quirky, but I've never experienced a friendship before like the one we share.

I hear the jingling of the door and November's loud snort. It took several months before the sound didn't make me cringe. "Hi, Doris. Make me a mocha, please. And just the Pluto Peach scone today. I'm starting a new diet."

They should study November Bean for her superhuman metabolism.

I peek my head around the corner. "Vem, give me a minute, I've got to find the mate for this saucer. That's my latte on the table."

When I return with a hand-painted rose china cup and its saucer mate, she has plopped down in front of my drink, her frizzy hair engulfing my mug. "What's with the almond milk?" she asks with disgust.

"Do you want to try it?" *I know better.*

"Maybe just a taste."

She gulps down half my drink in one slurp. My pride overrides my need to shop, forcing me to sit down and pull my cup in front of me. Without the decorative foam she has consumed, it's just an unappealing coffee. "It worried me when you called. Especially during your hour of giggle meditation, when you're not to be disturbed." *There's a significant event happening, Lanie. We need to speak immediately.* The word "significant" makes Vem itch, so she promised it would only be used for emergencies.

"Yes, I have an announcement." She takes a bite of my scone before hers is placed, blessedly, in front of her. "It was important and I was hoping your boyfriend could join us." She pushes a stray piece of my blonde hair behind my ear with her finger, and then begins primping my ponytail.

"He's not my boyfriend." I bat her hand away. "We're not fifteen."

"Fine. Your fee-ahn-say. Is that better? I wanted to tell him at the same time. I'm in the middle of Word Waste Not Month. Trying to fine-tune what comes out of my mouth. Word refuse is just as bad, mentally, as physical garbage. It can pollute the landscape of your psyche don't you know?"

She glances at her lime green watch, in complete color agreement with her lime jumpsuit, glasses and headband. "Okay, you'll just have to repeat this to Cos. Today I'm teaching a Mid-Day Moan session and I don't want to keep my students waiting." She looks at her watch again, and then sighs. "I'm going to have a houseguest soon. A very important one."

I try to picture someone who would willingly stay in her house, game for all of her peculiarities. I'd like to hurry home myself, to listen to all of her student moaners. Ten to twelve people attend her classes each week. "Who is coming? A friend from California?"

November rolls her eyes. "You're a terrible guesser, so let's not waste time on that game. We started a newsletter for former members of the Fallen Branch commune. It's called New Leaf. We keep track of everyone who wants to stay in touch. In the last issue, there was an article about one of our former members who needs our help. I've invited her here."

I feel soft lips on my neck. "There's a newsletter?" The hairs rise on my arm as I turn around to face Cosmo Hill, the other half of my first real relationship, holding on to my chair. It doesn't matter how long it's been; he still makes me molten inside every time I see him.

"Last night was delightful," he whispers in my ear as he sits down. I sincerely hope I'm not blushing.

"You don't know about the newsletter? You and your sister should be on the list. What's your email address?" November pulls out her phone and licks her finger before preparing to type.

"I don't have one. Seems like a waste of time. I've got better things to do," he pulls up a chair and stares at me admiringly. It used to make me uncomfortable; now I just expect it.

"That's the problem right there. I can help you get one. I'll bring my special guacamole with cheddar sauce and we'll make a party of it." She glances at him hopefully. Cosmo shakes his head.

"What about Cedar?" she continues. "She's got to have an email to be our marketing guru. Cosmo, do you have your sister's – forget it, I should know better than to ask you. Lanie, do you have her email address?"

"Um...I..." I struggle to focus on something besides Cosmo's ice-blue eyes. "Yes, I'll get it for you. Tell us about this person staying with you. An old friend?"

"No, not a friend. She was the last baby born in the Fallen Branch community two months before it disbanded. Zion anointed her his successor. After things broke apart, her parents tried to disappear like so many of us. A fringe group called Broken Branch, whose slogan is, 'Like Fallen Branch, But Better.' found her family. She's been harassed frequently ever since. Doesn't matter where she moves, they always find her. After years on the run, the poor girl and her parents came up with a great plan. Why not hide in plain sight, where people know her story already and will protect her from the crazies?"

"And why does this concern us, November Bean?" Cosmo's eyes narrow perceptibly. "You're not involving my fiancée and I in your crazy schemes. Lanie's busy with my sister, getting this place on the map as a tourist destination. And I've got the bakery–"

November stands up and puts her hands on her hips. "Cosmo Hill, you of all people know what it's like to be ostracized because of something you didn't do. This girl needs us!"

I hate when people remind Cosmo of his years in prison. After we found Zion and proved Cosmo hadn't killed him nine months ago, I thought it would end. It didn't. He's still known around town as the toxic guy who went to prison for twenty years for murder. Some folks drive to Tellum for coffee just to make that point. "Vem, you know this is a sensitive topic. Leave Cosmo alone!'"

She ignores me and continues. "Look into the chestnut-brown eyes of your beloved. Marvel at her alabaster skin and dainty, famous-looking nose. Tell her that you don't want to help another poor, lost, soul after all you've been through. Tell her, Mr. Baker Man."

Cosmo squeezes my shoulder. "It's okay, babe. I get her point. This kid needs help and I should help her." He looks up at November. "What do you want from me? I've got a couch she could sleep on, or maybe she could clean up around the bakery."

"She went to culinary school. I told her she could work in the bakery. She'll be here tomorrow."

"Did you, now?" Cosmo folds his arms and leans back in his chair. "Without asking me first?"

I can see him ramping up. I put my hand on his muscular arm. "This might be a good thing, Cos. You said Doris wanted to take some time off to bond with her new dog."

Cosmo looks out the door where the rain is now coming down sideways. "It's the off season. We don't tend to get lots of customers. She still might end up cleaning, at least part time. How old is this kid?"

"She's twenty-three. Piper Moonlight is her name. I'm sure she'll do whatever you need around here. Oh, Cos, may I hug you?" Vem is already approaching him with her arms outstretched.

He puts his hand out. "No. No hugs."

"And what is it you need from me, Vem?" I'm a little hesitant to ask this question, given that just last week when I offered to help her during a "crisis" I ended up polishing her incense lamps at two a.m. for an emergency meditation session to make her cats live in harmony.

"You did such a good job solving the mystery of Zion and the Flanagan sisters. Our very own sleuth here in Piney Falls. I'd like you to investigate these people. Find out what they want from Piper, so we're prepared."

"November, I'm not a detective. I'm a marketing manager. That's where I...*excel*. You're rubbing off on me." I wink but she doesn't notice.

Cosmo squeezes my shoulders. "We know what they want. To start a new cult with her as their leader. I don't have to get the newsletter to figure that one out."

"They do. But according to people who have been

following them, they already have someone in mind to guide her. We used to have a mole on the inside, but then he got bored and went on to do something else. Typical of former members, I'm afraid. Now he doesn't respond to our messages. He never had a chance to tell us who was in charge."

"Who would be stupid enough to be your mole?" Cosmo walks over and pours himself another cup of coffee.

"Jez Dillon. Year of the J." She quickly puts her hand over her mouth. "That name was supposed to be a secret. Rumor has it, he changed his name and moved when he didn't want to be a part of Broken Branch anymore. This is what happens when I'm trying to concentrate on too many things at once." Vem sighs and pushes her chair in. "I'll bring her by tomorrow afternoon. You can meet her and give her instructions. You'll be here too, Lanie?" She looks at me hopefully.

"Why?" I giggle. "Are you afraid the ferocious pastry man will tear her to shreds if left to his own devices?"

She looks at me tentatively before she repeats her question. "You'll be here, right?"

I have so much to do. It's not that I don't trust Cedar to do it all, it's that I still have control issues and I can't quite let it all go. "Ok, I'll be here. For a little while. But I'm not going to hang out every day to run interference between Cosmo and a harmless young lady."

Vem hugs me tightly before heading out to the door. "Bye, Blushing Beauty. See you tomorrow, Planetary Pal." The door jingles merrily as she exits, before the wind catches it and pulls it backward. There is another regular customer sitting adjacent who jumps up and pulls it shut.

Cosmo furrows his thick brow. "When did we get nicknames?" He bends over to wipe the raindrops from the floor that blew in.

"I made the mistake of telling her about a seminar I attended, *Treat 'em like you know 'em*. I think she really took it to heart."

He sighs. "I don't like any of this."

"It's okay," I assure him. "She'll get bored here. There's nothing for someone her age to do in this town. Eventually, your sister and I plan on changing that, but for now, Piney Falls has as much excitement as dry toast. I bet by the busy season, she'll be ready for different surroundings."

"That's exactly when I'll need more help. It's not dealing with her as an employee that has me concerned. It's having another connection to that hellish cult. There is something about this that doesn't sit right with me. She will stir up trouble and I don't want you in danger." Cosmo stands tall and puts his hands in the pockets of his faded blue jeans.

I smile. It's hard to get used to having someone in my life. In the months I've lived here, I've gone from being a workaholic to finding friendships and a man I never allowed myself to dream about. Things have been almost picture perfect. "You don't have to worry about me, Cos. Before I came here, I lived in the middle of a big city all by myself and I managed just fine."

"You weren't dealing with rabid cult members there. If they are half as crazed as the people in the original Fallen Branch, they are capable of anything." He walks over to the window and looks out at the sheets of rain battering the street, running his fingers through his thick, silvery hair. "Which is why I actually agree with Vem for once; you need to be here when she arrives to make sure I don't say something stupid. She's also got a point about investigating this girl and her family. See where they've been, what other things they've been up to since Zion upended their world."

"No, Cos. I don't have time. Cedar and I are working on selling Fallen Branch, and I—"

"Don't you think that is exactly why they would start to sniff around? I don't think it's an accident this kid is coming to town right now. Maybe Zion sent out a signal through someone at the jail to lure them back."

Not once in my life before moving here did I think of myself as a detective. But somehow, researching the Flanagan sisters—who founded of the town of Flanagan, which eventually became Piney Falls—got my juices flowing. It was like a drug, luring me in a little more every day. I had to keep going until I figured out Zion's connection to the past and all the secrets of Fallen Branch. Secretly, I'm intrigued by this potential new piece of the puzzle.

He comes up beside me, encircling me in his meaty arms. I feel at home in this space. "Think of it as a favor to me. You are my world," he whispers in my ear.

"Okay. I'll look into it. In my spare time. Just don't expect anything earth-shattering. This isn't going to be another big mystery to solve. Just a simple background check on a family that's probably as normal as you and me."

3

———

ONE MONTH EARLIER

Piney Falls, Oregon

Lance Peachtree leans back in his adjustable leather chair, crossing his legs and exposing a calf-length, tan colored sock. "Your marketing plan is very impressive. Piney People Savings and Trust is happy to have you on board." He folds his hands politely in his lap. "No one has shown interest in the Fallen Branch property in all of these years. If you convince a large corporation to invest in our community, that would be sensational. Just sensational." He smiles, revealing straight, yellow teeth.

My business suit feels scratchy and foreign against my skin. I stored away both the suit and this persona long enough to make them hard to revisit. "I've taken the liberty of making a call to a potential investment group, inviting them to come see our town and what it has to offer. They'll be pleasantly surprised."

"Of course, if there were to be other bidders, we might run into an issue. But I don't foresee–"

I lean forward in my chair, something I was hesitant to do up until now. He gives off the scent of a man eager for things I no longer offer. "What bidders? You've had possession of this property for over twenty years after Zion defaulted on his loan! You weren't even thinking about selling the land until I convinced you it was a good idea!"

"No need for concern, Miss Landers. It's something I have to say; you know, a formality. This will be sensational." He reaches out for my hand in an attempt to placate me, but I pull it back quickly and stand.

"Thank you again for allowing us to give historic tours of the property. I think its generating real interest. We've received thirty-seven positive responses on the feedback cards handed out. And one *I was told there would be ice cream.*

"Well no, it is I who should thank you for donating the signage for the tours. Seems a shame those will have to come down once the property becomes part of the resort."

I'm frustrated he's already forgotten my presentation. "No, the signage will become part of the hotel's theme. It will be a historic hotel with information strategically placed throughout for the guests to browse at their leisure. The rich history is one of the selling points for the investors."

"Yes. Sensational." He smiles again.

"I'll be in touch," I call as I walk out his office without shaking his hand.

It is only three blocks from the bank to the former tourist information center. Cedar looks up as I enter the newly renamed Piney Falls Welcome Center and smiles at me with the same startling blue eyes that drew me to her brother. Some days, it's still hard to fathom the change in her. From the robotic, vacant human who greeted me when

I first arrived in Piney Falls to a sparkly personality who can't wait to create. She is hungry for knowledge, information about marketing Piney Falls as a tourist destination, and creating a real career for herself.

"Sorry I'm late. I had to stop at the bank. Lance Peachtree just gives me the creeps. I'll be glad when our business with him is finished."

"Lanie! I got a call from the Sleepy Sounds Investment Group. A confirmation call that they'll be here soon to see the land. Can you believe it? Piney Falls will be on the map!" She grabs my arms and jumps up and down, causing her perfectly coifed silver hair to bounce in one solid motion.

I smile. "That's wonderful news, Cedar. But let's not get ahead of ourselves. Just looking at the area doesn't mean they will buy. They look at lots of places before they settle on the perfect location. How long do we have to get everything in order?"

"Sleepy Sounds executives will plan to visit your location in approximately six weeks," she repeats in a serious, secretarial voice as if she was reading from a script. "Please make sure all details are in order prior to their arrival. A helpful tip: Make sure your property and all concerned are prepared for our visit so there are no surprises. Our executives have only two hours to spend with you. Make it count! We look forward to seeing what your community has to offer." Regular Cedar returns. "Never in my wildest dreams did I expect to make such an impact on this community! Lanie! It's happening!" She giggles, touching her hand to her mouth.

Sweet Cedar acts like a twelve-year-old girl who got asked to the school dance for the first time. One more activity she didn't get to experience. "Okay, hon. Calm down for a minute. Let's go over all of this again, to make sure you've got it memorized. What are the levels of their hotel chain?" I motion for her to take a seat at her desk behind the counter.

"Well, there's the bottom level chain, the Groan Inn, for the budget-conscious traveler. Then Snore More, a medium level establishment that offers a few perks and free breakfast. And then…" she makes a drum roll sound on her desk. "There is the resort-level Hi Sigh chain. That's the hit run."

"Home run," I correct. After spending all of her childhood in a cult, she has no point of reference for sports and I have little interest in teaching her.

"The home run. A full-service restaurant, complete with Cosmo's pastries,"

"We hope!" I cross fingers on both of my hands.

"We hope," she repeats. "With a pool, local tours, and if we're lucky, a spa."

"Yes! You've certainly done your homework. I'm so proud of you, Cedar. It's a good thing we scheduled the community meeting. Now that we have a date, we can prepare everyone for proper behavior. We'll do our best to make sure there are no surprises from our end." I head to the breakroom and pour myself a coffee. "Wait. Did you say they are coming in a little over a month? We'll still be in the rainy season! And that's barely enough time to get the locals ready!"

The residents of Piney Falls aren't exactly well-seasoned tour guides. They have scared off their share of tourists, treating people coming to view the remains of Flanagan Hospital to smoke bombs and vandalized cars. It's a good thing I didn't know that before I arrived.

This is our shot at making this city a competitive tourist destination. If we fail, I'll have an even harder time convincing them to put on a show for the next interested party.

Cedar jumps up and throws her arms around me. "Oh, Lanie. It's going to be okay. I've already trained the people doing tours of Fallen Branch. I'm going to do whatever it takes to succeed. You've taught me so much already. We won't fail!"

"Thank you, Cedar. You've been a real gem through all of this. Your personal and professional growth has been exceptional–" I stop myself. This is what I said to my employees. Many times, it was followed by, "That's why it's so hard to let you go today." The Old Lanie rears her head once more and doubts creep back in. I don't know if I'm the right person for Cosmo Hill. He's never experienced a shark in the business world like me. There's still so much he doesn't know about my past.

"I have a good feeling about this." I paste my perfectly normal fake smile all over my face.

4

PRESENT DAY

Beginnings

My office space is the former home of a dirty mop and outdated cleaning products. Cosmo helped me paint this neglected closet sky blue, and even framed a picture of us together at the top of Piney Falls to hang above my shiny new desk. All of my supplies came at a full discount from my former employer, *Work Ahead Office Supplies - The Most Profitable Office Supply Chain in the World.* I'm still considered the top marketing employee in franchise history.

First, I search for Jez Dillon, the man Vem said was the mole inside Broken Branch. I lean back in my chair when the first search entry pops up. "Cedar! Please come here for a minute?"

She peeks her head in the door. "Yeah?"

"Can you read this and tell me if it's the person you knew from Fallen Branch?"

She leans forward, squinting as she makes out the words. "Age forty-six, brown hair, blue eyes... Yep; that's him."

I stare at her, hoping for a little bit more of a reaction.

"Is something wrong?"

"Doesn't it concern you that the person the New Leaf team put in place as a mole in the Broken Branch group is missing and presumed dead?"

She shrugs. "People who lived in Fallen Branch are a different sort. Lots are nomadic now. He probably just left his job and decided not to tell anyone. Can I go back out front? I've got a lot to get done today."

"Go," I say, motioning with my hand as my eyes returned to the screen. *Jez Dillon has been missing since 2015. He didn't show up for work one morning and when authorities searched his Missouri home, they found his cell phone and credit cards. There is no evidence of a break-in or a struggle.*

The doorbell squawks from a speaker above my head, the biting sound of an injured chicken. "Lanie! There's someone here to see you!"

When I reach the front, November, dressed in matching buttercup yellow attire, is standing behind a young woman with short, dark hair and peculiar, almost violet eyes. She has a round, pretty face and smiles shyly.

"This scrumptillyicious woman is Lanie, my best friend in the entire universe. No offense to you, Cedar."

Cedar opens her mouth to speak but changes her mind.

"Now that I've come into my own," Vem continues, "I found I needed a strong woman with business acumen to guide my inner being to the path of success. I've got so much to teach you about that."

"You're watching words this month, right?" I gently remind her.

"I'm sure I have leftover words from yesterday. Meditative mumbling doesn't count."

I resist the urge to roll my eyes and turn my focus to the young woman. "Hi there! You must be Piper."

She reluctantly takes the hand I offer and shakes it.

"I've heard so much about your bravery. We're so happy to have you in our community and we'll do our best to keep you safe."

"Thank you, Lanie. I'm pleased to meet you." She laughs nervously. "You're the one who solved the mystery of the floaters. Isn't that what they called them, Mrs. Bean?"

November blushes. "Yes, that's what the Townies called them. Former Fallen Branch members who were murdered by Zion. But that's all in the past. Just like Mrs. Bean. I'm just Vem now."

"Zion is in jail awaiting trial. His lawyers have delayed it for almost nine months. I'm telling you that so you'll know he can't hurt you here." I nod, hoping to reassure her. Instead, she has no reaction.

We stand for a moment in awkward silence. "There are many former Fallen Branch members here, but they're all good people. I promise you that. Can I ask you about your eye color? It's so unusual."

"Oh that," she giggles again. "I wanted to hide. One time, I even shaved my head. Anything to change my appearance to the Firestarters – that's what I called the bad people who always try and take me. Last year, my mom took me to an eye doctor who told me it was possible to turn green eyes violet. He gave me these contact lenses. I thought, you know, I wouldn't look like everyone else."

It seems like a strange choice for someone who doesn't want to be noticed.

Vem looks at her large-faced, pale-yellow watch. "We

have to get you over to the bakery. But first, I told my sacred rock guru I would bring Piper in so he could bless a rock for her. Will you go to the bakery and prepare Cosmo, Lanie? Try to soften him up a bit?"

"I could, for a—"

"Lanie and Cosmo are dating," she explains to Piper. "Not the way you kids do it, where you sleep with each other first and then decide you want a relationship. No sirree. They did it the old-fashioned way. It was months before they even held hands, and they could be well into their golden years before they share a bed."

"November!" I gasp. "That's not appropriate." I turn quickly so Piper can't see the heat flare on my cheeks. I shake my head at Cedar, who shoots me a knowing glance. "I'll go prepare Cos. Though I think he's already November-proof and Piper won't be an issue."

Cedar hands me my red umbrella and I slip out the door, trying not to think about the awkwardness of what just happened. The walk to the bakery, only two blocks, is hardly enough time to sort the issues of the upcoming visit by the investors and Vem's new boarder. When I arrive, shaking my umbrella free of the rain, Cosmo is in a dark mood.

"She said eleven, right? I've got enough to do without spending my life waiting on November Bean." He tosses his apron down on the counter. "Should have told her I wanted to take my bike out today."

I've grown accustomed to his releases of steam. He's a big, muscular man with an imposing presence, but for all of his bluster, Cosmo Hill means nothing by his outbursts. "Cos, it's pouring rain. It's not safe for you to be out on your motorcycle today," I gently remind him. "Make me another latte, half-foam, and I'll tell you about the community meeting Cedar and I are setting up."

I move to the new table he added in the antiques room. Business has been growing steadily because I set up a web page for the bakery. We post pictures of his Cosmic Scone of the Day each morning.

He silently obliges and soon I hear the espresso machine gurgling. Eventually he sets the frothy mug in front of me, a swirly "C" visible. I smile when I think about our discussions of branding himself.

"Don't we need to plan a wedding before you turn this town into the Monaco of Oregon?" He pulls the chair out beside me and sits down.

My heart drops with a thud.

"You said you needed a few months and it's been nine," he continues. "I haven't heard around town that you found someone else in that time."

"There's no one else for me, Cos." I stare at him admiringly. For a minute, I fantasize about running my fingers through his course, grey hair, our bodies entangled. "I never imagined I deserved to have someone as wonderful as you. I'm just not ready...yet." I wish I could tell him. I don't know how or even if I ever should.

"Couldn't we take a small step? Maybe move in together?" He rubs my hand with his thick, rough one. "You're always on the go these days. I'd like to know we could look forward to seeing a familiar face at the end of every day."

"You know I like my space." I squirm in my seat. "We need to find somewhere we both want to live first. I realize being next door to Vem makes you break out in hives. We'd need to look around–"

"Hellooo Friendly Falls Familiars! I bought company!"

"We're in the antique room!" I call. Cosmo rolls his eyes. "Be nice!" I admonish.

I notice Piper is wearing candy-apple lip gloss and her

hair is tinted purple on the ends. It wasn't visible in the darkly lit Welcome Center. As she moves closer to me, I can smell the scent of Adoring Body Spray. It's gently sweet with a touch of spice, the free sample I got in the mail reminded me.

"Piper, this is Cosmo Hill, he will be your boss here at Cosmic Antiques and Cakery."

Cosmo sticks out his hand. "Tell us what brings you to our little hamlet by the sea? We've got our suspicions, but I'd like to hear it from you."

I squint in disapproval.

Piper twirls her hair nervously. "Well, you guys know about Zion's naming me his successor. 'Amaris, Queen of Rebirth,'" she sing-songs. "So stupid. I hated that name, so I changed it. Most people forgot Zion's prophecy once they left the cult, except for Broken Branch. No matter where we've moved, they've followed."

"He knows, dear. He's just trying to be difficult," Vem interrupts. "It's been in the newsletter for quite some time. Really a shame some people choose not to read it." She shoots him a sideways glance.

"Your whole life? As far back as you can remember?" I ask.

Piper nods. "When we lived in Michigan, they tried hurting me for the first time. I was just four years old, playing outside with my little brother, Sawyer and my best friend, Hazel who was a few months younger than me. This car sped down the street and a big man jumped out, dressed in black and tried to grab me. He had me under one arm and Hazel, who was on oxygen because she was always very sick, pushed her oxygen tank in front of his legs and he tripped. I got away and he jumped back in the car and it sped away."

"What a quick-thinking friend!"

"She was," Piper puts her hands on her hips. "Poor Hazel. She died soon after that. I don't really remember her; I was so young. But Mom tells me she was wise beyond her years. From then on, we were on the run, trying to hide from them. When I got a little older, they started cutting off pieces of my hair every time they caught me. And then we'd move again."

Cosmo shakes his head. "None of this is what Zion taught. If they had a collective brain, they'd send him a letter. I'm sure he'd be glad to lead them in a chant."

"Oh, they don't believe that's really Zion." Vem interjects. "They think that's an imposter sitting in jail and you killed the real Zion years ago." She glances at Cosmo, knowing he'll react. "Don't be mad at me, it was in the newsletter!"

"That's just crazy is what that is." Cosmo lowers the tone of his voice, to keep from scaring Piper. "Lanie got this all figured out. There's DNA proving that's really Zion and the guy I threw over the falls was my–" he looks at me. "The guy I got rid of because I didn't know any better, was the man I thought was my father."

"I know all of that." Piper looks at him earnestly. "It's just what those crazies think. My mom has been my rock all of these years. She said we can't control those people so don't bother trying to change them. I know who I am. That's why I changed my name. Every time someone calls out, 'Amaris!' I know they're part of the crazies and it's time to move again. Normal people just call me Piper."

"Why didn't you change your last name though? Moonlight isn't a very common name." Vem is doing some of her calm breathing, only she's standing behind me and it's making me anything but calm.

"Mom insisted. She and Dad still believed in Zion's

teachings and he bestowed that name on us. My story united them. They legally changed their names to Olivene and Hal Moonlight so we could be a real family. I think it's kind of cute. At least it was until my dad couldn't handle it anymore and took off."

Vem stops her breathing and massages Piper's shoulders. Piper shifts her weight uncomfortably but doesn't complain. "Oh, sweetie, I know exactly where you're coming from. My husband couldn't handle me either."

"Completely different thing Nov–"

I discretely step on Cosmo's foot. He doesn't need to make trouble right now.

"We're happy to have you here now, Piper. I'm sure Cosmo will be pleased to have another baker in the back. Won't you, Cosmo?"

He nods. "Piper you can start tomorrow. As long as you're not one of them, you'll have no problem with me."

She nods. "I figured my mom and brother needed a break. They've had to live their lives looking out for me. Now that I'm here, where everyone knows my story, I don't have to worry as much. And they can live normally in California without constantly looking over their shoulders."

"Cosmo, don't you want to take her in the back and help her get started?" November encourages. "I'll stay and wait for you, Piper. Lanie and I can catch up for a bit."

After they move to the other room, November leans in close. "Poor girl. She's jumpy. On the way in today, she pointed out someone she thought had attacked her in Des Moines when she was younger. I jumped on his back and had him on the ground before he could explain he was on his way to Newport for a photography class. Did not understand who or what a Piper Moonlight was."

5

SEVENTEEN YEARS AGO

Des Moines, Iowa

"Hal, set those boxes to the right. You know the drill." Olivene Moonlight wiped her brow and turned to pull her curly-haired toddler son off the moving van bumper.

"Sawyer, you stay put. Amaris, I told you to watch your brother." She picked up a short-for-her-age, dark-haired five-year-old and moved her in front of the toddler. She placed the girl's small hand on the toddler's head. "You see? This is your responsibility. We talked about things expected of you, remember?"

"Yes, Mama." Obediently, she picked up a toy truck and began running it back and forth in front of the boy. "See, Sawyer? We play like this while they finish our 'venture.'"

The toddler squatted down and watched her momentarily before running off. "Sawyer! Wait! You're my 'sponsibility!'"

Hal Moonlight, a short, balding man with wisps of brown hair crossing his head and wrinkles that defied his age, stared at his children. "I wish we didn't have to uproot them so often. Kids need stability." He looked at the ground, waiting for what most assuredly came next.

Olivene took a deep frustrated breath. "Hal, we must protect these children. You don't want to stay in one spot and allow someone to hurt them, do you? We made a promise to ourselves to keep them safe and that's exactly what we've done. I understand it gets hard, but we must be vigilant."

"You're right, Ol. Sometimes I just wish we'd chosen a different life for them." He shook his head. "No, that's wrong. I wish the universe would have chosen a different path for them." He stared at his wife hopefully.

She bent down and picked up a box. "We can't change the universe. But we can change the state of this house. The last round, we were settled in two days. I think we can cut that down to a day and a half. As long as we follow my fool-proof system."

Hal nodded. It served no purpose to argue, but he always had to try.

The next morning, Olivene was in the kitchen scrambling eggs when her daughter wandered out, rubbing her sleepy eyes. "Mama? Where are we?"

Olivene bent down and gently touched her daughter's back. "Take a deep breath, baby. What does that smell like?"

Amaris took small sniffs. "Toast. And eggs. Scrambled with peppers, Daddy's favorite."

"And what did I tell you about those smells?"

"When I smell them, we're home."

"That's right. We're home. This time home means a place called Des Moines. We'll find a nice park and take our lunch there later. Would you like that?"

"Mm hmmm." Amaris looked around the room. "And

that's my home table and my home chair. And over there, my home towel with the red chickens on it."

"What about your nightgown?" Olivene went back to stirring the eggs with one hand and buttering the toast with the other.

"Princess Piper Proudstone. My home pajamas."

"That's right, Amaris. Home is where your family is."

"Mama? Do the Firestarters know we're here?"

"Not yet, baby. We're safe for now."

"And what about later? Will they know we're at the park?"

"No, baby. The Bad People won't know we're at the park. We're safe today."

Amaris, satisfied by the usual answers, scooched herself up to the table and waited patiently for a familiar breakfast.

By the time they reached the park, it was full of summer-time picnickers. There were children swinging, a giggling group playing tag, and someone playing a flute.

"Much better environment than the mortuary, right Ol? I don't know how you go there every day, working on the dead. It's too much." Hal lifted containers out of the picnic basket and placed them on the checkered cloth.

"Hal, you're being dumb. There's so much to be gained from every job. I'm glad I decided to do this again. When we lived in Cedar Falls, I observed the entire embalming process. At Freddy Dan's Mortuary I've discovered how important just the right makeup is for the family viewing. It's a fascinating business."

Hal smiled at his wife. "Glad you've found something to feed that extraordinary brain of yours, Ol. It needs stim-ulation."

"Mama? Can I go try the merry-go-round?"

Olivene stopped scraping bits of peanut butter sandwich

off her plate and looked up. The park was full of families, each immersed in their own activities. "Yes, but stay where I can see you. Promise?"

"Ok, Mama." Amaris walked over to the merry-go-round, where two boys were hanging by the bars, dragging their dust-covered shoes on the gravel as it twirled slowly around.

"I'm Amaris. What's your name?"

The boys shrugged. She leapt to the middle of the spot on the play equipment and sat down, holding one bar with each hand. "You're supposed to tell me your name. I'm the Chosen One."

They ignored her, continuing to drag their feet.

"MY NAME IS AMARIS! I'M THE CHOSEN ONE! Stupid heads!" she stood up and began stomping her feet even as the merry-go-round went faster and faster. "Chosen One! Chosen One! If you don't listen to me, I'll hurt you!"

The boys' mother ran to their side and pulled them away from the equipment.

"Keep your crazy kid away from mine!" she snapped when Olivene appeared, flustered.

Olivene lifted her daughter off the equipment. "What's going on, baby?"

"They don't know who I am, Mama! They're supposed to know!"

Olivene squatted down to her level and brushed the dirt from Amaris's blue jean skirt. "Remember what I said? We don't talk about that in public. That's a family story."

"I know." Amaris kicked the ground as she followed her mother back to the blanket on the ground where her brother and father were eating peanut butter and pickle sandwiches.

"Did you have fun, darling? Meet some new people?" Her father tousled her hair.

"They were stupid heads. They didn't know who I was."

"Amaris, we talked about this. It's a private thing. Not everyone can understand."

"If the Firestarters can know, why can't everyone else?"

Her parents exchanged a look. "Top secret. Like the cartoon you watch, Piper Proudstone, Superhero Detective?" Hal made sure she was out of bed every Saturday in time to watch her favorite show. "The Superhero Detectives know the story and they collects clues. But they don't tell anyone. That would ruin the story."

"I'm sick of my name." Amaris announced. "Can you call me something else?"

Hal chuckled. "What name would you like? Steven? Calliope?"

From out of nowhere, a woman ran up with a pair of scissors and clipped a chunk of Amaris' hair and placed it in a plastic bag. She was gone before anyone else in the park realized there was a problem.

Even though the scissors hadn't touched her scalp, Amaris reached for her head and cried. "Owie! Daddy! Make the Bad People stop!"

"Firestarters, remember, Amaris? You forgot to yell 'fire' today, that's what gets people's attention. They almost caught you." Olivene chided.

Hal jumped up. "She tried to hurt my baby!" he yelled, pointing vaguely at the nearby baseball diamond. He ran toward her but quickly stopped and put his hands on his knees, trying to catch his breath. Several picnickers ran past him trying to catch the woman, who by now was on the edge of the outfield, where a black car sat with the door open. She jumped in and it sped off.

Breathless, Hal returned to his family. He sat on the ground with a thud. "They must have been training, because they're getting faster. They're using scissors now, Ol! What next?"

"We'll get them next time, Hal," Olivene soothed. "Just one crazy. The rest haven't tried to hurt her."

"That's a record," Hal mused. "We weren't even here a week."

6

PRESENT DAY

City Meeting
Or
Patience doesn't live in Piney Falls

"Cedar is coming around to collect all of your name tags." I look around the room, surprised to see so many faces. At least fifty from the community sit patiently in the middle of the Piney Falls Welcome Center, an old bank that was once ominously used to process the Fallen Branch members after they left the cult.

Cedar borrowed extra folding chairs from the high school. As I gaze into the crowd, I see the owners of Just Dream of Fudge, Cantankerous Quilters, and Urica's Fine Art just to name a few. I've been getting to know them as I walk around town, introducing myself and handing out flyers about our growth plans for the community.

Long before I arrived, city council members, desperate to attract tourists, passed an ordinance that every adult in

town had to wear a nametag. *WELCOME TO PINEY FALLS!!
I'm Lavonne! Ask me about our antique pinball machines!*

Some people hated them so much they taped over their names or found other creative ways to disguise the information they shared with tourists. Cosmo tied his to his shoe. They made an already reluctant community appear even less friendly to outsiders.

"Okay, do we have all the nametags?"

Cedar nods.

"These will be sent to Portland, to a nice recycling facility. You'll never have to wear them again, at least if you don't want to."

A loud cheer goes up, followed by a standing ovation.

"Those were the dang dumbest things!" a man wearing a "Fishin' Fool" cap exclaims.

A timid hand in the back goes up. It's Emma Williams, the gaunt, barely-twenty-year-old manager of Cheese With Your Burger, a fast food place that just opened off Highway 101.

"Excuse me, Miss Anders? Shouldn't we wear nametags to be friendly? When I went to manager training, they said the customer should feel as if you're their friend. How can you be friends if they don't know your name?"

There are murmurs of agreement.

I raise my arms above my head, which eventually calms the chatter out of pure curiosity. I learned that little nugget in the *Calm the Masses* seminar. I slept with Doake, the seminar leader, that afternoon. That wasn't an unusual occurrence for me, unfortunately.

"You're right, Emma. We will encourage those of you in the service industry who want to continue to wear them to do so. The rest of us will use our warm and inviting voices to welcome others like they are old friends." I nod at Cedar, who dims the lights while I start the projector.

The first slide is a small town from 1950 with tall chimneys billowing smoke. "We all know what happened to Foamyville. It was a voracious logging town just twenty-five miles up the road. The community filled the void left by Scheddy Salmon Cannery when it burned to the ground in 1925." There is an audible gasp. "It's okay to talk about it, guys. We can all express our feelings about the horrible demise of Faye and Fiona Scheddy without Piney Falls crumbling. Just not right now." The town founders' suicide that same year hangs over every public gathering like stale cigarette smoke at a bowling alley. Old ideas die hard.

I take a deep breath before continuing. "There were over a thousand hard-working people, lots of businesses, and a cannery. Once the canning industry dried up, so did the town. Unlike Piney Falls, they refused to move forward. There was nothing left by 1955. Now, where a vibrant community used to stand, there's nothing but a few abandoned buildings. That's it." The slide shows the former cannery building, the only one still standing in its entirety, was covered in graffiti, things like "Fart" and "Can this!"

Gladys Petrie, the centenarian who works at the public records office, raises her bony hand. "Lanie, are you suggesting that we're doomed? Piney Falls will meet its ugly end? She's a smart cookie, folks. If that's what she says, you'd better get your homes on the market now."

The crowd buzzes with concern.

I push my blonde hair behind my ears. "No, no. We're doing fine. Unlike Foamyville, we're on the move. We've got new businesses coming in, like Cheese with Your Burger." I wave at Emma. She waves back enthusiastically. "And now, we've got an exciting idea to bring in more businesses and make Piney Falls a real tourist destination." I click the projector for the next slide. It falls halfway; stuck sideways.

Cedar runs to the projector. "I'm sorry, Lanie. I just practiced last night. It worked fine." Tears form in the corners of her gorgeous eyes. She's so nervous when she has to stand in front of a crowd. A deep scar from the night two decades ago when she had to speak in front of the city council and Zion humiliated her.

Back when I worked for *Work Ahead Office Supplies - The Most Profitable Office Supply Chain in the World*, this kind of slip-up would have sent me over the edge. Without hesitation, I would have quickly fired whichever quivering assistant stood before me. Here, I'm a different person.

"That's okay, Cedar. Next time, we can use my laptop. Modern technology will fight its way into Piney Falls. You'll see."

After a brief break, where Emma hands out buy-one-burger-get-the-second-free coupons, the slide is upright and there are more gasps in the room.

"That's downright handsome!" someone calls from the darkened crowd.

"This is an artist's rendering of the Fallen Branch property, not as a reminder of things that brought sadness and death, but as a shining possibility of a future that includes a giant resort and spa."

I give them a minute to marvel at the layout. The large square that contains four long, cement buildings will be replaced by four-story, white-stucco buildings, each with a covered entrance and connected by a Spanish tile walkway. In the middle, instead of the giant fire pit where Fallen Branch members sat listening to Zion's endless sermons, there is an indoor pool.

"Can we folks use the pool too? Does it have a hot tub?

Y'know we've only got one of them now." It's Ed Jr., who works at the run-down Spruce Bark Motel, the establishment I stayed in my first night in Piney Falls.

"We'll work out passes for the locals, and who knows? Your kids might get some swimming lessons."

I smile at the crowd. So open and receptive. What was I worried about? The back door of the room opens and I strain my eyes to see a muscular figure and a short woman with her arms wrapped tightly around her middle. It must be Piper alongside Cosmo, who is wearing a wide, welcoming smile on his face. He gestures two thumbs up. At least those two appear to be getting along.

"The Sleepy Sounds Corporation has three levels of hotels. The Hi Sigh is on the top level. It includes a spa and this nice pool. That's our goal. They've given us a very specific set of instructions for their visit. When they come here in a couple of weeks, we need to charm the pants off them."

"I'll bite. What do we need to do to dip our toes in that yummy-looking pool?" I hear Cosmo's booming voice. It still gives me chills.

"Thanks for asking, Mr. Hill. Cedar, would you care to explain?" I nod to her. We went over her speech several times. She looks down at the floor uncertainly. "Um... well..."

Deep breaths. Center yourself. Focus on the words you need right now. Everything I taught her in the last three months.

She clears her throat. "Well. We have an intensive training course. It will be on your lunch hours twice a week for the next four weeks. We're calling it 'Launch Lunch.' She makes a sweeping motion with her arm, a complete improvisation. "You'll learn everything you need to know to ensure Mr. Walters and his companions realize this location is a diamond just waiting for its polish."

"Aww. That don't sound like any fun. I like to shoot the breeze with my buddies over at Cosmo's place on my lunch hour." Fishin' Fool Hat Guy is going to be a problem. In my last job, they taught us to focus our lectures on the one person in the room who didn't want to be there. The more they are engaged, the more likely they'll persuade the entire crowd. I motion with my eyes and nod slightly in his direction, but she's looking nervously around the room.

"We'll provide lunch... something different every week. Something you'll like–" Cedar's voice is shaky.

"I promise I'll make your scone to go, and I'll kick your buddies out so they have no choice but to meet you here." Cosmo chimes in.

I touch her arm. "Go ahead, Cedar. They're listening." BE LOUD, I mouth. Just like we practiced.

"It will be fun." She's finally reaching the people in the back. "We start this Thursday with 'How do I Engage Strangers?' We'll do some practice sessions. Cosmo is making turkey sandwiches and brownies. I'll fix iced tea and lemonade."

"Sounds to me like you're trying to make us into something we're not. A little like that cult." It's the grumpy lady in the back who told Cedar she didn't want to be here longer than thirty minutes, so her husband didn't get too comfortable in her comfortably dented space on the couch. "How do we know these people aren't headed by a smooth talker, lookin' to move in and turn our little hamlet into another Foamyville? Like your old friend there, Zion. Didn't he try to change us to meet his needs?"

7

PRESENT DAY

All for One

"I can assure you; this is a legitimate corporation. We'll never allow another cult to take over–"

Cedar puts her hand up. "I've got this Lanie." She turns to the crowd. "The only cult that exists here now is those of you who consider yourselves 'Townies.' You were here before Fallen Branch and now, over twenty years later, you're still trying to keep us out. You're pushing good people away. Do you want to end up in a has-been town? You've already proven your point, that Fallen Branch was a mistake. Isn't it time to move forward as a group? Aren't we stronger together?" She pulls the one empty chair in front of her and climbs on. "Piney Falls Proud! Piney Falls Proud!"

At first there is an uncomfortable silence. I join in. "Piney Falls Proud! Piney Falls Proud!" Cosmo is next. His voice fills the room. Fishin' Fool Hat Guy stands up and does the same. Soon the entire room is on its feet, chanting and clapping. For several minutes, the room swells with local pride, whoops, and hollers.

I come to Cedar's side and help her down. "Good job!" I whisper.

Cedar turns crimson, but I can tell she's pleased. "Please pick up information about our lunches on the table as you leave!" she calls as the crowd begins to filter out.

I take the microphone, distracted momentarily by Cedar's big moment. "Wait just a minute, please. There's something else we need to discuss as a community." Motioning vigorously towards the back of the room, I try in vain to make eye contact with Piper. Cosmo nudges her gently and nods his assurance and finally she walks timidly to my side. Her violet eyes narrow as she surveys the room.

I place my hands on her shoulders. "This is Piper Moonlight. For those who don't know, she was the last baby born in Fallen Branch. There is a small group of former members–"

"Broken Branch! Read that in the newsletter!"

"Yes, thank you, Broken Branch. They haven't been able to leave the cult mindset and in fact, have been trying to re-form. They're trying to harm this young lady. That's another good reason to sell that land, before the fringe group finds a way to reclaim it. They think Piper should be their new leader."

There are snickers in the room.

"I can assure you, this is no joke. Study this face. If anyone notices she is being followed or is approached by an outsider, please step in. We're Piney Falls Proud. We can keep evil out if we work together."

There is a smattering of clapping before the rest of the group disperses. Piper lets out a whoosh of air.

"Sorry to put you on the spot like that. It was important

we address the situation before people see you working for Cosmo and rumors fly. Small towns are big on rumors."

She smiles politely.

"How was your first day?" I ask. "We didn't have much of a chance to visit."

Piper shrugs. "Fine, I guess. Cosmo thinks I'm an idiot. Basically, he won't let me do anything but take out the trash."

I study her youthful face. "He'll warm up. Just like you, he has a million reasons not to trust people."

"Excuse me, Piper? I was acquainted with your mother, Olivene."

The owner of one of fifteen local galleries, Urica Jolloby, appears by Piper's side. We know her around town for her unique stories about Fallen Branch and her multi-colored tunics. There are some former members who swear her version of events never happened. It doesn't matter to me. She's entertaining.

"Piper, I changed your diapers when you were born. We didn't actually have diapers, so we took some of our sand-colored outfits and tried to cut them down for you. Didn't work so well. I ended up pretty wet some days," she chuckles. Piper pulls the corners of her mouth in but says nothing.

"Dearie, I'm glad you're here. I can always use help at the gallery, if you need a job."

I gaze hopefully at Piper, waiting for her to respond. She doesn't. I guess she's not used to conversation after lifetime of hiding. "She's working for Cosmo, down at the bakery. Piper's got some experience as a baker, don't you, hon?"

Piper shrugs.

"Well, just keep me in mind. I knew your parents well. If you don't mind my saying so..." she leans in close, her long braided hair falling on Piper's shoulder, "your mother was a little out there. I always thought she'd follow Zion down the falls, if you know what I mean."

Piper stands a little taller. "My mom had a hard life. Before she came to Fallen Branch, she had a very strict father who kept her like a prisoner in her house. She didn't know good people until she came here and met my dad. At least that's how he was in the beginning—"

"You don't have to say anymore if you don't want!" I jump in. "Urica, I'll make sure we have your information just in case Cosmo thinks he can't afford to pay another staff member."

Urica leans in close to Piper and squints. "Them eyes are beautiful. Exotic. I remember getting lost in them when I took care of you as a tiny baby." She doesn't wait for a response. "You'll know where to find me," she calls over her shoulder.

Piper touches her face absently. "Thank you!" she calls out.

We move to the now-empty folding chairs. "I'd like to talk to you about your family if you don't mind."

"Sure, I guess."

There is another presence beside us. It's good people are taking an interest. "Piper? I'm Emma Williams." The young lady from Cheese With Your Burger sticks out a small hand, waiting for Piper to shake.

The two young women share dark hair but Emma is taller and so thin extra fabric from her tiny shirt folds like an accordion across her chest.

"I'd love to hang out with you sometime. We're practically the only young people in town." She smiles widely, displaying braces on her top teeth.

Piper eyes her suspiciously. "I don't really...hang out."

Emma throws her head back with laughter. "Aren't you

darling? I'll give you my card and you can call me when you get bored. Which will be about this time next week! "She sticks a diminutive hand in her fanny pack and pulls out a pink business card with a picture of a giant hamburger in the middle.

Piper watches her walk away and then looks at me, unsure.

"Don't worry. People here seem strange at first. You'll get used to it. I wanted to ask you a little about yourself. Can you tell me a little about your parents? What are they like?"

"Well," she concentrates for a minute. "My mom is very strong and sensible. She always knows what to do. Every time one of those crazies followed us to a new town, she had a system. 'Pack it up, Piper. Adventure awaits,' she'd say. It was never negative. My dad on the other hand, he was always second guessing her. 'Maybe we shouldn't do that, Olivene. Don't tell her those things, Olivene.' I was only a little sad when he left us."

"That had to be difficult. I'm so sorry."

"No, don't be. This life can be hard. My brother Sawyer, my mom and I were a good team. It just got to a point where my dad wanted a normal life. We couldn't give that to him." She itches her petite nose.

"My father left too. I was four. He found his secretary more to his liking. I know how painful that can be."

I feel guilt for a moment about Cosmo's desire for information. This poor girl has been through so much already. But if there is something I can uncover that might help all of us to stay safe, it's worth the discomfort. "Cosmo wanted me to write down other family member names, for contact information, just in case."

"There's just my mom. She doesn't allow Sawyer to have

a phone. Though now that I'm gone, maybe he's got a little more freedom."

"Where is your mom now?"

"Ferndale, California. We've been there almost three years. That's our longest stretch anywhere. No one approached me at all. I felt like I wasn't special anymore." She giggles. "It gave me time to figure some things out, go to culinary school to be a pastry chef. I even made a few friends. It's hard to trust anyone, though."

"How do you think they found you all of those other times?"

Piper crosses her arms and leans on one leg. "After my dad left us, I thought it was him. He was always arguing with my mom about moving us around so much. I was sure once he left, we wouldn't have any more problems." She shifts to the other leg. "And then we were in Santa Fe, New Mexico, eating mint chip ice cream like all the normal people. Someone grabbed me from behind. He snipped my hair and just like that, it was time to move again. Dad wouldn't have had any idea where we were."

"Oh, Piper. What a life you've—"

Her eyes grow wide. "STRANGER! FIRE! FIRE! She points to the back of the room, where a heavy-set bearded man is talking rather informally with Cedar.

"Is he one of them?" I ask helplessly. "Cosmo!" I'm not yelling, but the sound I'm making is not a normal one. When he hears us both, I point to the back of the room, where he and the remaining townsfolk tackle the stranger and bring him to the ground.

Piper is calm but ghostly pale. "I have to leave again," she says dully.

"No, you don't. We will protect you. And we'll get to the bottom of this, once and for all."

8

___

PRESENT DAY

Dilemmas

"You're sure he's not a threat?" November is wearing her favorite chartreuse-themed ensemble complete with chartreuse-framed glasses. Her canvas shoes sport laces in the corresponding shade. I always marvel at her ability to accessorize every jumpsuit so seamlessly.

As we round the steepest curve, headed to the top of Piney Falls I feel a sense of pride that there's no need to stop and catch my breath. It took months before we could walk side by side at her brisk pace. City life wasn't exactly conducive to exercise.

"Hawk Beechum swears Piper's mother sent him here to check on her. Piper called Olivene and she confirmed. Hawk Beechum will not be a problem." I grab Vem's arm. "Can we go further? There's something about the site of the old Flanagan hospital that always brings me clarity."

She pumps her fist. "Go Lanie! You've becoming a hiking

beast.

"What do you remember about Hawk from Fallen Branch?"

"He was weird. We were all into Zion's teachings at one point or another, but Hawk trailed him around like a puppy. Even when he was forbidden from contact, he waited outside Zion's quarters. Some of us were so relieved when it all ended, but it devastated Hawk. The last time I saw him, he was sitting in the middle of the fire pit, sobbing. Thought for sure he'd end up taking the long walk over the top of the falls, too." She closes her eyes and open her arms to the heavens, waiting for further thoughts to enter her head. One of the many things Vem does that seemed strange nine months ago, but now it's a normal part of our hiking routine.

"Do you know how he ended up at Fallen Branch?" I never know how long to wait for these rituals to end.

She brings her arms back to her sides and opens her eyes. "It was very sad. His parents dumped him at the gate like a pet they didn't want anymore. As far as I know, he had no further communication with them, at least while he was one of us. But I can tell you he had a thing for Cedar. Left her notes covered in hearts and flowers. She liked him too."

"Cedar was talking to him after the meeting. She was smiling in a way I'd never seen her smile before. I wonder why he and Piper's mother are still in contact? It sounds like he's someone she would want to avoid."

"He's a clinger. Probably needed someone from the group to stay in contact with after he lost Zion." Vem stops and points to a Rhinoceros Auklet, a brown bird with a tiny horn protruding from its beak.

I don't know if this means we stop for a bird admiration meditation or if we keep going. I nod and move ahead slowly.

"Cosmo thinks Piper should move in with him temporarily, until she understands she's safe here. Would you be okay with that? Or maybe she should stay with you a little longer." Jealousy is not an outfit I've worn before and I don't like how it fits. But I still wish she'd protest.

We reach the top of the falls and pause to feel the spray on our faces. This, too, has some positive effect on our well-being, according to Vem. I follow her lead and lift my chin so that my face can become fully immersed in the light mist.

After a few minutes, Vem turns to face me. "It might be a good idea, her moving. I'll talk to her about it."

"Really? I mean, if it offends you, I can talk to him."

"Lanie, I've got to tell you something difficult."

I gaze at her more-than-average serious face. "What is it? Are you sick? Has one of these 'firestarters' tried to hurt you? Whatever it is, I'll be here for you!"

"You remember I told you about my husband? Franklin Bean? He's the toilet paper king, owner of Klean and Komfy toilet paper."

"I don't remember your telling me exactly what he did to make his money. Is that why my toilet paper goes missing every time you visit?"

"Nobody needs that scratchy inferior sheeting." She huffs. "It's cheaply made and unhealthy for the skin. When it's not Word Waste Not Month, I'll give you some background on that factory and the unhealthy things workers told me about. There was the time–"

"Waste not, remember?"

She nods. "When we separated, he convinced our son I was at fault for breaking up our family." She crosses her arms in front of her chest, something she's told me repeatedly not to do when we're absorbing Piney Falls' good vibes.

"We were always a broken family, but Franklin relished

his control over me. He blamed everything that was wrong in his business, in his life, on a young woman who was climbing the tallest mountain; trying to live life normally. He showed our son that was how a man should treat his wife." She rolls her eyes. "In hindsight, I married someone just like Zion." She lets out a loud howl. Her own patented stress reliever.

I wait patiently until she finishes. "You told me you've had limited contact with your son for several years. I'm sorry. That has to be very painful."

"March Franklin Bean. Calls himself Frankie these days, at least that's what Franklin Senior says. He's just graduated from college and decided he's going into business with his father, unfortunately. There's nothing I can do about that. His father offered him a trip to Europe for graduation. He told Franklin he wants to visit me instead."

"Vem! That's great news!" I look at her emotionless face. "Isn't that great news?"

"March – Frankie – is very much his father's son. He doesn't understand the power of meditation or how howling clears the cobwebs from the soul." Her voice quivers. "He thinks I'm a garden variety nut."

"He's also YOUR son. He wanted to see you. That's a very good development!"

She concentrates on my face. "I love your nose. I know you said it isn't organic. But I love it nonetheless."

"Vem! Concentrate!" She can't ever seem to get over the fact that I had ill-conceived plastic surgery to make my features even closer to forties movie star, Tulip Sloan. Changing the organic me.

"It is a very good development. He'll only be here a few days. Just long enough to upset his father, I'm sure. That's probably what this is about. His father made him mad, so he's getting back at him the best way he can. Since he hasn't spoken to me in two years, he made his father call to tell me." She pulls out her rainbow water bottle and drinks half of it in one gulp. "It's good for Cosmo to take Piper away. March was inappropriate around girls the last time I saw him."

I frown. "That doesn't sound like a son you would raise."

"No more Bean business. Let's get to the important stuff. Have you told Cosmo about your sordid past yet?" She waggles her eyebrows suggestively.

No matter how I think I am prepared for her random, rapid-fire questions, she always catches me off guard. "When you put it that way, it sounds like I'm a real mess!"

"You WERE a mess, Lanie. You've changed since moving here. I think you lead with that statement." She motions toward the new path we've been creating through the brush, toward the remains of a giant home that was converted into the town's first hospital in the early 1900s. "And then you crush his soul with the fact that you slept with every man you ever worked with."

I push tall weeds out of my way with ease, something I've recently mastered. "I was afraid of relationships. It was easier to sleep with a man and discard him. But then I met Cosmo Hill and everything changed. I just don't know if he'll see it that way. He views the world in a very black-and-white manner. He doesn't like surprises, at least not at his expense." I find a ladybug on a tall strand of grass in my pathway and gently move it to another stalk. Vem is rubbing off on me. "He also doesn't know how relationships are supposed to work. He thinks us not sleeping together is normal. I suppose I don't know how they work either. I'm not sure I'm ready to marry someone when I don't know what that looks like." I stop when I realize I don't hear Vem's controlled breathing behind me. "Vem?"

It used to frighten me; walking alone in nature. There are all sorts of creepy, crawly unknowns. Vem has helped me understand it's okay to embrace what I don't know. Backtracking, I find her crouched over a bug on the path.

I sigh. "Is this something we need to do right now? There are plenty of bugs. I doubt you can save everyone."

"No, look at this. It's an Asian Lady Beetle."

I bend down to view what looks like a ladybug on the body, but on the head there are butterfly-shaped black marks. "Wow! That's remarkable!" I reach out to touch the branch and let it crawl on me, but she bats my arm away.

"NO! Bad luck! If these things get in your house, they multiply so fast you can't get rid of them. We'll both have to take our clothes off outside and put them in a bag so we don't drag them inside. That's common knowledge."

I wonder for a minute if she's joking. Then I realize November Bean, while delightfully odd, doesn't make it a habit to tell jokes. "I'll be glad to do that. But what do you mean about bad luck? It's a bug, not a sign from the heavens above."

She stands up. "Lanie Anders, you haven't heard the story of the Asian Lady Beetle who ate a town?"

I giggle. "Not that I can remember."

"It's a rather long, but since I'm careful with my words this month, I'll give you a condensed version. The story goes, if you let one sweet-looking bug into your heart, she'll take over the space until you're drowning in bugs. No more heart but her own. Even if they're cute, you must be wary."

I gaze at her skeptically. "And you believe this?"

"It all makes sense, Lanie. We let Piper in, now she will poison us. Try to keep up."

"Oh, Vem. She's a sweet kid. Let's not make this bug problem about her."

"I don't know why I missed this before. This girl will be trouble. I only wish I hadn't invited her to stay with me. Good thing she'll be moving in with Cosmo."

There is no point in arguing with her. "We'll see. In the meantime, please remember you're keeping your words to a minimum and only kind words at that. Don't scare this poor girl."

By the time we reach the bottom, I'm late for a promised check-in with Cosmo to see how things are going with Piper. Downtown Piney Falls is a short, five-minute drive down the mountain and into town.

When I open the door, I can smell the intoxicating scent of blueberries and chocolate comingling in the oven, the key ingredients for my favorite Scorpio Scones. I can hear a high-pitched, sweet voice in the back. It's out of place in Cosmo's bakery, where his deep voice and that of former smoker Doris usually fill the air.

"My best friend, Hazel, was born with a terminal illness. She was like our family. My mom said she could sense when Hazel was having trouble breathing. She always came running, no matter how far away we were playing. After Hazel died, I never had another close friend. Mom said that was normal. Once you find perfection, you stop looking."

I hesitate before ringing the bell. Her dark head pops around the rack of cinnamon rolls and scones, a purple polka-dotted ribbon holding her dark brown hair. She is wearing a Cosmic Cakery and Antiques apron that is two sizes too big. Her cute, round face belies youth and innocence, despite the life she's had. "Oh, sorry Lanie. I was just chatting with Doris. It's so nice to talk about myself without worrying someone will use it against me."

"That's partly why I'm here." I point to the fluffiest cinnamon roll on the rack, rationalizing the scones can't possibly be ready before I go and a girl needs some nutrition after a hike. "One Centaurus Cinnamon Roll to go, please."

She turns and grabs the tongs from a metal holder.

"I wanted to talk to you about that. I'm sorry to bring this up because I'm sure you're upset by last night, but do you remember seeing that guy, Hawk Beechum, before? Did your mom say why they remained in contact?"

She places the thick roll in a paper sack and sets it in front of me. Her demeanor changes. "Yeah. My mom says he's kind of a goof, but completely harmless. They all have those beards and a dull look in their eyes. I really thought I'd heard the name 'Hawk' before, but Mom says we've never met. It happened once before, when we lived in Sandy Salts, Iowa. I thought I saw a man we'd chased off in Montana. It turns out he didn't even speak English. Poor guy was a tourist, just minding his own business." She wipes the counter in small circles, not returning my gaze. "Your usual too?" She holds up a note, written in Cosmo's handwriting, "Standing order for Lanie: Latte, half-foam,"

I smile. "Yes. And whatever you saved for Gladys today. Oh, did Cosmo talk to you about moving in?" The words don't want to come out of my mouth.

She smiles a half-smile. "I'm not moving in with your man, Lanie. That's creepy. Besides, I'll be just fine. Cosmo promised."

I think about Vem's warning about her son. For many reasons, Piper shouldn't feel safe there, but I still couldn't stop the words from falling out of my mouth. "Well, if you're sure."

9

PRESENT DAY

Hidden Resources

I take my roll, along with Gladys's favorite, Pegasus Peach, and walk to the public records building. When I arrive, she is in the middle of her twenty-five-minute power nap. I sit in the dark leather chair and sip my latte patiently. Piper's version is almost as good as Cosmo's. I won't tell him that.

When Gladys comes to, she sits up abruptly in her desk. "Why d'you scare an old woman like that?" she snaps while reaching slowly for the drawer to her left.

"It's okay, Gladys. Leave your knife in the desk. It's just me, Lanie. I'm here to get some information." We went through this last week too. She's paranoid now that she knows someone may come after Piper.

"The whole town is on edge, what with crazies after that poor girl. I heard tell on Sunday night Pete Fortner was walkin' his corgi when a bearded nut job came up behind him and wanted to know where Piper was staying. Can you imagine? Good thing Pete has that karate training."

"I don't think I heard that story, Gladys." There are so many fake Broken Branch member sightings, I feel sorry for the small police department. They don't have the manpower to check out each and every report. People here don't let former Fallen Branch members live in peace, even over twenty years later. "We need to focus on preparing for the investor's visit and stop worrying about Piper. There are plenty of people watching out for her. I do have some questions though."

She takes a huge bite of her scone. "Sure, toots. What did you want?" she spits scone on my hand and all over my purse. I put my offended appendage down by my side and try to shake the crumbs off without being noticed.

"I'm trying to find information on Piper's family. I need resources. Maybe not the kind the average person would use."

Since my search for the Flanagan family secrets, I've learned Gladys is quite the internet whiz. She gives classes every week for the elderly on how to use the internet. She also keeps files on everyone from Fallen Branch, not trusting they have become legitimate, productive members of society.

She leans over the counter and whispers while spitting more bits of scone. "You want the good stuff? I have my sources. Give me the names and I'll do a check."

"I had a sense I could count on you." I force a smile though I feel a bit queasy on the inside.

"You know about those files the police found in Zion's place when they cleaned it out?"

They uncovered lots of disturbing material at his cabin deep in the woods. He was watching everyone in town, it seems. "I've been so busy training Cedar and trying to get this marketing package off the ground; I lost track of Zion. I know his trial is coming up. What did they find?"

"Well, you didn't get this from me," she leans her elbows on the desk and motions for me to move in closer. I'm a little afraid of what might literally spill from her mouth, but I lean in nonetheless.

"They bagged up many documents. Some of them were statements people had to write when they joined Fallen Branch. Why they wanted to be there, what they hoped to gain from the experience, etcetera. My son-in-law Boysie, who is the police chief, knows I have all these records on the kooks. He took pictures of each document and sent it to me. Who're you looking for?"

"Olivene and Hal Moonlight. They've lived all over. You'll probably have a file on both of them. Oh, and Hawk Beechum, the man who came into the meeting the other night." I'm slightly surprised she didn't do this the moment she learned Piper was in town.

"Let me fire up old Matilda." She pulls an ancient laptop from a large drawer and sets it beside her. She stares at me sharply. "You know this will take about twenty minutes, right?"

The large clock on the wall says 2:45; Cedar's been working by herself and may need help. "I may just leave and come back."

"You're always on the go, toots. I think you're running away from something. Maybe you and the boyfriend need to have a heart-to-heart?"

Caught off-guard, I stand abruptly. " I need to check on Cedar and make sure she has everything ready for the first Launch Lunch. Don't believe everything you hear, Gladys." I shake my head as I let the door shut softly behind me.

My eyes haven't even adjusted to the outside light when I hear a familiar voice. "We're going to every business in town so you, March Franklin will feel at home. This is my best friend and soul sister, Lanie. Shake her hand, son."

The two shapes that appear in front of me are Vem and a well-dressed young man with dark hair and Vem's distinctive nose.

"Frankie Bean. Pleasure. I'm here looking at properties, for investment purposes. Dad and I want some vacation property."

His sticky hand grabs mine, pulling me uncomfortably close to him. My nostrils are assaulted by a body drowning in expensive cologne.

"Nice meeting you, Frankie. I'm on my way to the Welcome Center, but I'm sure we can talk later."

He releases my hand and makes a clicking sound as he shoots his finger gun at me. "Counting on it, Lanie."

Just as Vem said, he's nothing like her.

The Piney Falls Welcome Center, recently the beneficiary of a shiny new sign thanks to my grant-writing efforts, is the oldest standing building in Piney Falls. As soon as the door is opened, the sound of giggling echoes over the squawking of the doorbell. Hawk Beechum is draped over the counter, deeply involved in a conversation with a deeply enthralled Cedar.

I clear my throat, though I know the screeching of the doorbell was too loud to miss. "Excuse me, I don't mean to interrupt. I just wanted to check on Cedar and make sure everything is ready for tomorrow."

They both look up at me, and Hawk seems slightly annoyed. Cedar's face has so much color she might seem ill if I didn't know any better.

"Lanie, did you meet Hawk? We're old friends from Fallen Branch."

"I heard a lot about you in all the confusion the other night." I stick my hand out and he looks at it with uncertainty before waving with the opposite one. "Hawk Beechum."

"Now that you've seen Piper, is there a reason you're sticking around Piney Falls?"

He looks bemusedly at Cedar. "Thought I might reconnect with old friends."

My pocket buzzes and I pull out the phone. *Printer's on the freetz. Only printed Hawk B file. Come by and get it and I'll get the others tamor. G*

It's a good thing I speak Gladys. Her texts are often illegible.

"We're going on a date tonight," Cedar announces proudly.

I've never once heard her talk about dating or having an interest in anyone. "That's terrific! Where are you going?"

"The Seashell. Over in Tellum. Cosmo said we'd leave around six."

"Cosmo is going with you?" I know he is protective of his sister, but this is a little overboard even for him. She's forty-three years old for goodness sake.

"You're both coming. It's a double date."

10

———

TWENTY YEARS AGO

HAWK BEECHUM - INTAKE FORM

Fallen Branch Commune

Sponsor: *Olivene Durning*

About me? I'm five-seven, curly brown hair that's kind of a mess, brown eyes you can't find under all of my hair. Probably weigh around two hundred-fifty. I'm pretty thick around the middle. Is that what you wanted to know?

Oh, why I'm here. Okay. Well, it's a long story. You probably get lots of those.

My dad and I got along just fine on our own. My mom left when I was six. He never told me why, only that the two of us would figure things out. We did. I got into trouble here and there, stealing the neighbor's wrench set and writing bad words with a permanent marker on our fence for everyone to see, typical stuff boys get into.

When I was ten, I came home from school one day and Dad's sitting on the couch with his arm around this lady. A short round woman with thick glasses and grey streaks of hair. Not good-looking in my mind. He said, "Hawk, this is your new mommy."

"Hello young man." She had a deep voice, almost as deep as Dad's. I thought that was funny for a short woman like that.

She said her name was Marlene but I wouldn't call her that name, it wouldn't be decent. From that day on, everything in our lives became about being decent.

She wasn't there more than a week before she'd gone through our cupboards, cleaning out all the fried noodles and canned meat; things we bachelors liked. It wouldn't be decent for a family to eat those, she said. She filled the shelves with creamed corn and gelatin for her casseroles. What a decent family ate.

I wasn't allowed to have friends over. I hung with the outcasts at school – long haired hippies and some who only wore black. You can imagine what she thought the first time they came over. Not decent at all.

I resented my dad for inflicting this woman upon us. Turns out, he'd been dating her for almost a year. Never said a word. Then he just shows up with her...man. Can you understand how that'd make a kid crazy?

I guess I decided I wanted to show Dad how I was such a good kid and he'd missed out on that part. Now I was gonna be a hellion and make him long for those times. That's what Marlene called me, not my words. I ditched my wannabe angry friends and started hanging out with the we-don't-take-it-from-no-one rough crowd. The kids who spent their after-school time trying to outdo their last crime. One day we knocked over every bottle of wine at the grocery store. There were only twelve bottles on the shelf, but still we felt like we accomplished something.

We started stealing candy from Ted's Quick Mart. He was always high in the afternoons, so if we got there after two, he'd be staring into space. We cleaned out the candy aisle every time. This pretty much describes my high school years. The only joy I had was walking away with something I didn't rightfully own.

Marlene didn't care what I did, as long as I showed up for

dinner, folded my hands nicely and said the right things around her friends. We were decent.

One of the kids, Bret, spent time in kiddie prison for car theft. He'd heisted about ten cars in his life, but stupidly decided he wouldn't be cool until he heisted the governor's personal vehicle. Stupid Bret didn't think about security cameras and they caught him before he was a block away.

Anyway, Bret taught us how to hotwire a car. It wasn't hard. We stole our first car from an easy mark – a guy who was too drunk to care.

We took that car and being kids, drove it three blocks, got out and ran. After that, we got braver and planned a night of car thefts so big the town would talk about it for years to come. Later, I heard Marlene telling Dad we'd never live this one down in the eyes of the townsfolk. No hope at all of being known as decent folks.

My friend knew of a place we could take the cars where they would pay us in cash, more money than any of us had our whole lives. Selling the candy we stole made us each some nice pocket change, but nothing like stealing cars.

I decided I'd take my next-door-neighbor's Jeep. Awful Aughton washed that thing every Saturday without fail. My buddies said that would be an easy get. We made a plan where we'd meet up after the biggest carjacking in the city's history, carried about by a bunch of clueless fifteen-year-olds.

It took months to plan. By then, my sixteenth birthday came and went. Dad forgot until bedtime. He expected Marlene would tell him; he said. In my mind, that was his last chance to make things right with me. His last chance to prevent me from becoming a big time criminal.

The next night we all went to our locations. I knew exactly what time the neighbor took his hairy little dog out for his late-night crap. Sorry for that word, is it okay to use? I knew what time he turned off his light and went to bed. He was more reliable than a clock.

He always left his keys in the glove-box, 'cause it was a small town and that's what people do. I thought it would be easy. Well, what I didn't know was that stupid Jeep had an alarm that could wake the dead.

Dumb kid like me, I panicked; fell on my face, trying to get away. That was just enough time for Awful Aughton to come out of his house. His yippy dog was nipping at my face and when I shoved him off, the neighbor clocked me right in the nose. That's why my nose is a little crooked, as you can see.

He and Dad made a deal. He wouldn't call the cops if Dad wouldn't press charges for him hitting me. Marlene said it wouldn't be decent for a kid like me to stay in their house. She planned to send me away to a reform school.

I was at Villman Academy for six months. The only reform that happened there was that I stopped caring. I learned how to steal cars with alarms in them and planned to try out the new method when I got home.

Marlene had something different in mind. I wasn't home an hour before she told me to come and sit in the living room. It wasn't really a living room anymore, Marlene covered everything in plastic, so it was more like a hospital room for one of those kids who gets sick all the time.

She pulled out this list she'd made of the things I wronged. None of them were what I was sent away for. "You've never bathed properly; I'll be timing your showers from now on, to make sure you aren't missing something. We'll be checking the length of your hair every other week." Things like that. Then she pops the big one. "Your father and I decided you'll be living with my spinster aunt, caring for her this summer. We'll figure out a place to put you after she's been placed in the care facility."

Can you imagine? A sixteen-year-old kid stuck with an old

lady all summer? Wiping her gross lady parts and stuck inside the house all day? I thought about running away, but I didn't have anywhere to go.

They drove me to Pendleton, Oregon, where this copy of Marlene was waiting on the porch. They could've been twins. When Marlene said she was almost 90, I laughed.

Bettine was a great lady. Every Saturday she had bridge games with the other old ladies in the neighborhood. She taught me how to steal from people without their realizing anything was gone. 'Keep 'em engaged, son. They'll never notice.' We made enough each week to take us out for pizza, where Bettine toasted my slippery hands. For the first time, I felt like someone cared.

The summer ended and I knew our time together was almost over. I did everything she asked me to do, even giving her a bath. It wasn't so bad, as long as I thought of something else. I was pretty confident she would give me a good report and Marlene would decide I could come home.

That Saturday we sat in her living room, waiting for Marlene and Dad. We joked about our favorite television show and what we thought would happen during the next season. Then, out of nowhere, she pops this one on me: "Hawk, you know Marlene controls all of my money now. What I don't lift from the bridge group's purses. She's a real piece of work, but she's all I have. When she gets here, I have to tell her you were awful. That's what she wants to hear. She doesn't want you living there and needs me to tell your father you aren't safe to have in the house."

That was a real kick in the pants. I waited in the driveway while she listed all the evils I'd done, at least the ones Marlene wanted. When they came outside, Dad shook his head in disappointment. "Don't know what's gotten into you, son." There was a time that would've cut me like a knife. It relieved me there was nothing left to feel.

Marlene had already painted my room and moved her

crocheted animals on the bed. She told me I could sleep on the couch for the night. The next day, they were both happy and full of smiles. A united front. I didn't know Dad anymore. Marlene pushed the Fallen Branch brochure in front of me. She said it was a labor camp for troubled youth. I could come back and visit once I could behave decently. There's that word again, who determines what is decent anyway?

The drive up here was quiet. Winding through the trees, Dad playfully leaned into Marlene as we went around the curves. They were probably nice people to the public. I bet they had friends who thought they had the perfect life if it weren't for me. When we pulled up, I got out of the car, waiting for them to follow. Dad popped the latch to the trunk and rolled down the window. "Get your things. We'll expect a postcard soon." After I got my suitcase, the one Marlene only gave me as a belated birthday gift because she knew it meant I'd be out of her life, Dad rolled up the window. They turned down the road without looking back.

11

PRESENT DAY

Date Night

My knees are touching my chest in the back seat of Cedar's compact car. She and Hawk chat about old times in the cult during the forty-minute drive, blissfully unaware of my agony. I retreat to examine important information on my phone, trying to block out their childish conversation. When we arrive, Cedar pulls into a parking space but leaves the car running.

"We can just wait out here for Cos. I don't see his motorcycle yet."

"There's adult supervision in the backseat, so no funny stuff," Hawk remarks, squeezing her knee.

"I think I need to stretch my legs. I'll see if the restaurant can seat us early." I push on Hawk's seat forcefully, trying to remove myself from this physically and mentally uncomfortable situation as quickly as possible. He makes an irritated sound, but opens the door and gets out eventually.

As I walk along the pier, the breeze lifts the turquoise earrings Vem made me in harmony. The peaceful feeling is disturbed by a buzz from my pocket, hopefully Cosmo. *Gotcher things prnted, G.*

I chuckle to myself thinking about thinking about the irony of Gladys being paranoid. "You never know who might be lookin' at your email, Lanie."

I took pictures of each document, though she insisted they be printed, and read Hawk's file on the drive over. It was a nice diversion from the gooey mess in the front seat. A sad childhood, a glorified life in the cult; Hawk's file showed he was the perfect minion to carry out Zion's bidding.

The timing of his arrival doesn't make much sense. If he's still in touch with Olivene, he must know how scared Piper is when people are following her. Why would he purposely spook her like that?

"Watch where you're going, pretty lady!" A familiar, manly scent hits my nostrils and I look up to see the wall I've encountered is Cosmo's strong chest, followed by his dazzling smile.

"Cos!" I kiss him quickly. "We should go in. They're in the car making goo-goo eyes at each other. It's nauseating, just to warn you."

"Hold on. You're always in a hurry." He pulls me close and hugs me tightly, gently caressing my neck with one hand. One of his permanent scars from twenty years in prison, being falsely accused of Zion's murder, is his constant need for affection. Vem pointed that out on one of our walks. I hug him back, half-heartedly.

"What's so interesting?" He points to my phone.

"Hawk's intake form from Fallen Branch. I'll fill you in later." I wave to Hawk and Cedar and the four of us walk out on the pier, to a small, yellow building sitting at the very end. Once inside, Cosmo and I slide into one side of a red, vinyl-covered booth, and Cedar and Hawk the other. The waitress hands us four large menus, shaped like clam shells, and Hawk pinches Cedar's hand as he picks his up. She giggles.

"Is that the Fallen Branch version of a secret handshake?" I ask sharply. *I'm not Cedar's mother,* I remind myself.

Cedar laughs girlishly again. "No, we used to pinch each other as we walked by in camp. It was our way of saying hi, with no one noticing." She looks at Hawk adoringly.

"I knew nothing about that. Who else did you pinch without telling your brother?" Cosmo snickers.

Cedar rolls her eyes. "No one I'd tell you about."

"What can I getcha?" the baggy-eyed waitress asks, pushing a lock of dark, stringy hair from her face.

"Sexy Seafood Pasta for myself and the lady and two beers, whatever's on tap," Hawk announces boldly.

I hope ordering for his sister doesn't make Cosmo come unglued. Instead, he glares at Hawk who doesn't seem to notice. "You sure you don't want to order for yourself, sis?"

"I'm fine with whatever Hawk wants to order," she responds sweetly.

"I'll have the burger, rare. I can order for you too, Lanie. But I'm thinking you are a woman who likes to use her own mind."

I squeeze his knee under the table, our own signal for calm. "Just the spinach salad with scallops for me, please." I've got to steer this conversation to a more neutral topic quickly, or Cosmo will lose his temper. "Hawk, tell me about your life after Zion disappeared. I find it fascinating to hear everyone's stories."

Hawk clears his throat. "Well, I believed in Zion's message. He wanted commune members to transform into beings as close to nature as possible. That was how humans began and Zion preached we could correct all of our past mistakes, including other family members' mistakes, by becoming one with the earth and with Zion, of course." He leans his head back dramatically, lifting his chin high in the air. "The day they found his body, I was down at the river washing clothes when I heard a commotion."

"You mean the day he ran away like a coward," Cosmo interjects.

Hawk ignores him and continues. "When I got into the camp, it was complete chaos. People were running, screaming, some even suggested a mass suicide. I calmed them down and asked what produced that kind of frenzy. Sister Millicent, Year of the M, told me Grand Elan was dead. She didn't know where to go or what to do." He pauses, as if he's telling a dramatic story none of us have heard before.

"I told her, 'The sun is your direction. You know Grand Elan promised he would always be here, by our side. When the time is right, he'll give us guidance.'"

Cosmo snorts. "He made a whole lot of promises. Did he ever tell you in your private sessions how he was planning to push all of those people over the falls?"

"Cos, I'd like to listen to his story," I mumble. "We already know the ending, but we haven't heard the middle." I nod to Hawk. "Go ahead, finish what you were saying."

He takes a sip of his beer and looks at Cedar, who nods encouragingly. "I walked into town, positive this was all some kind of mistake. Zion would never leave us. He knew how important his mission was to the world. When I found a Townie willing to tell me what had happened, that Brother Cosmo had killed Zion in a fit of rage, I fell to my knees, bereft."

I put my hand on Cosmo's arm but thankfully, he's quiet.

"I sat by the firepit, making plans to break into the jail and kill Cosmo myself." His eyes dart between Cosmo and Cedar. "That's when I took off, into the woods so I could plot my break-in. Everything negative about the old Hawk came flowing back, tarring me from the inside from head to toe. I collapsed from exhaustion. At the end of the fourth day, Zion came to me in a dream. 'Don't waste yourself on hate, Brother Hawk. It's up to you to lead my people now.'"

A large chuckle escapes from Cosmo's mouth and then he composes himself. I look at him and frown. "I know," he mouths.

"That's brave of you, Hawk. Deciding to carry on," Cedar sips her beer, looking out the window and purposely avoiding Cosmo's gaze.

"I wasn't prepared for what I found when I returned to camp this time. The place was covered in debris, our common garb strewn everywhere. I looked around but didn't find another soul. Finally, I summoned the courage to walk once more into town. I went into the tourism center, which had been turned into a processing station for former Fallen Branch. There, behind the desk, was a sweet, familiar face. Do you remember, Cedar?"

"I do, Hawk. You asked me what happened to my clothing." She tilts her head. "You were shocked that I could move on so quickly."

"Then I remembered your pain. I said I was sorry about your brother. What a betrayal. You stared at me as if I were a stranger, not a comrade in this fight to make a better world."

I can feel Cosmo's knee bouncing. I place my hand on it firmly.

"It was hard on all of us. I was in shock." Cedar runs her fingers up the back of his neck, pulling the mass of brown curls away from his large head.

"I know, sweetie. You were choosing to make a life with the Townies. You said, 'Unless you decide to get a job and assimilate like me, I don't want to speak to you again.'" Hawk stares at Cosmo defiantly. "Trying to be brave after what your brother did."

Cedar is oblivious to the standoff happening right in front of her. "I gave you money for a bus ticket. So many members just wanted to leave this place behind. Where did you go?"

Our meals arrive and we eat in silence for a few minutes, Cosmo moving food around his plate.

"You know, maybe you forgot that we all suffered. I was arrested for a murder I didn't commit. Cedar was left alone, without family. We were still teens, without any direction in life and we were scared. You weren't the only one who struggled."

Hawk glares at Cosmo for a moment and then turns to Cedar. "For several years I moved from town to town, state to state. I was lost," he continues, ignoring Cosmo entirely. "I didn't understand what or who I was without Fallen Branch. I got a job at a library, restocking the shelves. One day, a cover with gold leaves intrigued me. *Essays on Renewing the World through the Eclipse*. The author, Felix E. Gaummond, felt every time there was an eclipse, the earth was reborn in some way. Children born during such times were especially powerful and could be the biggest instrument of change. Just like Zion said after Amaris was born. There was confirmation of his path, right in front of me."

"Is that when you contacted Olivene?"

"Olivene was a great comfort to me in Fallen Branch. Not a mother, but..."

Cosmo drops his fork and leans forward. "I know exactly

what Olivene was. You tracked her down and then you stalked her daughter?"

I stare at Cosmo sharply.

Hawk swirls his pasta meticulously with his fork. "I still believe in Zion's cause. He wasn't wrong, Cosmo. I'm not here to hurt Olivene's daughter; as a favor I told her I'd check up on Piper while I was visiting a friend. More importantly, I realized this was an opportunity to find my way back to the only person who has truly cared about me my entire life." He takes Cedar's chin in his hand and gently kisses her lips, his thick, curly hair engulfing her face.

"This is about all I can take for one night." Cosmo pushes his plate away and stands up. "Lanie, do you want to ride on the back of my motorcycle, or would you rather waste the rest of your evening with these two?"

I wipe my mouth with my napkin and look up at Cosmo's troubled face. "Give me a minute and I'll ride with you."

"Suit yourself." He drops a hundred dollar bill on the table and leaves. It's more than he can afford, but his pride won't allow him to split the bill with the likes of Hawk Beechum.

"Hawk, quickly, can you tell me more about Zion's thoughts on Amaris? Why she was chosen?" They continue kissing, ignoring my words. I wish this restaurant had a long hose that could reach to these booths. "Hawk?"

He wipes his mouth with the back of his hand and smiles at me. "Zion took a special interest in her. Even though it was the year of the W, he named her, "Amaris, Queen of Rebirth."

He leans back in his seat and puts his arm around Cedar. "He predicted she would have a big impact on our group, maybe even becoming his successor. She even had a birthmark in the shape of a crescent moon on her upper arm, reinforcing his vision of who she was. I shamefully confess I didn't believe her to be that savior. I was his chosen successor. My vanity overtook my sensibility and I couldn't see Zion's prophetic words for what they were."

Now it's my turn to suppress a giggle. No one has mentioned Hawk as a successor. "And what about the book? What did it tell you?"

"Gaummond? He had six tenets: Number one, respect the words spoken by the earth; natural disasters and eclipses are telling us something..."

As his speech stretches past ten minutes, I stare longingly out the window at the gentle waves rolling in and out. There is no polite way to make him stop.

"And finally, number six, recognize your leader and help them to achieve all the great things they are born to accomplish. I could give you examples, but I can see you're growing weary."

Cedar giggles. "You are windy."

"Mmm. I see. So you decided to start your own group with these teachings?"

"When I found Olivene, I sent it to her. She said Zion was dead and we had to follow his teachings to the letter, if we were going to continue our group at all. But I found others who were interested. We put together an online page and began discussing this book and how it related to Zion's idea of a perfect society. You never know where that might lead."

I'm thankful Cosmo is waiting outside and I have a reason to leave this disturbing conversation. I put my napkin on the table and scooch to the edge of the booth.

"Before you go, there's one more thing you need to know," Cedar wraps an arm through Hawk's elbow. "I've asked Hawk to move in with me. He has nowhere to go and we've wasted too much time apart already, I hope Cosmo can come around to the idea eventually."

I smile weakly and stand. It will be up to me to break this to Cosmo. "Thanks for the ride. It was an interesting evening."

I can feel the heavy cloud of stress lifting as I walk down the pier. When I reach the end, Cosmo is leaning against his bike with his arms folded. "Was it necessary to spend more time giving this mess your approval?"

"You wanted me to get more information about Piper. He's part of this puzzle. As much as he nauseates both of us."

"What else did you find out?"

"You're not going to like it."

He puts his hands in his pockets and walks toward the sea.

"Cos! Wait!"

He pivots quickly. "What?" he snarls.

"The extra helmet. It's in Cedar's trunk."

"I've got a set of keys to her car. Let's get it quickly and get out here."

As we walk to her car, I take his arm and rub it gently, trying to calm him down.

"I don't like this at all. It's okay for my sister to have a boyfriend. I'm not weird or anything. Hell, she probably had several while I was in prison and was just too afraid to tell me."

She didn't. Like me, she had issues.

"I've never seen her act like this before. All stupid and silly. Isn't it bad enough I have a teenager working at the shop, without dealing with my sister acting like one too?"

"Piper's over twenty, but I know. That's why this will be difficult–"

"And that guy. He gets under my skin. I never liked him. Too intense and self-righteous. Full of himself for no reason."

Cosmo opens the trunk and pulls out a constellation-covered helmet.

"He's got lots of problems, that's for sure." I smooth my hair down, removing all signs that I spent time fixing and hair spraying it tonight.

"How do you know?" He eyes me suspiciously.

"What? I've been trying to tell you. Gladys found his intake form from Piney Falls. He was ripe for Zion's words from the start. I think Olivene was his sponsor. It says, Olivene Durning."

"That was her last name. Well, Hal's. Before Zion anointed them Moonlights." Cosmo scoffs. "Stupid. Changing your name because some idiot proclaims it should be so."

"What did a sponsor do?"

Cosmo's face twists into something I've never encountered before. "They were supposed to guide you. Give words of wisdom, like an elder." He rubs the back of his neck. "Instead of acting as some kind of mentors, they turned into extra pairs of eyes and ears for Zion. Any time someone got out of line behind his back, the mentors all went and told him. They got extra punishment. I don't want to talk about this anymore. You ready to go?"

I nod.

We turn around and Cedar and Hawk are standing behind us. I can't tell if they've heard anything we've said because they both have goofy smiles on their faces.

"Just grabbing the helmet." I pull it from Cosmo's hand.

Thanks for the ride, Cedar. It's a lovely night. So nice meeting you, Hawk."

He throws his chubby arm over Cedar's shoulder. "I make the best pasta. Better than the subpar meal tonight. Cedar and I will have you both over for dinner soon. Won't we, sugar?"

Cedar smiles quickly and nods.

I don't wait for Cosmo to respond, but pull his arm beside me as we walk.

"What did he mean by the 'we'll have you over for dinner' comment?"

"Get on the bike, Cos," I order. He hops on and tilts it slightly so I can follow. It used to be a challenge for me to get on his motorcycle, but hiking has given me muscle strength where I didn't even realize I had muscles.

We are just to the edge of town when I put my lips close to his ear. "They are moving in together."

The bike warbles slightly, causing me to lean forward and cling on to him tighter.

12

THIRTEEN YEARS AGO

Sandy Salts, Iowa

"Daddy? Will you take me out sledding again?" Amaris touched her snow-crusted mittens, dripping on the heating vent.

He smiled at his daughter as he pulled a dry, red thermal shirt over his head. "Punkin, we've barely thawed out. Go work on your homework now. I'll bring up a plate of those cookies you made with Sawyer last night."

The only good thing about living somewhere so desolate in the middle of the winter was that none of the Firestarters would try to hurt her. She was safe, warm, and completely bored out of her mind.

Amaris climbed the stairs to her attic bedroom. As good as living in desolation could be, homeschooling was even more intense. There was no escape from the constant expectations of high achievement. Supper and chores and then back to work.

She sat down and stared at the blank screen, wishing there was a way to turn the internet on without her father knowing. Last week, while Olivene and Hal were "out for coffee" as they called their serious conversations that always resulted in two non-speaking days, Amaris and Sawyer turned on the internet and took turns looking up forbidden information. They lived for those stolen moments.

"Kids? Your mom wants me to meet her in town. I'll be back soon!" Hal called before slamming the large wooden front door.

Amaris ran to the top of the stairs, trying to contain her excitement. "Okay, Dad!" As soon as he left, she ran back to the computer room. Her brother had already been busy.

"Sawyer, did you turn the timer on?"

"Ten minutes. Then it's my turn," he called from his bedroom.

When these preciously short opportunities arose, she kept a mental list of things important to know. Today, it was the origin of her mysterious name. The page loaded quickly, to her surprise. "Amaris - means 'child of the moon.' Great. So, original. Child of the Moon Moonlight." She hesitated for a moment and then typed in Broken Branch Leader. There was only time to view two web pages before her turn was over. The library internet was so much faster, but Olivene always stayed right by their side as they studied.

A sliver of the moon at the top of the page began filling in slowly. "Argh! Hurry up!"

"Almost my turn! Remember, we have to make our time even or it's not fair."

She sighed as loud as she could. "Okay, Sawyer!"

Some days, she fantasized about being an only child. Then she thought about Sawyer singing in her ear or them both telling jokes to take their minds off their parents' screaming bouts. Having a best friend like Hazel to tell secrets would ease the loneliness. At least that's how she thought it would be. Amaris didn't admit to her mother she no longer remembered Hazel.

"Finally!" The first two paragraphs filled in.

On the magical date of September 27th, 1996, as we all marveled over the lunar eclipse, a child was born. Our Grand Elan (Elk) told of the great good fortune of such a birth. It meant a future leader for Fallen Branch. He planned to train this child in his principles to continue his legacy. This child he named Amaris, Child of the Moon, will be assisted by Sister Cedar, Year of the C, and others to be found in his favor in her ascendance to a place of leadership within our community.

Her parents, Hal and Olivene, were bestowed the last name Moonlight as a position of honor. It was barely two months later when Zion was taken from us by a violent, untrained soul named Cosmo, Year of the C. Zion's destiny as a leader of a world-wide Fallen Branch community was thwarted, but our Amaris is still growing and learning...

"Dad's back already!" *Thwap, thwap, thwap.* Sawyer's thick slippers hit the wood floor hard as he ran to Amaris' side. "Did you hear me? They're coming down the road!"

"It takes forever to get through the snow. Mr. Smith plowed yesterday and more snow fell last night. Turn off the router. I'll shut this and cover it."

By the time Olivene and Hal opened the oak door, Amaris and Sawyer were dutifully studying World History in their respective rooms. After her homework was done, she walked down the narrow former servant's staircase to the kitchen where her parents were drinking tea and speaking in hushed tones. Soft voices almost always fueled loud arguments.

Amaris glanced quickly at her parents, trying to gauge their moods. Her mother's cheeks were still rosy from the below-zero air. Hal had a sparkle in his eyes. "I want to talk to you about something. It's important."

"Did you finish your homework?" Olivene looked past her daughter, like there was something much more interesting on the other side of the room. A stare that had become a normal way of life. "I brought loose meat sandwiches home for dinner."

"I got most of it." Amaris sat down at the table and folded her hands in front of her, as she'd seen her parents do every time they have something important to say. *We're moving again. You can't say goodbye to any of the people you've met. Upset? Don't bother making any connections next time.*

"What do you want to talk to us about, sweetie?" Hal gently rubbed her arm.

"The Firestarters know where to look because they know our name. Why don't we change it? Moonlight is a weird name."

Hal glanced at his wife. "That's who we are. We can't change that because people are hunting us. If you don't have a name, you're afloat in the world."

Olivene nodded and smiled quickly. "Your father is right. We have to maintain something normal in our lives. You were born a Moonlight, you'll remain a Moonlight."

Amaris cleared her throat. "Then I will change my first name. From now on, you'll call me Piper. It's Piper Inez Moonlight."

Hal chuckled. "We're playing pretend, are we? Maybe my name will be Phillip. Prince Phillip, that is. Did you get this idea from that coffee shop in town, Jack's Beanery? Fairy tales?"

"This isn't from a coffee shop." Piper scowled. Why was it so difficult for them to take her seriously? "I don't want to be Amaris anymore. It's too easy to recognize. All the

Firestarters have to do is locate a family with a daughter who has a weird name. Easy. If I have a different first name, at least that will throw them off for a little while." They stared at her skeptically. "And if you don't let me change my name, I'll hurt myself."

Hal looked at her with concern. "I thought you finished that talk? Ol, didn't you tell me she was over that kind of talk?"

Olivene tapped her finger on the table. "We need to discuss this for a bit. You go upstairs with your brother and we'll come and see you when we're done with our conversation."

Amaris studied them both warily. "No fighting, though. Please, just talk about this quietly. I'm firm in this decision."

Olivene looked startled. "Firm? I don't think…"

Hal put his hand on his wife's arm. "We'll talk about it and be up in a few minutes. No arguing, we promise."

Amaris meandered up the stairs, hoping to catch a few words of their conversation. She stopped on the top step.

"She may be right. At least she'll have a little sense of safety even if it's not—"

"She shouldn't feel safe. We all need to be on our guard at all times. Remember?"

There was a silence. "Amaris? Are you still listening?" Sometimes Olivene counted her footsteps so Amaris has to do extra pretend steps to make it sound like she's upstairs.

Amaris realized she'd been holding her breath. She let it out in a big huff. "Fine!"

She found Sawyer on the floor of his room, working on a State of Iowa puzzle they found in the attic of this old farmhouse.

"It's missing two edge pieces, the one connecting it to

Nebraska and the one connecting it to Missouri," Sawyer announced.

She flopped down on his bed. "Don't you want to go to school? Have some friends?"

He shrugged, not bothering to glance at his sister. "Maybe. I don't want the Firestarters to get us. That's most important."

She reached an arm over the side and hit his head. "Hey. Look at me."

He ignored her for a minute, but she began shaking his arm so he couldn't work any longer. "What?" He looked up, annoyed.

"The Firestarters aren't after you. They're after me. Someday, I'll go out on my own. You won't have to worry anymore. Okay?"

"Okay. But they want us, too. Mom said."

"What? She never said that." Amaris sat up and crossed her legs.

"One day we were making meatballs. It was spaghetti night. She said, 'Sawyer, you've always got to be on the look-out. Things are coming. Big things. You can't be complacent.' Then she asked me if I knew what that word meant. Of course I did though, it was part of my vocabulary lesson last year when I was ten."

Amaris thought for a moment. "That doesn't mean she's talking about the Firestarters. Maybe she wants you to be prepared to go out in the world on your own. She doesn't want you sitting on the couch eating cheese balls when you're forty."

Hal knocked on the frame of the door. "Sounds like there might be a serious conversation happening in here. Mind if we join you?"

Sawyer and Amaris looked at each other. Their parents appeared calm.

They both sat on the bed, one on either side of Amaris. They each took one of her hands. "You've had a rough time. We all have. Toronto was hard." Tears welled up in Hal's eyes.

"It wasn't your fault, Daddy. We lost focus." Sawyer stood up and patted his shoulder. "We should have been watching to our right. We forgot to watch the right."

Amaris's mind raced back to that day, three months ago. They were on a beautiful wooden merry-go-round, with ornately carved circus animals around the top. It was a public place, but there were lots of people around. Amaris and Sawyer were on the same horse, too old for such a small seat, but it was still fun.

The woman slipped her arm around Amaris' waist and pulled her off the horse in one swift motion. With her other hand, she took scissors and attempted to snip off a lock of her hair. Sawyer screamed, but the merry-go-round had stopped with their horse facing the corner of the room where no one stood. Amaris tried screaming, but the woman covered her mouth, scissors pointing dangerously close to her eyes. Amaris grabbed for poles as they ran, trying to find a way to slow them down.

There was someone in the back room they were running through, someone the Firestarters hadn't counted on. Amaris grabbed her hair and held on. The woman's head jerked down and she grabbed at the legs of Amaris's abductor, causing her to trip. Amaris got up quickly and ran.

"Call the police!" the bystander yelled. There was no calling the police. It meant staying longer, answering questions. The Firestarters would have more time to plot and hurt them. It didn't matter if they arrested the abductor, there were plenty more, just waiting for their chance. It was always best to move again.

"You deserve some peace," Olivene began. "We've decided to allow you to change your name temporarily. If it makes you feel good, live your life as someone else for now."

"What made you choose that name, if I may ask?"

"Piper Proudstone. Remember the pajamas I had when I was little? She is the superhero princess from my favorite show. She's strong and smart. No one can touch her because of her brains, beauty, and strength." Piper smiled, thinking of all the nights she'd dreamt of herself dressed as Piper Proudstone, defeating the Firestarters.

"And what about Inez?"

"That lady at the hair salon who told me I was beautiful. Her nametag said Inez."

"Just remember who you really are. Amaris Moonlight." Olivene patted her leg. "There's strength in the Moonlight name too. You'll be amazed when you grow up and realize what's inside you."

Piper smiled. There was definitely something growing inside her. Piper Inez Moonlight sheltered a deep, seething rage.

13

PRESENT DAY

Dinner is Served

"**E**xcuse me, ma'am!"

I'm bending down, tying the orange-and-black sneakers Vem gave me when March called them "prison quality." I guess I should've been thinking about the fact that people actually do walk down the street now, instead of worrying about Vem and March. They've been bickering non-stop for three days.

So much for not wasting words on her part. I can hear them easily from my front yard, each conversation dotted by her howls and yelps.

When my head snaps up, it lands directly under the chin of a local realtor. I've seen his ruddy, oblong face on the one park bench in town, but never met him in person.

"Sy Romington. Romington Coastal Realty! Sorry we had to meet under such 'bumpy' circumstances!" He slides his thin, clammy hand eagerly into mine.

My head is throbbing, but I force a smile. "Lanie Anders. Marketing coordinator for the city. You've been working with my partner, Cedar Hill. I suppose we should sit down soon and discuss our plans for expansion."

"Oh, my." He stands back and eyes me up and down. "Has anyone ever told you how much you resemble Tulip Sloan, the great movie actress from the forties? Her old movie posters hung in the local movie theatre when I was a lad. Did you know she visited once? It was in the 1940's. She came as a favor to a wealthy local entrepreneur, to celebrate his daughter's thirteenth birthday. My dad always said she was the last of the great dames."

"Do you know how many times I have been called a dame?" I can't help myself. "Not only did they call me that offensive name but also felt it was appropriate to squeeze my backside just as a 'dame' would have experienced during those years." I straighten my top and pull the sea air deep into my lungs. *Just breathe, Lanie. Let it come out in air, not verbal barbs.*

He puts his hand to his chest.

"I'm sorry. That is a particular trigger of mine. My therapist pointed out that people didn't know any better. Probably why I couldn't hug anyone until I was in my thirties."

He leans in closer and I can smell the pungent aroma of liquor on his breath. *It's only ten-thirty.* "Your nose is remarkable. I secretly studied her face so closely I dreamt about her features. I watched every single one of her movies. *Fondly Remembered* and *Her Secret Husband* are my favorites. She once threatened to expose a director's affair with his cousin if she didn't get pay equal to her male co-star."

I sigh. I wasn't really in the mood for this conversation today. "Yes, I know all about her. I studied her too. *Gabby Gilly* is my favorite. She co-wrote that one. A truly remarkable woman." I think about all the days I spent alone in my dark basement, watching the movies my mother rented for me before going out to see her man of the week. *Don't forget to rewind the tapes. Any extra fees when I return them and it will come out of your allowance. Make sure to put yourself to bed at nine, dear.*

"Have you considered becoming a platinum blonde? Anyone around town who saw one of her movies would drop dead." He chuckles. He has a thin, dark mustache like villains from some of Tulip's movies. *I wonder if that's on purpose?*

I hear someone behind him clear their throat and realize Mr. Romington isn't alone. I'm surprised to see Frankie, dressed in an expensive, grey pinstripe suit, olive shirt and grey tie.

"March? I mean, Frankie? Why aren't you with your mother?" Immediately I regret my tone. "I'm just surprised you're not spending time with your mom, since you came to see her."

He smirks and though his eyes are shielded by Plex sunglasses, the kind even I thought were ridiculously expensive, I can tell he's rolling his eyes.

"I'm looking at some properties. Remember? I told you that's what I was here to do." He snaps. "My dad and I are planning to invest."

I'm taken back by his attitude. I'm not Vem and I haven't involved myself in their problems. "You don't have to worry. I won't tell your mom anything. That's between the two of you. I need to get to work. Good luck to you both."

I move on abruptly, not interested in further confrontation, though I'm rattled by his snotty-ness. *He's still young,* I tell myself. There is barely any time to reflect on Frankie's troubling attitude as I open the door to the Welcome Center and the bell squawks. The second surprise of the morning awaits me.

Cedar looks up from her human entanglement, somehow perplexed by my presence. "Lanie? I didn't hear you come in." She pulls her shirt down and smooths her hair. "Hawk and I haven't been able to stop talking ever since our date the other night. I wish we hadn't wasted so much time apart." She strokes his face lovingly. He giggles softly and kisses her hand.

"I'm glad you found each other." I give them a fake smile; one I perfected in my previous life but try not to use often here. "We've got about two hours before the rain starts again. Last week we had to cover the back room when the wind blew so hard it came in through the windows. Maybe Hawk could join us in a bit for coffee?"

Cedar stands up and ruffles his hair. "Do you need money?"

"Nah, I'm fine. I'm going to meet up with someone and then I'll go to the store. You just wait – this goulash will make you cry. It's that good." He pulls on his jacket and walks out, winking and shooting a ridiculous finger gun at me as he passes by. That makes twice I've been assaulted by a finger gun this week.

I work hard to leave the emotion out of my voice as I set my bag down on a folding chair. "Looks like you two have really connected." I pull out the plans for the new event center we're hoping our investors will include in their plans for Fallen Branch.

"Sorry, Lanie. I know you and Cosmo are still struggling. I didn't mean to be insensitive."

I glare at her sharply. "Did Cosmo say something?" Of course he did. They share everything. "I didn't think we were struggling. We're just taking things slow."

"I...um...you're not intimate. That's all I meant."

I want to run and scream. "He told you that? Why would he tell you something like that? Does everyone in this town know? That's none of your business, Cedar. None!" Tears are streaming down my perfectly made-up Tulip-Sloan-alike face and I hate myself for that. Old Lanie never would have shown emotion in a work environment. Sometimes New Lanie is so irritating.

Cedar throws her arms around me as I continue working. "Oh, Lanie. I'm so sorry. I don't really know how these things are supposed to go. I've been reading self-help books for years, waiting for my first real relationship. If you need advice...?"

I pull her arms away. "I don't. Thanks, though." A horrid mental picture forms in my head; one where I have a conversation with Cosmo about the things he shares with Cedar. "We need to drive out to Fallen Branch to see how the new tours are going. Can we do that after lunch? I want the whole town viewing this as a historical event and not a black eye by the time the investors arrive."

"Absolutely. We'll join a tour group at one-thirty. They purchased disposable rain ponchos like you suggested and the pop-up gift shop is now up and running with all the Welcome to Piney Falls...what do you call it?"

"Merch. It's called Merch by the pros. Short for merchandise."

"Okay, merch. We've got t-shirts, caps, fanny packs, mugs and some umbrellas. That's funny to me. It's so windy here when it rains, they won't get much use out of them." She smiles the trademark family smile that can send even the staunchest soul to their knees. I think about it every time either one of them uses that weapon. So gorgeous. So powerful. So frustrating.

"The Launch Lunches are going pretty good," she continues. "Bill Smythe asked if they would compensate him for his time spent being 'unusually kind.' I told him this was just behavior that would be expected of him from now on. Haven't seen him back since."

I shrug. "We can't expect everyone to be on board. As long as the majority will be nice to strangers and willing to share some of the town history, we'll do fine."

There is a subject that is always hard for me to bring up. "Cedar, have you been able to start a discussion with any of the former Fallen Branch folks? How we need to think of ourselves as one town united instead of two?"

She shakes her head. Working at the tourism office, she has learned to have an outer shell whenever she has to use a public face. Underneath that, she's still a wounded bird, trying to limp out from under the dark shadow of her child-hood. "I tried. I used the examples you gave of big cities overcoming diversity issues. People said they looked that up on the internet and it wasn't true. And then everybody started arguing."

"I don't get it. You had a mayor, November's brother - may he rest in peace - who was former Fallen Branch. What happened since then?"

Cedar puts her hands on her hips and walks around the large space for a minute. She finally stops in front of me. "He was one of those people who didn't see barriers. He had no trouble talking to anyone and if they were to ask him about Fallen Branch, he didn't feel guilty about it. The rest of us can't look anyone in the eye without feeling embar-rassed. I don't think there's been anyone since who had the ability to do that."

"I know people who do seminars on these kinds of things. When the hotel is done, maybe I can schedule one of them to do a conference here." There is a long list in my head of conference speakers who have shared my bed. Finding one who hasn't could be a huge challenge. I'm glad I've never accidentally offered that information to Cedar; It will be my burden alone to tell Cosmo.

We work on our little model of the new Breezy Road Luxury Spa and Resort,(as we've taken to calling it) each in our own space of reflection. I step back, admiring our work when the large round clock above us catches my eye. "It's time to meet Cos." I have my coat on and my purse is over my shoulder when I realize Cedar is not moving. "Aren't you coming? To see your brother?"

"No. I want to check on Hawk. He says he's an expert cook. But so far, I've only seen him burn eggs. This dinner means a lot to him. It's the first time he's making an entire dinner for me."

A humid gust of air, heavy with the scent of baked goods and soup, meets my nostrils when I open the door to Cosmic Cakes and Antiquery. The place is packed. Often on especially blustery days people find themselves tired of being cooped up inside. They come to Cosmo's place and stay for the afternoon playing chess or reading a book. He's even added two folding tables today, just to accommodate the additional customers.

Working my way through the closely packed crowd, I find Cosmo at the back of the room and plant a kiss on his cheek. He pulls me in tight for a hug, something I still find makes me uncomfortable when we're in front of people. My previous "relationships" all took place behind closed doors.

"You're a sight for sore eyes." He taps my nose lightly.

"I never tire of you saying that. I found some of the information you asked for. It doesn't look like we can talk now though."

Piper appears from the kitchen carrying two steaming bowls of the soup of the day: pureed carrot and ginger. Under protest, Cosmo agreed to a limited lunch menu of her choosing. She asked Cosmo if she could make bread to go with it, a type she learned in culinary school. It's round and fluffy and smells fresh-from-the-oven.

"Hi Lanie! Can't wait to come to your place for dinner tonight!" she calls on her way by.

"Me too!" I yell, too loud for the space. "She's a sweet girl. I doubt any of this will involve her."

Cosmo raises his eyebrows but says nothing.

"Lunch seems like a hit."

"I guess. Right now half of these people are just here to gawk at the girl the cult thinks is their second coming."

"I re-read all the background information on Hawk. He sounds like a fanatic. You were right."

"Should I be even more concerned than I already was?" Cosmo crosses his arms and leans against the wall.

"I'm afraid so. For Cedar's benefit, at least. She's completely lost herself in this man. I walked in this morning and they were all over each other."

I feel a little guilty. *Is this just jealousy? Have I devolved into schoolyard tattling?*

"I don't like it one bit. There's no point in my saying more to my sister though. She'll dig her heels in. Decide this clown is a genius."

Time to change the subject. "I'm headed over to get the intake files for Hal and Olivene. Gladys says she can get me more information on Hawk too. I'll call you after Piper comes for dinner." I kiss him on the cheek.

"Let's make a plan to slow down one day. Promise me?" He reaches for my arm.

"Promise!" I slip away through the swarm of people

again. As long as I keep moving, I don't have to think about us; how I've kept my past a secret and how I don't deserve him.

"THE DARK WEB'S a great resource for all kinds of things. Hacked into the encrypted Broken Branch site and found this speech, originally posted when the site first went live in 2005."

Gladys pushes two pages in front of me. "No scones today?"

"They were in the middle of a lunch rush. Didn't see much in the case. I'll bring you some tomorrow."

The old woman looks at her oversized watch. "Time for my nap anyway. You pull up a chair and read what you want. Won't bother me any." She promptly places her black orthopedic shoes on her desk and leans her head back without waiting for my response.

I find a folding chair and sit down.

Who We Are

What if we could re-create his words and make a new Fallen Branch? We all remember excitedly that Zion predicted his successor, Amaris Moonlight. A perfect child born during the eclipse who would bear the mark of change and would go on to lead us all into a new realm. We'd have to find her, train her and allow her to become our new leader. That would involve regrouping, bringing only the most dedicated followers together.

A Broken Branch is a wounded part of the tree that remains strong in its own right. That is our new identity – Fallen Branch's wounded offshoot, still sturdy and proud. The first order of business is to buy back our sacred land.

As Zion's most trusted associate, he ordered me to recover funds collected throughout the glorious days of our Grand Elan. People came from all over the world, bringing whatever they treasured the most to share with our community. When he was brutally murdered by once-trusted Cosmo Hill, there were rumors Mr. Hill took the money. Thankfully, I know that isn't true. Because Zion speaks through me, I know exactly where to find this money to bring our community back to life.

The most important part of our journey, though, will be planting the first seed. Amaris Moonlight, will join us as prophesied. For now, my Brothers and Sisters, we must keep her close at hand, collecting pieces of her clothing and sharing locks of her hair for good fortune. We were once broken, but are now like the phoenix, rising from the ashes to rebirth.

In peace and harmony,
Your Secret Servant

14

PRESENT DAY

PINEY FALLS, OREGON

Drowned Rat

She looks so tiny and vulnerable standing on my porch drenched from the rain. "Come in, hon." I open the door and the familiar bakery scent wafts through the room as she passes by. "I hope you like enchiladas. I'm not an expert in the kitchen like you." I take her wet things and hang them on the coat rack Cosmo made for me from a dead tree we came across out at Fallen Branch. He chopped it with such vigor I was sure he was envisioning Zion's head and not a hunk of dead wood.

"That sounds terrific!" her voice is a high-pitched, fake-excited sound.

"Sit at the counter and relax a bit. They're almost finished." I push a plate of cheese slices and crackers in front of her and she nibbles furiously. "So, tell me how things are going with November and March — err — Frankie." Cosmo has been slow to move Piper to his place. Maybe he senses my reluctance to have her there.

"Oh, it's fine. I don't like Frankie. He's asked me out

several times. I keep telling him no, but he doesn't seem to get the hint. Now I ignore him." She sighs. "I missed out on being a teenager, so maybe I don't understand how it all works."

"You're definitely in the right place. Most of this town is full of people who missed out on some of the important rites of passage." I chuckle and then realize she has no idea what I'm laughing at. "Just go with your gut. If you're not interested, tell him. That's how it works. You are in no way obligated to date someone. Cosmo's moving you soon anyway, right?"

"I guess. He hasn't said anything lately."

As I dice vegetables for the salad, I glance over at the empty cheese plate.

Piper looks down. "Sorry. November makes these strange salads with things she grows and then slathers them in fake cheese spread. I'm not sure they're real vegetables. The only identifiable food I get comes from work."

There is another plate in the refrigerator for Cosmo. I place it in front of her and make a mental note to talk to Vem about providing recognizable meals for her guest. "I've been so curious about your life. It's hard to imagine being on the run all of those years. How did you do it?"

Piper folds her arms in front of her and leans her elbows on the counter. "My mom is responsible for all of it. She made a list of everything we needed to do when one of the Firestarters tried to take me."

With a finger, she scoops all the cracker crumbs into a corner of the plate before pushing the whole pile into her other hand and into her mouth. "For several years, we pulled the list out and checked everything off. Then we started moving so often, we didn't need a list anymore."

"Your mom sounds like a treasure. She must've had so much patience."

"Um...not really. Mom has a bad temper. My brother Sawyer and I always understand when to stay out of her way. Dad hated all of Mom's bad moods." She sucks in her cheeks.

I frown. "Vem – November – gave me old newsletters and they never mentioned your dad. Where is he now? Surely he still wants to see his kids?"

Her face twists momentarily with some unread emotion before she regains control. "He didn't want to move so often, but never complained. The thing that drove me crazy was that he never stood up to Mom. He had practical ideas for us, like putting us kids in a regular school. But you can't tell her anything. Just once, I wanted my dad to put his foot down and tell her no. Iowa, Nebraska; he was always asking if we could stay put for a while. He thought we could find a way to put down roots but she always said no. He's not strong enough for this life and I think he's ashamed. That's why he hasn't contacted us."

I chop the last of the carrots for the salad. "My mom was very controlling, too. She had me working in the mall every weekend, signing photos of Tulip Sloan. Tulip was a famous actress from long ago. Everyone hung her poster—"

"I know her!" Piper pops up excitedly. "My brother and I watched all of her movies. There wasn't always a lot to do. Sometimes my mom wanted me to stay out of sight. I don't know how she knew they were around, but she did. Anyway, while we were living in Cedar Rapids, Iowa, we had a Tulip Sloan marathon. My favorite was *My Girl Wednesday*."

"Oh, yes! She runs errands for a famous movie studio and they discover her while delivering sandwiches to the wrong building." I wore that green-and-white checkered dress for over a year. Even after it was too tight around the bust. *You can't totally embrace the part, can you Lanie?*

"Mom said she liked *A Spider on the Wall*."

That movie centered around Tulip's ability to hear through walls, always knowing what was going on with other people. "Tulip gave an interview years later and said this was her least comfortable role because she always wondered if someone was watching her after that." The timer on the oven goes off, causing us both to jump. We move to the table where I place the cheesy casserole pan in front of her and scoop a large portion onto her plate, gooey strings of yellow and white cheese following.

As we eat, she gazes at the ocean view. "This is so pretty, I hope I can stay for a while. The Firestarters shouldn't be able to take me here, right?" I pick up the serving spoon and scoop more on her plate without waiting for her to ask.

"Most everyone knows your story here. You'll be safe. And you've got Cosmo—"

"He hates me." She sets her fork down and looks at her hands. "It's got to be hard having someone like me around."

"Why do you say that? He let you implement your lunch menu."

"He always seems angry to have me there. I think that's why he really doesn't want me moving in with him."

I feel slightly guilty. "Cosmo Hill is fair to everyone. Even Vem, whom he still doesn't trust since their Fallen Branch days. Doris gets shot down once in a while, too. Her idea for a chocolate mint scone didn't go over well."

Piper stands up and walks over to the window, pulling the curtain back further and displaying the full view of my yard. "It's not that. When you're taught not to trust anyone, you learn pretty quickly how to size up a person. Mom called it 'drinking in their air.' It's a throwback from her

Fallen Branch days. Whatever someone breathes out is their negative energy. When Cosmo breathes out, he releases spite for me."

I'm in complete shock. "This doesn't sound like Cosmo at all. If you feel unsafe at the bakery, I can put you to work. We have lots of marketing materials to—"

"No Lanie. I want to bake. That's my passion. For the first time in my life, I can do something just for me." Her sweet face is tight with emotion. There are tears at the corners of her eyes, but they don't fall.

"Do you want me to talk to him? I know how to crack that tough nut."

In a surprise gesture, she throws her arms around me. "Thank you. Please ask him what I can do or what I need to say. I'm trying to start fresh and I don't want to mess this up."

Impulsively, I stroke her hair. She jumps at first but then eases into my touch. "Just be you. And relax a bit. We're all good people, even Frankie." I'm not entirely positive about the last one, but with Vem as a mother he has to have some good qualities.

"Hey, something came to mind. When I moved here, I wasn't entirely ready to let go of my old life. I brought all kinds of expensive clothing. It's just hanging in my closet. Since I hike, I'd like to think it's 'muscle mass' that has made them uncomfortable to wear these days and not the scones and delectable baked goods at Cosmo's. Would you like to try them on?"

"Okay!" she clasps her hands together. "I've never worn expensive clothes before. This will be fun!"

I pull out four silk tops and a flowered, sleeveless, designer Mark Sanderson dress. Immediately, she picks up the dress. "We never dressed up. There was nowhere to go." She caresses it softly.

"Try it on. I'll wait in the living room."

I pour myself a glass of Sassy Lasses Rebel Riesling and wait on the couch. In a few minutes, she appears, transformed from a frumpy girl to a stylish young woman. Her smooth, muscular arms compliment the dress in a way mine never could. "Turn around."

She twirls, the emerald and peach skirt lifting with the artificial breeze. "Oh, Lanie. This is just perfect. Are you sure you want to give it away?"

"I'm positive." I smile. "It never brought me the joy I see on your face. We'll find you some matching shoes. If you don't mind, I'll see where it needs taken in. You are smaller than I was even at my top office form."

She nods enthusiastically and I move to her side, where I pull in the fabric underneath her arm tight. To have such smooth, flawless skin again. "This won't take much. I found a lady downtown who does alterations. Tomorrow on your lunch hour you can take it there and I'll pay to have this fixed up for you."

We both return to my bedroom and she bounces from one leg to the other as I throw more options on the bed. After much consideration, she takes several tops and skirts. I fill two large bags with clothing, and all the leftovers I have.

"These," I jingle a *Welcome to Piney Falls* keyring with two keys, "are keys to my place. November made extra sets in case I wanted to pass them out randomly and see who experienced a cosmic pull to me. You are welcome to raid my refrigerator any time."

Piper walks down the front steps, but then pauses and turns around. "Thanks for inviting me over, and everything else. You're like the mom I wish I'd had."

I'm drawn to her too, but I don't have the words to express what I'm feeling. "Come over any time!" I repeat, trying not to show inappropriately motherly feelings.

Cosmo pulls into the driveway, here for our weekly movie night as I watch her walk up the steps of Vem's house. He kisses me gently on his way by and I pat his arm.

"How did your dinner go?" he asks, placing the leftover Cosmic Cranberry Cream Cheese Scones on the counter.

"Cos, you've got that poor girl so upset. She thinks you don't like her."

He pours himself a glass of wine and one for me and sits down on the couch. "She's right. I don't. You already know I don't trust her."

I curl up on the couch beside him, tucking my feet under me. "But why? She is such a sweet kid. She's been through so much. Don't you think she deserves the chance to learn the world can be a kind place?"

He stares at me with the coldness that used to send shivers down my spine. "Everybody deserves a chance. Some of us need the second or third. There's something about the girl that doesn't seem right to me. She's wound up tight, and sometimes those are the ones who snap without warning." His gaze softens and he pats my leg. "You know me, after living my life in that place I never figured out who to trust. Now I have to be wary of most everyone. That's why I asked you to look into the family. Did you come up with anything, by the way?"

I set my wine down on the table. I've struggled all day with whether I should tell him what I found out about Hawk Beechum. I don't want Cosmo losing his cool before I have everything I need to bring Hawk down. "Not a lot yet. Gladys says she can get access to Hawk's group through the dark web. Can you imagine that?" I stroke his neck softly.

"As far as Piper goes, neither she nor her brother were ever enrolled in public school. The boy did some kind of scouting program, but nothing else to speak of. Olivene does odd jobs, milking cows, painting houses, lots of funeral home work. It doesn't seem like enough to live on. And Hal hasn't had a job in three years."

"Hmmm. And these Broken Branch people? How do they find them?"

"Probably the same way I did. They have their Gladys." I take a sip. I never knew good wine until I moved here. "Gladys will try and get more information for me. But there is another way. I can visit—"

"No, Lanie. We're not going down that road."

"He probably doesn't even remember me."

Cosmo leans back and puts a hand under each armpit. "Oh, he remembers you. That guy doesn't forget a face. You don't want to put yourself in front of him or he'll never leave you alone. Is that what you want for you? For us?"

"Of course not. I won't contact Zion if you don't want me to."

"I don't want." He takes my hand and kisses it. "You mean too much to me. I can't afford to lose anyone else to that monster." Someday we won't have any secrets. On that day I'll feel safe when he says things like that.

Nightmares about Olivene and my mother keep me up half the night. When I finally fall asleep, it is so sound that my alarm doesn't wake me for over an hour. It is the constant buzzing of my phone that finally rousts me.

Cedar has been texting me for almost two hours.

What's going on? Are you okay? Nothing. She chided me once for calling her instead of texting, but sometimes there aren't options.

It rings just once. "Cedar? Are you hurt? What happened?"

There is only the sound of sobbing.

"You're worrying me. Tell me what it is or –"

"It's Hawk. He's gone."

15

PRESENT DAY

PINEY FALLS, OREGON

The Disappearance of Hawk Beechum

I pull up the chair beside her and lean in. I didn't even bother to put on makeup or day clothes; I'm sure it will hit the town gossip chain in less than an hour. "Oh Cedar, did he hurt you? I knew he was a bad seed."

She shakes her head as she delicately wipes her nose. "Not physically. Something was off with him while he was making dinner. He kept saying he'd been tricked, but we could figure it out. 'After dinner, we're reading the book together, Cedar,' he said."

"The one with the crazy manifesto? Cedar, the ideas are very similar to Zion's. He just twisted them to make himself come out on top." I put my arm on the back of her chair, touching her shoulders. "Is he really one of those crazy Broken Branch members?" I ask innocently.

She shakes her head. "Not THE Broken Branch. His own version. He started to explain it all and that's when the smoke alarm went off; his goulash didn't work in my inferior pans, he said. From that point on, things got weird."

Nothing about Hawk Beechum seems normal to me.

"As we drove to Cheese With Your Burger, he told me how Zion had gotten it all wrong. Piper wasn't the perfect person to lead them after all, it was him. Whatever happened today really upset and confused him, but he was positive about that. He had an epiphany during another eclipse, Zion came to him and told him so. Piper needed to see him as the leader of Broken Branch so the rest of the group would follow him too."

I pull her in close and hug her tightly. "You didn't know he was disturbed. He was a crush you never got the chance to explore and now you did."

"Yes, I suppose you're right." She blows her nose hard. "We had such an awful fight. I tried to change the subject after we sat down to eat. I wanted to tell him about our plans for the Fallen Branch property. I do love my job, Lanie!" Cedar laughs. "All of a sudden, he launched into this tirade about how no one would listen to him and that he came here for a purpose. It made me so uncomfortable." Her bottom lip quivers. "Everyone stared at us, but I didn't care. He started in about *his* big plans for the Fallen Branch land. I told him that was impossible. A light switched on in him and he exploded."

"Oh, Cedar." I ache for her.

She lifts her shoulders up with a deep breath and then lets them down slowly as she breathes. "He called me a traitor and shoved all of our food on the floor. Someone yelled, 'Fallen Branch freaks making a scene as usual!' from across the room. Emma threw us out of Cheese with Your Burger and threatened she could make phone calls that would ruin us both."

I'm going to warn Piper away from Emma. She sounds a little too immature.

"As we were walking out, I told him I never wanted to see him again. He grumbled about picking up his things from the motel and leaving town as he stomped past me." She wipes her nose one more time. "We never even had the chance to move in together."

"He got the message, then." We share a knowing glance and laugh. "Piper will be relieved he's gone. As much as it hurts, you're so much better off without him. It's for the best for everyone involved."

As much as Cedar needs support, we have to stay focused. "I hate to change topics, but we have little time to work. We've got Launch Lunch today and we need to make sure everything is on schedule at Fallen Branch."

"Oh, I forgot. Some realtor called. Someone else wants to look at the property."

"What? After all these years? Lance and I had an agreement!"

She shrugs. "That's what I said. Maybe they're curiosity seekers."

I remember back to my chance encounter with the realtor earlier in the week. "No, I know exactly who it is."

There is a loud commotion in front of the building and we both look to see what's going on. Cosmo opens the door, ashen faced. He is breathing hard and leans over and puts his hands on his knees.

"Cos? What's going on?" Cedar rushes to him, checking him over for injury.

He stands up again, looking up at the ceiling. "I'm fine, sis. It's Piper. Someone just tried to attack her."

"Hawk!" Cedar and I say in unison.

16

TEN YEARS AGO

Kansas City, Missouri

"Not with your gun, Sawyer. Use your hands. Knock them to the ground and then put your knuckles in their windpipe." Piper pulled the half-dummy from their CPR class over closer to demonstrate. She jammed her fist into the windpipe of Mo, the mascot of Kansas City Self Defense and Karate. Once she started, she couldn't seem to stop.

"Quit, Piper. This thing costs them thousands of dollars. Remember last time? You almost got us kicked out." Sawyer stood in front of his sister, shielding her actions from the rest of the class, who were now filtering out of the room.

"I can't," she whispered.

Unflappable, Sawyer ambled to the other side of the room, where Olivene was talking to Mr. Tanaka.

"You don't think shaving her head was cause for alarm?"

His face displayed no emotion. "No, ma'am. Kids, especially at this age, will find ways to rebel. You said yourself, your husband's job takes you all over the country. That kind of upheaval can cause a general sense of unease. It's good you enrolled her in my class. She's tough and this gives her a healthy outlet for her anger."

Sawyer transferred his weight from one leg to the other, trying to wait patiently for the conversation between the adults to end. Olivene would be livid about the cost of the damage. When Piper punched holes in the walls of the last home, she only stopped when her knuckles were so bloody they had to be wrapped in bandages for weeks.

"Do you want her to practice at home? She gets her studies done quickly. Both of my kids are fast learners. I don't allow them to watch much television, but they seem to find their way to a screen no matter how hard I try to tear them away." Olivene laughed a deep throaty laugh, placing her hand on Mr. Tanaka's well-defined bicep. Sawyer looked at the ground and tapped his mother's foot with his own.

Olivene snapped her head to her left. "Sawyer! You know better than to break into adult conversations!"

"Mom, I'm sorry to interrupt! Piper's causing problems." He pointed to his sister, who was punching Mo with such gusto they could hear her from across the large gymnasium. A group of observers formed; kids energized by the show of force. "Kill it! Kill it!" They chanted.

Olivene and Mr. Tanaka ran to the other side of the room. She shoved the enthusiastic group out of the way, two students at a time. Olivene bent down when she got to her daughter, but Mr. Tanaka shook his head furiously. Usually this opposition to her authority would cause Olivene to make a statement about how men never insert themselves in front of her, but this was his domain, not hers.

He lifted Piper by the elbows and away from the mannequin. Her small body was stiff and contorted, her eyes sharply focused on something far away. "Off now. You have better ways to control your anger. Miss Piper."

She struggled to release his grip, but he held her tightly. "Yeeeahhh!" Piper screamed.

Olivene watched silently.

Red-faced, Piper refused to give in. Mr. Tanaka held her patiently until her tantrum had subsided. The other children in the room watched in rapt silence. He set her down gently, changing his grip so he could face her. "Look me in the eye, Miss Piper."

Defiantly, she stared across the room.

"I can wait. I don't have another class until two."

Sawyer wiggled impatiently. He tried to walk out of the room with the other kids, but Olivene pulled him back. The one freckle-faced boy who spoke to him in class meandered by them, staring at Piper but saying nothing.

Finally, Piper let out a large breath. Her eyes softened and became recognizable once more.

"Where do we direct our anger when we're upset?"

"We put it into our moves. Controlled moves. Violence is for those who don't have control of their minds," she replied, repeating word-for-word what he told the special class of social outcasts and angry teens each week.

"That's right. Be respectful of your parents. Be respectful of others. I will see you next Saturday." He stood up and bowed. Piper did the same. He looked at Olivene and mouthed, "I'll send you a bill."

The three Moonlights walked outside and toward their car. "Did you have a good class today?" Olivene asked, as if her daughter hadn't just beaten an expensive piece of equipment to a pulp.

"I met a boy I liked. I think his name is Francis. Or Pete."

She straightened her *Kansas is for Lovers* t-shirt and pressed down the small nibs of hair on the side of her head.

Sawyer giggled. "You don't know their names?"

"You're an idiot," Piper retorted.

Olivene stopped. "What did you just say to your brother?"

"I said he's an idiot. Are you going to throw a fit right here? Like you do with Dad? I don't cry like he does." She tilted her head to the side.

"It's okay. I don't mind," Sawyer took his mother's hand and tried pulling her ahead. "You promised we could get ice cream today, Mom."

Olivene shook his hand loose. "This isn't about your dad and me. This is about you. How are you going to prepare for your place in the world if you don't at least pretend to respect the people around you?"

"HA. Ha ha ha." Piper put her hands in the air, pulling leaves from the trees as she passed under them. "You don't respect Dad. 'Shut up, Hal. You keep forgetting the big picture.' What is the big picture, Mom? That we move around until someone takes me and I die? Is that my place?"

Olivene rolled her eyes. "You will not die, Piper. If they wanted to kill you, they would have done it already. When we were in Houston, they accidentally pushed you in front of a car and then when they saw what was happening, that idiot jumped in front of the car to protect you. Do you think he would've risked his life to save you if he wanted you dead?"

"That was so gross. His arm bone was sticking out–"

"Shut up, Sawyer!"

Olivene shot her daughter another warning glance. "So many kids would love the life you have. You've seen ten times more of the country than most of them. You never have to worry about typical kid problems like schoolyard fights or teachers you hate. Remember your little friend, Hazel? How much that sweet little thing struggled? You'll never have the worries she did."

Piper shrugged. "You say that all the time. Like she's your kid. I don't even remember that stupid girl."

Olivene slapped her daughter across the face, something she'd never done before. All three of them stood in shock, waiting to see what happened next. Piper's hand went to her cheek as she ran from her mother and brother. The one thing that was highest on the list of prohibited activities in the Moonlight family. Since the only public outing she had was going to her karate class, Piper did not understand where to go. It made her angry that she didn't know how to get home, if that's what it was. She walked for three blocks, alternating between crying and screaming.

A woman with curlers in her hair stood behind a chain-link fence with her hands on her hips.

"Are you okay, young man? Do I need to call someone?"

Piper shook her head. She reached the corner and a familiar dark blue sedan pulled into her path, blocking her from going any further. Olivene rolled down the window. "Get in, now! This is a reckless move on your part!"

Piper stood at a crossroads. If she did what her mother said, Olivene won again. But it was getting chilly and she had nowhere else to go. No friends, no life. She got in the back seat and slammed the door shut.

They drove seven blocks to Phil's Creamery, where Piper order three scoops of Rocky Road, knowing full well her mother would lecture her on healthy eating and what that meant to a body that had to prepare for a long and strong life. The three sat in silence, each lost in deep concern.

"What well-behaved boys you have," a woman at a neighboring table commented.

Piper turned around and glared. "I'm NOT a boy."

The woman rose and stood beside their table. "Oh, my. I had no idea. I saw your shaved head and thought... I'm so sorry. Are you in treatment? My nephew is recovering from cancer, too."

"My daughter is healthy. She made the choice to shave her head. As a way to upset me." Olivene's glare towards her daughter went unnoticed.

Piper took an especially large bite of ice cream, making sure to chew with her mouth wide open.

"Ohhh... I get it." The lady winked. " Well, she'll grow out of it. Before you know it, she'll have hair down to her waist and be looking at prom dresses!"

"People on the run don't go to prom."

"Piper!" Olivene and Sawyer said in unison.

The lady gathered her things and walked toward the door. "You've got a real challenge on your hands," she commented.

Olivene raised her hand in the air in acknowledgement. She waited until they were on the way home before tackling the ever-present issue. "I don't know what to do with you. I'd say you know better, but anymore, I'm not sure that you do."

Piper stared at the happy families playing in their yards as they drove by. Sawyer put his lips up to her ear and hummed his favorite song from the radio, *Look on the Bright Side*. She punched him in the shoulder, hard. "You're such an annoying person. You're thirteen and you still act like an infant." As usual, he didn't react.

Hal was waiting in the yard, raking up the few leaves that had fallen as they drove into the driveway.

"I found this handy piece of equipment in the garage."

He put his hand out for a high five. Sawyer obliged as Piper continued by him. "Rough day?" He looked at Olivene, shading his eyes from the late afternoon sun.

She sighed. "The usual. She went crazy on the CPR dummy. The teacher had to pull her off."

"He's so strong, he lifted her up by her elbows!" Sawyer jumped off the porch step into the small pile of leaves. "I want to be that strong too!"

"Why is the door locked?" Piper jiggled the doorknob and then did it again. She began kicking the door repeatedly.

"Piper!" Olivene called.

"Stop it, sweetheart!" Hal jumped on the porch and tried pulling her away. She smacked him in the face.

"Leave me alone!" she screamed.

Hal let go of his daughter and touched the red welt on the side of his face. "That's not how we act. I know you're angry –"

Olivene shoved Hal out of the way and grabbed Piper by the neck. She pulled her to the porch swing and pushed her down. "Do you want the neighbors to come running? And then what will happen? They'll look at my crazy daughter who shaved her head when she didn't get her way and start asking questions you don't want to answer."

"Why am I crazy? Because I didn't want to leave Illinois? Because I want to be a regular kid for a while?" Tears that she knew were only the product of weak people began running down her face. "All I wanted was some time to be like everyone else."

"Oh, babe. You're not normal. You're a Moonlight. That makes you special."

She rolled her eyes. "That's crap. We're just a dumb family from a dumb commune that fell apart."

Hal sat down beside her. "Did we ever tell you the story of how we came to be Moonlights?"

"I know!" Sawyer wriggled in beside his father. "We are Moonlights because when Piper was born, it was a lunar eclipse. Zion gave all the babies first names, but he wanted our family to have a special last name, too."

"That's right, son. Partially, at least." Hal patted his son on the leg. "But what you don't know is that not everyone is bestowed a new last name. That right is usually just reserved for royalty. We were the only family allowed to live together, treated respectfully every single day. Zion, for all of his faults, was a clever man. He could see the Moonlight family should always be held in high regard."

Piper looked away. "What does it matter what Zion thought? He's dead. There's no more Fallen Branch. Just Broken Branch crazies who follow us everywhere. That doesn't make us special. It makes us hunted like animals."

"I promise you, that will end. The day will come when they won't come after you anymore. They'll grow old and tired." Hal wrinkled his brow.

"You've got a very special position in this world, Piper."

"Both of us do," Sawyer chimed in.

Olivene smiled. "Yes, son. Both of you. Maybe you started off in a cult, but all of this adversity has only made you strong. You just have to get through these awkward years first. If you want to be average, you'll be disappointed because Amaris Moonlight's luminescence shines through. That I promise you."

"It's Piper Moonlight."

"Okay," Olivene sighed. "You win this round."

After dinner, Piper slunk to her bedroom and sat in front of her mirror, staring at her perfectly shaped round head. The hair stylist mentioned that many people who shave their heads hated the results. "When they realize they have slightly misshapen noggins," she commented, "they regret what they've done and resort to whatever they can to cover it up. Not you, honey. Your head is perfect. Put a bow around it and celebrate yourself."

Piper plucked a purple ribbon from the drawer and tied it around her head. The last time they moved, she took some makeup from her mother's box and hid it. She pulled the mascara from the drawer and applied it lightly before adding a touch of dark red lipstick. "I could pass for sixteen," she said proudly to the defiant image in the mirror.

"My queen. Amaris. You don't need makeup. You are perfect to us as you are."

How did she forget to check her closet when she came upstairs?

Instead of screaming or waiting for him to come for her, she grabbed him by the arm and flipped him on the ground, putting her foot in the middle of his body. She brought her other knee to his chest and flopped, hard, on top of him, falling forward, inches from his face as he expelled air

For the first time, she was in an intimate position with one of her potential abductors. His eyes were blue. His pupils were wide and she saw deep down, he was frightened, or maybe confused. He couldn't be over twenty, the age of the karate assistant. It felt good to squeeze his neck. His arms flailed helplessly.

17

PRESENT DAY

Piney Falls, Oregon

"Are you sure it was Hawk? It's an obvious move, attacking Piper when he's been in such close contact with Cedar."

Cedar nudges me.

"I meant nothing, Cedar, other than that Hawk has spent a lot of time with you lately." My face is bright red. They aren't children, but Cosmo is very protective and thinking about his sister doing things with Hawk Beechum always sets him off. "What happened, Cos?"

He wipes his sweaty brow on his brown t-shirt. "She was finishing up the sandwiches for your lunch meeting. I was cutting apples. There was a loud noise at the back door, like a cat got in a terrible scrape. Piper ran for the back door. The next thing I know, she's screaming 'fire!' By the time I made my way through all the catering boxes, she was lying on the ground, holding her head. I saw someone running off. A chubby goon, all in black. Even with his face covered, I knew who it was."

"Did you run after him?"

"I did." Cosmo rubs his hands together. "I almost had him. And then this car with tinted windows comes out of nowhere. Someone reached out and grabbed him by the front of the shirt, while the vehicle was still moving. It was like I was watching a movie; I stood there in shock. When I got my senses back it was too late - they were already rounding the corner. The things you never figure you'll see in a small town."

An ugly feeling slides through my chest, permeating the all of my extremities. "Is she all right?"

Cosmo nods. "Just a little shaken. I told her she could take the rest of the day off if she wants. She said she'd have nowhere to go but November's house, and you know she's performing some kind of naked voodoo, figuring she's alone."

I'm a little insulted she decided not to use my key. "I need to check on her. Can you handle things for the lunch, Cedar? I'll be back as soon as I can."

"Sure. I can do it." She looks at me a bit helplessly. "Maybe. You know more about this than I do."

"You'll do fine. Go over the notes before you begin. And tell your brother what happened."

"Cedar? Did something happen to you, too?"

She rushes to her brother and dissolves in his arms. "Oh, Cos."

LANIE ANDERS DOES NOT RUN. When I was in the 6th grade, my mother upgraded my Tulip Sloan outfits, from the calf-length formal dresses to silk floor-length dresses for my mall performances. Just like Tulip wore for her formal interviews. They were a low-cut style that was incredibly inappropriate for a girl at the tender age of ten and downright embarrassing. My long, thick, honey-colored hair had been painstakingly styled with "victory rolls" on the sides, pinned with over thirty pins on top of my head I looked just like Tulip Sloan in all of her publicity stills from 1939.

During one event, someone thought it might be funny to pull the fire alarm. Everyone, including my mother, ran out of the building, leaving me to fight my way in a dress fitted to my legs, wearing high heels. I tripped and fell several times, ripping the dress. My hair fell on one side. I was crying as I stumbled outside, unable to block out the giggles of my classmates who huddled in the comfort of their small groups. By the time I got to the parking lot, I was no longer the replica of a forties star. I was a dirty, forlorn child needing comfort from her mother. *Don't just stand there, Lanie. Run to me. Just like Tulip Sloan in* Pursued. *Scream and wave your hands around.* She got in the car and locked the door. She refused to let me in until I performed to her specifications.

As I scurry down the street, I envision those ugly times. I'm not completely opposed to running now. I should be over my mother's damage. But, as hard as I try, I can't bring my feet to move that quickly, even if Piper is in danger.

The *Shut for Now* sign is up over the door, so I rattle the knob until Doris comes and lets me in. "Where's Piper? Is she all right?"

"Got some ice on her head. Didn't want to see the doctor though. She's in Cosmo's office." She ushers me to the back of the store, where Piper squirms on Cosmo's swiveling brown office chair, one knee bouncing up and down nervously. She is holding the ice pack on her head and whispering something.

"Piper! Are you okay, honey?" I bend down in front of her and she hugs me tightly.

"Oh, Lanie. I was supposed to be safe. Everyone promised to protect me here." Her body is shaking against mine. I press her firmly to my chest until the movement slows, as much to repair my memories as to comfort her.

"We need to call the police. I'm sure Cosmo got the license plate number." I smooth her hair, taking care not to touch the side she is icing.

She pulls away abruptly. "No cops. We don't involve police. Then there will be questions and I've had too many fake IDs. My parents, too. Promise me, Lanie. You won't call them, right?"

There has to be something I can do. "Can you tell me exactly what happened?"

"I thought someone injured an animal. I should have remembered. They pulled this one when we were in Mankato, Minnesota. I think they have some kind of app on a phone and a speaker. Anyway, I ran out there and as soon as I opened the door, the guy was standing there with a bag he tried to throw over my head. I know self-defense, so I punched him in the throat. He fell back and I kicked him in the groin. My mistake was thinking he was down. I turned to run in and get Cos. That's when he got up and cut a piece of my hair."

"Your hair? I still can't get past that." Broken Branch members *share locks of her hair for good fortune.* Hawk and his friends are deeply disturbed.

"They took Zion's prophecy and twisted it, deciding to make me their lucky charm. That's what my mom has always said, anyway."

"Do they cut your hair every time?"

She smooths down the side of her hair closest to me. "Not every time. I never knew when they would have scissors. At one point I shaved my head. Mom said I was being defiant. When I let it grow back, I decided THAT was me being defiant."

I smile over the top of her head. "You're such a brave young lady."

"I suppose," her voice quivers, "I'll have to move again. Nowhere is safe."

I take her hands in mine. "Look at me."

She is staring at the bare cement floor. Eventually, she lifts her violet eyes to meet mine. Her knee slows and then stops.

"You are not going anywhere. This is where you belong. If you won't go to the police, we'll take other measures to help you. Cosmo will have some good ideas, I'm sure. I'll take you to my house and you can rest there until Vem's done with her – whatever she's doing right now. I'll call her to make sure."

She nods.

"Before we go, can you tell me a little about the person who attacked you? Do you remember anything about him or her?"

"It was definitely a 'him.' He had an earthy smell that was familiar." She pauses, staring at the dozens of notes clipped to the shelf above Cosmo's desk. "I think I've smelled that before. He has attacked me more than once."

We drive to my house in silence. After I get Piper settled on the couch with the television remote and every bit of comfort food from my cupboards, I return to check on Cedar.

Cosmo is serving the last person their boxed lunch, and Cedar is stumbling through the presentation. "We'll be bringing in an etiquette expert for the next Launch Lunch. You'll be so happy to have someone tell you what to say, so you don't have to worry you've said the wrong thing to a tourist."

A smattering of chuckles spreads throughout the room. "Who says we need lessons in etiquette?"

"Haven't kicked my mother-in-law to the curb yet," Someone yells from the back of the room. "That sounds polite."

Cedar's cheeks are crimson. I want her to do this on her own, but it's apparent she needs some backup.

"You'll know exactly what to say to your mother-in-law the next time she drives you crazy," I move to Cedar's side. "A cranky tourist can be a lot like a mother-in-law. Dual purpose." I look at the notes. Cedar has been shuffling them out of nervousness as she's done when we practiced.

"Thank goodness you're here, Lanie," she whispers. "This is too much for me."

"You're going to finish. I'm just here to support you."

All the color drains from her face. "What?"

"You've practiced this for weeks. You probably know the information better than I do. Just keep talking. You'll be fine." I wink at her - the one thing I promised myself I'd never do to another soul after I left my marketing job. "I'll be in the back, with Cosmo. You've got this."

Cosmo is pouring lemonade and iced tea in the corner. As I walk back to greet him, I can hear Cedar's voice, more confident each minute. When I reach him, he leans over to give me a peck on the cheek.

"Piper's back at my place," I whisper. "She's shaken up, but I think she'll be fine. She wouldn't let me call the police.

I told her she could go back to Vem's house when she was ready."

He hands the last lemonade to a lady I recognize from the beauty salon and then turns to face me. "She's not staying with that kook. The apartment next to mine is empty. I'll put some furniture in it and move her over there. I need to keep an eye on her."

What a relief they won't be in the same place. I force the smile off my face. "You'll be in danger too. Can't we get law enforcement involved?"

"Fallen or Broken Branch—no matter what part of that system they follow, they all think the same. They don't trust authority. I'm sure Olivene has pounded that into the girl's head. Those walls are paper thin. I'll know every time she sneezes."

"Did Cedar tell you about Hawk?"

He squints. "I'm going over there when I'm done here. That punk better hope my aim is off."

"If you hurt him, we'll never get information from him. Beyond Gladys, this is the only way to figure that situation out."

He shrugs non-commitally.

"We'll go together then. But if things get rough, you wait in the car."

There's no way I'm going to let him do something that might get him arrested. After Cedar finishes her presentation, we help her clean up quickly. "We're going over to Hawk's motel room," I announce.

Cedar's mouth falls open. "Are you sure?"

"Oh, I'm sure," Cosmo affirms.

"He wanted me to help him move his things into my place. He said the first act of trust was giving me his key." She hands me the key reluctantly. "It was too fast."

"Probably a good idea if you don't go, sis. I'd hate for us to find something else upsetting."

I know he's thinking he may end up hurting Hawk if we find him. "The purpose of this visit isn't to discuss your relationship. We want to know why he's trying to hurt Piper."

She looks at her brother and then at me. "You're right. Let me know what you find."

By the time we reach the Spruce Bark Motel, Ed Junior has the cleaning cart in front of the door and is half-heartedly wiping things down. He salutes Cosmo when we enter and backs up against the wall. It amuses me that some Townies are still a little afraid of former Fallen Branch members, especially Cosmo.

"Has Hawk been here?"

"Haven't seen him. I'm goin' fishin' soon. If you two need the room, can I go ahead and leave? You know, so I don't have to wait around for you to finish up your business?"

I blush. "There's nothing going on that you—"

There is a slight smile on Cosmo's face. "We'll be really loud. I mean, REALLY loud. It's probably best you leave. The missus gets embarrassed."

It takes Ed Junior less than a minute to pull off his gloves and push the cart away.

I look around the barren, olive-green-themed room. "How does someone travel with so little? One bag and two changes of clothing? It doesn't make sense."

"He's always on the run. You travel light when you don't want to be noticed." Cosmo pulls two shirts and a pair of dark jeans out of his bag. At the bottom is a book, the one he was telling Cedar about. "Feel like some light reading?"

He hands me the well-worn copy of *Gaummond's Essays on Renewing the World through the Eclipse*. "Sure. I took a speed-reading course in high school. Tulip Sloan wasn't much of a reader beyond movie scripts, so I thought it would distinguish me from her. My mother didn't care." I start to walk outside, but Cosmo isn't moving. "What are you going to do? Are you going to stay here and wait for him to come home?"

Cosmo is silent.

"This doesn't sound good to me, Cos. You're no better than him and all the other Broken Branchers if you handle things like that. Come with me to tell Piper she's moving to the apartment. She'll probably love it."

He shakes his head. "I won't wait long. I have a business to run."

18

EIGHT YEARS AGO

Scottsbluff, Nebraska

The grit in her teeth was the one thing that took extra adjustment. Living on the outskirts of this small, treeless town, there were few obstacles to block the constant wind, but three large poplar trees in the backyard of the two-story brick home offered a brief respite from the summer sun. Piper took a sip of her iced tea, picking tiny bits of blossoms from her glass. There were worse things, worse places.

"Sawyer? Will you bring me some carrots and dip?" The sound of the wind chimes, up three notes and then down, sometimes drove her crazy. There was no answer. "Sawyer? Are you messing with me?" He had recently begun hiding and trying to scare her. An irritating trait for an almost-grown boy of fifteen.

"Okay, I'm getting out of the hammock. If you are standing around the corner, you'll really get it! I don't care if you cry this time." Still no answer.

She swung to the side and put both feet on the ground, knocking over her tea on the way up. Luckily, the glass didn't break. She chose not to pick up her glass and stepped over the wet wood. One of her many passive-aggressive swipes at her mother, at least that's what Hal called it.

She opened the screen door and stepped into the massive kitchen. "Sawyer? C'mon. You know the best gag is one that's over in thirty seconds or less."

After she shaved her head, the Firestarters resorted to more twisted tactics. They started cutting her clothes; taking a portion of her sleeve or a chunk of her shirt decidedly close to her neck. They'd never tried to take Sawyer before, but each disturbing act topped the last.

Bats rested at strategic points around the house. She quietly opened the pantry door and pulled the closest bat from the bottom shelf. Piper crept up the wooden stairs, pausing only when she heard the curtains blowing in the landing window. Olivene wouldn't allow open windows, she'd have to remember to close it.

When she reached a bedroom, she paused before opening the door. She entered each one, swirling around fast with the bat to hit whatever might be in her way. Only once did she hit an actual dresser item, Olivene's Kansas City Chiefs signed helmet. Piper paused momentarily to view the scuff mark on the side. It would be another reason for an argument to erupt tonight.

She opened her door, the empty beige walls assaulting her senses. The Moonlights stopped bothering with decorations. When she was angry, that was one of the things that upset her the most. Piper Moonlight was a nobody with no personality. How could she be destined for great things?

After searching every bedroom thoroughly, a thought came to mind. "Dad? Was that you? I won't be mad."

Hal didn't move with them this time, choosing to stay in Santa Fe. He promised he would come soon. Olivene called him weak and stupid and even though she didn't want to be without him, Piper secretly agreed with her mother.

Carefully, she walked back down the ornate staircase. She reached the bottom, wondering what she should do next. Call her mother? That would cause unnecessary panic. She might decide they have to move again and Piper was rather enjoying the barren plains.

She grabbed the doorknob, and held it for a moment. The front yard was always risky, but they were out in the country, with one neighbor. The knob turned on its own and she jumped back, pulling the bat up, ready to pummel whatever was on the other end.

"Piper? Don't be mad."

"Sawyer? Where the hell have you been?"

She pulled him inside and hugged him tightly. "Stupid kid. You know better."

"It was our fault, actually."

She glanced up, surprised to see a blonde woman and a young boy standing on the porch.

"We're the Newsoms. Chiara and Chas. Your next-door neighbors." The petite woman, who had a large, deep purple birthmark extending from her left ear to her jaw, offered her hand.

Piper looked at her with skepticism. She didn't look like any of the Firestarters but they could be sneaky. In Louis-ville, one of them pretended to be a door-to-door makeup saleswoman. "Piper Moonlight." She stared at the outstretched hand. Handshakes were for normal people.

"We just moved here from Denver. My husband is a doctor at the hospital. It was so nice of your brother to spend time with Chas. He's been extremely lonely." She ruffled her son's hair lovingly.

Piper stared at her brother. How could he be so careless? "Mmm hmm. He's friendly like that." A devilish thought popped into her head. "Do you...want to come in?" Olivene would not be happy about this. Or anything else that had transpired this afternoon.

"We'd love to. Just a few minutes anyway."

Piper stepped aside and guided them to the living room, avoiding Sawyer's look of concern.

"Do you want some tea?"

"Sure, I'd love some. I'm rather addicted to the stuff every summer." Chiara pulled her the straps of her thin cotton top up on her shoulders.

"Do you want to see my cars, Chas? I've got three different collections."

Sawyer's voice recently deepened an octave, making him sound like more of a man than his father.

"Can I, Mom?" Chas turned his curly blond head to his mother.

"Okay, but just for a few minutes. I'm sure Sawyer has more important things to do than entertain a little boy."

They ran up the stairs, chattering loudly as they went. Piper poured two glasses of tea, handing one to Chiara.

"What brings your family to town?" Chiara asked.

"My mom's business. She sells insurance." Piper thought for a moment trying to remember the backstory for this move. Yes, that's right. Insurance.

"We'll have to learn the town together then. It doesn't seem like there's much to do for someone your age. That has to be a challenge."

Piper nodded and took a sip of her tea.

"It's so nice of your brother to spend time with my Chas.

Few boys his age would take an interest in a little kid like that."

"He's very friendly. He was the most popular kid in his Salmon Scout troop. He wanted to stay—"Piper took another sip of tea.

"What grade is he in?"

"High school. We home school, so he takes classes from several levels." This was getting uncomfortable. Maybe Olivene had a point when she said making friends was a liability and not worth the time.

"You've got to have some interests outside of school, Piper. Tell me what you like to do."

She searched her mind. Most days these made up personality traits came up quickly. *Horseback riding, acting classes, weightlifting...*

"I like to paint. I took a painting class last year."

Chiara leaned forward in her seat. "Are you serious? I'm an artist. Just unpacked all of my supplies. I'd love to have a partner in crime. We could paint that gorgeous monument. I've been reading a lot about the history behind this place. The monument and—"

"My mom wouldn't like me spending time at your place." Piper squirmed uncomfortably in her chair.

Chiara pushed a chunk of highlighted blonde hair behind her ear. "I'd be glad to talk to her if you want. I taught art classes in Denver before Chas was born."

Piper shrugged non-committally.

"Tell you what, we can make this a legitimate situation. I'll be your teacher. It can count toward your credits for high school."

It would be nice to do something that involved human interaction. Those months of therapy made her realize she desired friendship. Playing dolls with Hazel was the last time she felt free and alive. At least that's what Olivene always told her. The therapist agreed it was most likely true.

"Okay. But I need to talk to my mom first. She can be stubborn about new ideas."

Chiara stood. "Sure. You let me know, okay? Can you get my son? I forgot I need to go to the store before dinner. There's not much here in the way of variety. It'll probably be spaghetti again."

Although she spent hours rehearsing her speech, It wasn't as hard as she thought to convince Olivene she needed art lessons.

"That sounds like a good idea. It'll give you something to do. Much safer than getting a job like you wanted to do." Olivene opened the cupboard and took out a box of crackers.

Piper's heart sank. Another boring meal of crackers and cheese. "I'll run over and tell her. I'll only be a minute." She moved quickly, so her mother wouldn't have time to change her mind.

When she got to the end of the next long driveway, she knocked excitedly on the large knocker of the two-story Victorian-style home. From the few drives around town, it appeared these large homes only dotted the area on outside of town. Mostly occupied by doctors, Olivene told them.

A tall, red-haired man with a hint of a beard and kind, blue eyes opened the door. "You must be Piper. I've heard all about you. Come in!" He smelled like cloves and something musky. "I'm Steven, by the way." Piper stood in the doorway just inside the door, unsure how to proceed. She hadn't thought about what came after the door opened. "We don't bite, Piper." Chiara called from the kitchen.

"Follow me." Steven motioned.

She walked down a small hallway, resisting the urge to put her hands in a defensive position.

At the end of the hall, the house opened up into a very large kitchen and dining area where rich, savory smells enveloped her. Chiara was wearing an apron that said, *Artist by Day, Chef by Night*. Her cheeks were flushed; she was almost pretty. She looked up and smiled. "Piper! How nice!"

"What are you making?" Her stomach growled.

"Spaghetti ala Chiara. It's got all sorts of surprises. Mostly whatever I can find in the store. Do you want to stay for dinner?"

The words came out of her mouth before she could stop them. "Okay."

She sat on a stool and watched everything Chiara did; Crafting homemade garlic knots, rolling fresh-smelling dough into a rope before twisting it into a chain and painting it with melted butter and garlic salt.

Chiara, lost in thought, looked over at Piper as she was beginning the last one. "Do you want to try?"

Olivene had never spent any time teaching her to cook. When Piper stood helplessly and stared at the dough, Chiara took her hands and guided her. "See how easy that is?"

Next, Chiara showed her how to make a vinaigrette for the salad and finally she grated cheese for the pasta. They sat down at the table and passed dishes the way it was always done on television. The food was so much better than anything she'd eaten before. Ever since Hal left, there was no conversation and barely any dinner.

"Do you know why the man got hit by the biker every day?" Steven put his hand lightly on Piper's. She wanted it to stay there forever.

"He was stuck in a vicious cycle."

"Good one, Dad!"

Chiara clapped. "Best one all week, dear."

Piper couldn't stop staring at his open, friendly face.

There was a knock at the front door and Piper looked up at the large, octagon-shaped clock. Seven o'clock. Her heart sank. "It's probably my mom. I didn't tell her I was staying."

She stood. There hadn't been such an act of mutiny since Kansas City.

Steven put his hand on her shoulder, causing something electric to run down her spine. "It's all right. I'll talk to your mother."

Against her better judgement, Piper sat back down. It would only be a matter of minutes before her mother made a scene, ruining everything in her perfect fantasy family. She shoveled more spaghetti into her mouth as quickly as she could, trying to revel in these last few moments of culinary joy.

Steven returned to the table with a smile. "Everything was fine. I explained we insisted you stay for dinner, and being the polite young lady you are, you agreed. We've got your art lessons set up for tomorrow afternoon and I'll walk you home after we're done eating."

Piper smiled at him in admiration. "My mom rarely likes people."

Steven chuckled, a low sexy laugh. "Well, I am a doctor. I have to find a way to deal with difficult patients every day."

She never imagined she'd fall in love with someone who had red hair. In the romance books she read, all the male leads had dark hair and mysterious faces. Steven had a pale complexion and a kind, open face without a hint of subterfuge.

After finishing two helpings of Chiara's secret-recipe brownies, Chiara showed Piper her studio, a large, bright yellow room with lots of windows. There were paintings of flowers, mountains and some with faceless people walking down busy streets.

"I can feel the joy in your work." It wasn't just her paintings, it was the entire home. A real home and a real family. She ached with jealousy.

Steven knocked on the door frame. "I negotiated your release, but if we don't have you back soon, you'll never have the trust of the warden again."

He had no idea how true that statement was. On the way home, sweat ran down her neck from the mugginess of irrigation filling the summer air. At least it was dark enough he wouldn't be able to see.

"You'll really like art lessons. Chiara's talent in the kitchen is only exceeded by her painting. Piper Moonlight will be a changed woman after that experience."

Piper giggled.

"Did I say something funny?"

"No...it's just...I've never heard anyone talk like that before. She's lucky to have this life. And someone like you."

"Aww." Steven patted her back. "That's so kind of you. And you're right. She's damn lucky. If it weren't for me, she'd be living in a condo in the middle of a bustling city with a vibrant nightlife and lots of friends."

Piper stared at him.

"Now THAT was a joke."

She dreamt about Steven that night. It was wrong to feel that way but she couldn't help it. The next day and the weeks after, she couldn't wait for her art lesson. Chiara was unlike anyone she'd known before. Not that she knew many people. When they finished painting, they'd clean up and Chiara would show her how to bake. Espresso macaroons, tender sugar cookies and fluffy lemon cake. It wasn't art that filled her soul; it was baking. Chiara sent her home with all of her recipes.

On the days she had permission, she brought Sawyer with her and he would play cars with Chas for hours.

"I don't want to hurt your feelings, but your brother needs more socialization." Chiara said one day as she massaged the dough, motioning to the rolling pin they would use for their cinnamon rolls.

"He does. We've moved around so much, he hasn't had time to cultivate friendships." It was fun to use the words she'd read in her many books when having a conversation with an actual person. If they weren't right, Chiara said nothing.

"I'm sure there are lots of clubs he could join. I've been looking into swimming lessons for Chas. A young man his age should be out if not causing trouble, at least thinking about it. That goes for you too, Piper. You need to be around people your own age, thinking about college."

Piper blushed. "It's complicated."

"There's nothing complicated about doing what's best for your children," Chiara replied firmly. "There, you can roll these out now. I'll melt some butter."

That evening, she approached Olivene with rolls smothered in thick cream cheese frosting. "Try these, Mom. We made them today after my art lesson."

Olivene took one in her hand and eyed it from every angle. "You did this? I'm surprised. You've never shown an interest in baking before. At least anything that didn't come from a box." She took a bite and sat back in the recliner. "Good. You're developing a valuable skill." She closed her eyes.

"Mom, do you think I should spend some time with kids

my age? As a part of the learning process? So I can be ready for what's ahead."

Olivene sat up abruptly and set the plate down on the end table. "Where is this coming from? Don't you remember what happened in Kansas City? The mess from being involved with others?"

Piper pulled her arms around her chest. "I had therapy. I — got better. I understood what you were trying to do for me. For us."

She stuffed another bite of roll into her mouth. "If this woman persists in causing problems, we'll have to end these classes. I can't see the benefit outweighing the risk here. I don't want to make you feel bad, but all of this, the extreme life we live, it's not for me. It's for you."

Piper turned to walk away, knowing there was no use in arguing with her mother. "You should see them together. They laugh and have fun. Steven is the perfect father and husband," she mumbled.

"Nobody is perfect. Underneath the surface, they're struggling just as much as the rest of us!" Her mother called after her.

"Is this brown enough?" Piper carefully pulled the pan of sugar cookies from the oven and held them in front of Chiara.

Chiara glanced backward from her corner of the kitchen where she was stirring pink frosting. "Perfect! Set the timer for three minutes and then we'll take them off the pan. They'd stopped doing art altogether, once Chiara realized Piper was more interested in baking. Even though no words were exchanged, she seemed to understand the closeness of the walls in Piper's world.

"We're going to Denver to see family next weekend. I was thinking about asking your mother if you could go along. I could use the help with Chas. He hates car travel and would love someone to keep him occupied."

Tears formed in her eyes. "I'm sorry. I don't mean to be melodramatic. That's a sign of weakness. I'd love to go, but my mom will never let me."

Chiara dropped the spoon and pulled Piper in close for a hug. "Your mom is stern, but she's not unreasonable. I bet if I send Steven over and he asks nicely, she'll say yes. You need to enjoy life a little."

Piper nodded and wiped her eyes. "We aren't like normal people."

"Of course you are. You just have to move around because of your dad's job. You haven't told me much about him, but I'm sure he's—"

"We're on the run," she blurted. "We always have to move so the Firestarters don't get us."

Chiara's chin dropped.

"Forget what I said. I didn't mean it! I didn't mean it!" Piper ran to the door where her jacket hung on the ornately carved coat hook Steven gave Chiara for their anniversary.

"Don't go! We won't talk about it anymore, I promise!" Chiara begged.

Piper ran all the way home and then stood outside, letting the dusty wind dry her tears. At least she'd have a little time before her mother got home. She sat in her bedroom listening to music for hours. Trying to make the feelings go away. She wasn't strong if she let herself feel them.

She didn't even make dinner as she'd been doing excitedly every night since Chiara began instructing her. After dark, she heard a noise in the front yard. She opened her window a slit and recognized Steven's voice. It wasn't the lighthearted man who told her a new joke every time she saw him. It was a stern man.

"We can contact authorities if we need. Chiara is rightly concerned — "

No. No. No.

He was ruining everything. This perfect man who knew how to do everything right was making the biggest mistake of his life.

She heard the door slam a few minutes later, and her mother tromped up to her room. As usual, she entered without permission. "How dare that man question my parenting? And how dare you tell them ANYTHING? I thought I'd taught you to be stronger than that? After all the sacrifices I've made for you, are you a weak child?"

Piper threw herself on her bed, sobbing into her pillow. "Leave me alone!"

"You know what comes next. You also know why. We could have avoided it." She closed the door quietly.

"I don't want to do this!" she sat up and screamed. "Do you hear me? I don't want to do this! I want to be normal!"

The next three days were so quiet she felt dead. Maybe she was. She tried baking cookies, letting the eggs come to room temperature the way Chiara taught her. They tasted like dust in her mouth.

Piper was out on the patio on the fourth day, clearing the last of the nasturtiums out of the planter she'd begged her mother for in May. There was a knock at the door. She ignored it, but Sawyer opened it anyway. A policeman appeared in the doorway to the kitchen.

"Piper Moonlight? We're looking into the disappearance

of your neighbors, Chiara and Chas Newsom. We'd like to ask you a few questions."

She turned around slowly, giving herself time to display the vacant face she'd mastered so well.

"Yes?"

19

PRESENT DAY

Gladys Talk

"Cedar, I don't believe he's coming back. Your brother has been watching that hotel room like, well, a hawk. Nobody has been there since your argument. He tried and failed to kidnap Piper and now he has to figure out some other way to start his new cult."

Her blank stare is a clear indication she hasn't heard a thing I've said. This conversation happens at least once an hour and it is has become tiresome. "I'm going to take a walk and stretch my legs a bit."

I don't wait for her response.

After walking with purpose around the block twice, I continue on, until I reach the public records building. I have the overwhelming urge to share all of the past two days' events with Gladys.

"All a bunch of gypsies, is what they are," Gladys removes her swollen feet from the top of the desk and her black, orthopedic shoes land on the floor with a clunk. "Documents are all printed out for you. I've got more searchin' that can be done and plenty of time to do it."

Shame on me. I'm becoming a small town gossip, no better than anyone else here. "How are you so good at this?"

"We're practically family now. I'm sure he wouldn't mind my telling you." She leans forward and places a brown-spotted hand on my arm. "My son-in-law, Boysie Lumquest has been in law enforcement all of his life. He should've retired by now, but he loves it too much. Taught me how to do all of this. Got sick of me buggin' him about the cult and told me to do it for myself. 'I have a life, Mom. I don't have time for your foolishness.' He didn't realize I'm like a dog with a bone when it comes to nonsense on a stick. Both he and my daughter thought I'd get tired of it and go back to looking in my neighbor's basement with binoculars." She chuckles. "They underestimated me, Boysie and Sandra. Thought I'd give up. Do you wanna hear how I broke them?"

I shrug.

"Up at two, up at four. I started calling them every night. Every time an old lady makes a nighttime call, they don't know if I'm on my way to the grave, so they've got to answer. It only took two weeks of calling, every time I got up to move my bones or other nonsense. Boysie knocked on my door one morning with big bags under his eyes and offered to teach me everything about research." She cocks her head to the side and smirks. "Never underestimate the power of an old lady's bladder."

I stifle a giggle. "Or the power of you, Gladys."

She shoves a thick pile towards me and I thumb through the pages. "This is an impressive list. They lived in forty-two locations that I can count. Why are they so afraid of these

'Firestarters' as Piper calls them? If they stayed in one place and let the police handle things, Piper would be safe."

Gladys scoffs. "Oh, honey. When the Fallen Branchers were talking about taking over our little town, they wanted to abolish the police force and set up their own."

Scanning the documents further, there is something that becomes obvious. "In each location, there were people who came into contact with the family. In Kansas City, Piper took karate classes. In New Orleans, Sawyer did Skipper Scouts. Someone has to know something."

"There you go, Lanie." Gladys squeezes her chin. "You just put that detective hat on and get to work. We all depend on you."

I blush at this unexpected compliment. "I'm flattered and a little concerned that you trust me that much. I'll do my best."

We both stare at the ream of paper, separated with large clips.

"Hold on a minute and I'll get you something to carry all that." She disappears for a moment before returning with a large box that says Klean and Komfy.

"Did you know November Bean's husband owns that company?"

"Mmmhmmm." She sets it on the desk in front of me and drops the papers inside. They make a loud thunk sound as they hit the bottom of the cavernous box. "Knew her mister. He came several times by himself before they were married. He was more interested in the cult than he was that girl, if you ask me."

"Why do you say that?" Maneuvering the box to the floor, I realize I won't be able to carry it. Shuffling it along the sidewalk with my feet until I reach the Welcome Center seems to be my best option.

"Oh, he was in here a few times, asking us Townies about November and all the former cult members. A weird kind of obsession, it seemed to me. Course, the cult members kept their heads down. Didn't know yet if they'd be arrested for their crazy activities. When they got married, it was clear as day he was just looking for a trophy from that freak show."

Poor November. She wanted to run as far from Fallen Branch as she could. She forgot to open her eyes and see what was in front of her.

"I understand when this initially happened, you were all wary of what might come next." I'm a little afraid to ask this question, but it's been hanging over our conversations for months. "But now, it's been two decades. Why are you still keeping track of everyone?"

She wraps her knuckles on the counter as if pondering my question. "It's time you heard." Gladys reaches under the counter and pulls out a dusty scrapbook. She takes one gnarled hand and wipes a thick layer of dust from the pink cover.

"Way back when Zion first came to town, he was a friendly man. Handsome as a movie star. He had a commanding presence too. He mosied into every business, making friends and getting intimate enough with each family that he had ten to twenty invites every holiday. Never seen anyone so popular in this finicky town."

When I searched his cabin, he had lots of papers under his bed. Names and dates that didn't make any sense to me. Maybe they belonged to these people.

"He took a real liking to our family. My husband Carl, rest his soul, and my three grown children. I had a daughter who worked over at the supermarket, called Lucky Chuck's at the time. He came in and saw her every day, making his rounds. She latched on to his every word like a hungry pup to its mother." She opens the scrapbook to reveal pictures of a beautiful young woman, with honey-colored hair and round, blue eyes.

There are photos of her as a young child, hugging a similarly featured girl and a boy with a buzz cut and freckles. "This is her?"

"Mmmhmmm. Carlene. She was such a sparkle. When her dad and I were having problems, she was the one to say, 'Now, Momma, you and Daddy have to think of the big picture. What'll you be doing in twenty years if you don't have each other?'" Gladys looks up and stares at me, her eyes wet with emotion.

"What happened to Carlene? Did she join Fallen Branch?"

"She did. One of the first Townies to succumb to his charms. Dumb girl." A storm settles over Gladys's wrinkled brow. "At first, she came in to town to see us every Sunday. The nonsense she was spouting seemed harmless. 'Listen to the ground, give your power over to someone who knows what to do with it.' That kind of thing. We thought she probably needed to clear her head, that maybe we'd pushed her too hard to be self-sufficient. Once she realized how silly she sounded, we'd have our girl back. That's what Carl said, but things didn't happen like that."

"Where is she now?"

"Our dinners progressed from once a week to once a month, and then it was yearly. After that, she stopped coming into town altogether. I always took my ladder over and watched out that window there," she raises a thin arm and the loose skin flaps as she points over my head, to the small window at the top of the wall. "I watched them go through many crazy outfits. For a while they could only walk single file. I looked at every face, trying to find my girl. Never saw her."

"Oh, Gladys..."

"We had a spy who pretended to be one of them but would report back. He told us our girl was too radical even for them. She was questioning Zion publicly. Awhile later, she just disappeared."

"What do you mean, disappeared? Where is she now?"

Gladys shrugs. "Don't know. A lot of them just vanished. Don't think she jumped from the falls though. If she did, we never found her. I keep track of all of them in case the day comes I can pinpoint who she left with."

I walk around the counter and hug her frail body. "I'm so sorry. You must've been so tortured by all of this."

She squeezes me back. "Well, thank you, dearie. We lost her the minute she went out there to live with him. A sneaky man who manipulated everyone, and I do mean everyone."

My phone buzzes in my pocket. "We'll talk again soon. Cedar and I have a million things to get done. Thanks, Gladys!"

The box does not shove down the street easily, but when you're in a hurry, you achieve superhuman strength. The last few steps, I put the phone to my ear, expecting to hear my partner's voice. "Cedar? What's happening? Did the printer come through?"

"It's not Cedar. It's Piper. You've got to come to the bakery. Cosmo is freaking out."

20

PRESENT DAY

Darkness over the Ridge

"What do you mean, freaking out? Did something happen to Cedar?" My stomach is in knots thinking about him yelling at this poor girl, in one of his dark moods.

"Just come here, okay?"

I ponder what could have possibly gone so wrong. Piper seems to be happy living in her own place. After some initial grumbling about being told where to live, she appeared to enjoy the independence. Cosmo keeps an ear out for any problems, but doesn't bother her. He doesn't understand the temperament of women under thirty, so he's more comfortable staying at a distance. The living situation has worked out fine for them, and for me.

When I arrive, there is chaos in the back.

"Can't you do it? I'm frosting these tarts!" Piper snaps at Doris.

"Piper? Where's Cos?" I don't want to come behind the counter. Cosmo told me once that's like going through a man's drawers.

Eventually, Piper comes to the front counter, her face ablaze with emotion.

"Nothing is going right today!" She dissolves into tears and runs into my arms.

"Tell me about it, hon." Impulsively, I kiss the top of her head.

She pulls away and wipes her violet eyes on her apron. "My mom surprised me. She came in this morning and said she'd be in town for a few days. Probably to convince me to leave. But I'm not going anywhere."

"Your mom is–*here*?"

Piper nods. "She's staying at the Spruce Bark Motel. She was trying my Lunar Chicken Sandwich and Cosmo came in and blew his top. He said Mom wasn't welcome here and he wasn't sure if I was either."

This doesn't sound like Cosmo at all. "Where is he now?"

"Outside. Pacing furiously. Doris said not to bother him."

"You do whatever you need to do to prepare for the lunch crowd. I'll check on Cosmo. It's probably just some kind of misunderstanding."

Piper grabs my arm. "Lanie? Will you tell him I'm sorry?"

"What are you sorry for? You have done nothing wrong."

"I brought chaos. I always do. He didn't want me here in the first place and now my mom is upsetting him, too."

I cup her chin with my hand. "Listen, young lady. You've been through enough. Cosmo and the rest of this town owes you the comfort of feeling safe. We'll get this all smoothed over."

The back door to Cosmo's bakery leads to an alley where he's made many cat friends. He feeds them when nobody is watching; one of the many things I adore about this man. He is sitting on a crate, spooning food into the mouth of a fluffy, butterscotch kitten.

"I call this one Lanie Bug. She reminds me of you because she refused to leave when the big Tom came and scared the others off. A little too full of herself but kind enough humans can see past it."

I bend down and hug him tightly. "You're kind of crazy. Maybe that's why I love you." Those words just slip out of my mouth like melted butter.

He pivots and pulls my hands aside. "You what?"

"I–didn't mean that. I mean, I think I did, but–"

He sets the cat food down on the ground to the happy relief of Lanie Bug and stands up, pulling me with him. "I love you, too. These words should have come before I proposed, but I'm new to all of this romance kind of stuff."

We kiss tenderly, my arms falling to his waist. I can feel Lanie Bug rubbing her fluffy body against me. "Cos, as much as I'd love a make-out session next to your un-dumped garbage bin, you've got quite a mess inside. Why would you throw such a fit about Piper's mother coming to visit? Shouldn't she be able to spend time with her family?"

He looks down at the old pizza box beside me. "If it were anyone but Olivene, I'd agree with you. That woman is pure evil. I don't want her anywhere near my shop. The deal was we would help Piper. Her mother wasn't part of that package."

"You've said that before. So far, Gladys has uncovered

nothing to prove your point. What happened at Fallen Branch? Why do you hate her so much?"

"Things that are still too painful to talk about." He puts his hands in his pockets and rocks back and forth on his heels.

"Things worse than killing your father? Just explain why Olivene can't see her daughter now, two decades later."

Cosmo sighs. "She was a hard woman. I never understood why she was in that camp. She was just as manipulative as Zion. She should've been running her own place. Hal, her husband, was too soft. He did whatever she said, even if it wasn't what Zion wanted. I was a zombie like everyone else, so when Olivene said to jump, I jumped."

"And what did this jumping involve?"

He directs his gaze across the alley, away from me. "Taking personal effects from other people. We didn't have much, but what we had, we treasured. She pooled them up and said she'd give them to Zion as personal donations of gratitude if these people didn't agree to do things for her."

"What kinds of things?"

"Oh, little things, like working in the laundry house, or tending the fields, things like that. But also, she wanted their complete loyalty. She spouted some mumbo jumbo about knowing Zion's mind better than he did. Behind his back, of course. Lots of people thought they had the inside track with him. I s'pose she wasn't any different, just better at the game." He re-ties his cream-colored apron and wipes the orange cat hair from the front.

"When she gave birth to the eclipse baby her status went up with everyone, not just the people hanging on her every word. People who don't believe in Zion's teachings anymore still revere Olivene, because she gave birth on one specific day."

We stand in silence, both of us trying to make sense of the past.

The back door flies open. "Cosmo? There's a police officer here to see you." Piper doesn't look him in the eye, instead keeping her gaze pinned to her shoes. "I'm sorry about my mom."

Cosmo ambles to the door. "You're okay, kid. Whatever is between your mom and me should stay that way. Don't worry. You and your job are safe here."

I follow them inside to the front of the store, where two officers are waiting. There are only four on the entire force, so this must be a big deal.

"I didn't save you guys anything today. Should've called ahead." Even though Cosmo has a bad history with the police, he always tries to be polite.

"We're here officially today. Bordering on official, I guess. Giving you a courtesy call, Mr. Hill." Officer Briggs itches his nose. "Can we talk privately?"

Cosmo laughs. "There is no privacy in this town. I've done nothing to be ashamed of. Tell me what's going on."

He glances at his partner, Officer Mount, who nods. "We found a body outside of town earlier this morning."

"Not a whole body, exactly," Officer Mount corrects him.

Cosmo puts his hands up. "I was never in the murder business. I thought you guys knew that."

"We don't think you did anything," Officer Mount replies. "It's your sister we need to speak with."

"You think Cedar had something to do with this? C'mon guys. Have you seen her? She wouldn't hurt a fly."

"She was the last person to see this particular individual, sir. We stopped at the Welcome Center and she wasn't there. Thought you might be able to help us locate her."

"We made an informal identification, based on – you

know – this being a small town and we recognize all the faces." Officer Briggs interjects.

"Definitely not much more than a face," Officer Mount adds.

"Who is it? Who would Cedar be seen with? Oh, no..." I blink furiously. "You found Hawk?"

21

TWENTY-FOUR YEARS AGO

FALLEN BRANCH COMMUNE

Olivene Durning - Intake Form

If you need specifics, I'm 30, just like my husband. I have brown hair, deep-set brown eyes, a square face and thin lips. Some people say I'm homely. Luckily, Hal Durning thinks I'm the most beautiful woman he's ever laid eyes on. But that's not what you asked.

Why am I here?

Hal and I met seven years ago, when I was a student at Oregon State University. I was going to become a bookkeeper and erase everything about the sad little girl who grew up in Kansas. Instead, I met Hal and my world abruptly shifted on its axis.

It rained that evening. Night classes were finished and I was heading for the parking garage, carrying my flashlight that doubled as a weapon. I didn't trust anyone out that late. When I got to my car, tired from two jobs and a class I hated, I saw this little, beat up Honda parked at a funky angle, blocking me in. I had to be up at five the next morning to begin my waitress job and I didn't have time for some clueless kid taking classes to fill time without a care in the world.

That's what I decided while I was sitting there, trying to figure my next move. I searched for something to write on to leave him a nasty note. How could anyone be so careless? I like to be in control and something like that left me feeling pretty helpless.

As I finished writing the note, I heard someone walking up behind me car. "I'll pepper spray you if you get any closer!" I yelled. I couldn't afford pepper spray, but a classmate told me if you threaten using it, it was usually enough to scare them off. Realizing I had a flashlight in my hand, I shined it directly in his face.

He took his hood off and in the dim light of the garage; I saw this gorgeous skinny kid, with an angular jaw and thick, curly brown hair. His eyes were a deep brown and were so intense they made me weak in the knees.

"Did I block you in? I'm so sorry. I was late for class and my professor docks us one letter grade each time that happens. I've already gotten one when I was stuck in traffic. If I get another, I may lose my scholarship."

I crumpled the note in my hand. "I'm Olivene. I work at five in the morning."

"Me too. Three jobs and I'm still struggling, even with my scholarship. I'm Hal Durning, by the way." He offered his hand and I shook it. Hard.

We didn't waste a lot of time talking those first few weeks. Since this is about honesty, I'll say that Hal Durning was my first real boyfriend. He'd seen the world and had stories about everywhere I'd seen in books but never dreamt of visiting. He was a kind, intellectual, well-traveled man. I couldn't understand why he wanted me, though.

Coming from Cottonwood Falls, Kansas, where my life revolved around my father's church and my three, equally plain, *lookalike sisters, I craved something more. We weren't allowed to think for ourselves and I dreamt of the day I would prove to them I was destined for greatness.*

I secretly applied to Oregon State, using my friend's address. When I was accepted, I had to leave before my father found out. He would've forbidden me from doing something he didn't know about beforehand. I packed my suitcase in the middle of the night and didn't stop driving until I reached Oregon.

After living on campus one semester, I dropped out. The people were too strange and I couldn't adjust to life away from my small-town rules. I started working in a café six blocks from campus. The tips were good, especially when everyone came in on a Friday night, high or drunk.

Waitressing wasn't enough to pay the bills. I did phone solicitations at night and worked in a pet store every Saturday. I couldn't spend the rest of my life like this.

I tried once more to take one class just to see if I was even smart enough to finish college. It was an entry-level course, Mythology 101. Of the 32 people in the room, only myself and a guy who looked like Jesus attempted to take part. Maybe I could make this work.

The night I met Hal was my third week in class. My ego was a little bruised from being the oldest person in the room, not in on the jokes or the frat parties. Maybe that's why he was so appealing. That and his incredible smile.

Hal liked me to make decisions for him. I told him what to eat and when to eat it. I picked out his clothes. It seemed to make him feel secure. He was opinionated about one thing: his version of a perfect world. A place where everyone worked together to make things better. No egos, no drama. Just support, love and order. A well-defined plan for success. I pictured him building huts while I gave lectures on things like wilderness survival and sewing our own clothing.

Hal came to me excited one day. "Ol, there's a place not far away where the people are building something great. Making their own clothes, growing their own crops. There's no drama, just a man who truly wants to see what humans are capable of when they set their egos aside."

I looked at the brochure. Right beside the ocean in the middle of tall evergreen trees. It was everything we needed. "The three of us will be happy there," I told Hal, rubbing the small rise in my belly.

From the moment we walked through the gates, I could tell this was the place for us. My stomach was upset every day since I found out I was pregnant. We made the long drive in our reconditioned minivan, made longer by my constant need to pull over.

A nice woman took me aside right away. She said she could tell I wasn't myself. She gave me some tea with ginger, I think? And other things I hadn't heard of before. While I was waiting in line to fill out this form, I had a warm feeling. All the queasiness went away. I can picture myself as a leader here.

22

PRESENT DAY

In a Quandary

"Cosmo paced outside the police station for over an hour. I tried to keep him calm, but the whole time I couldn't shake this feeling that something terrible happened between the two of them." I set the plate of pastries in front of Vem, careful to take one for myself first. She has been known to bite fingers that got in her way. "You know Cos has an aversion to police stations because of his arrest. I ended up going in myself to bring Cedar home. Poor girl is just a mess."

November breaks off a piece of a Black Hole Boysenberry Scone before shoving rest in her mouth in two bites. "I'm trying to eat slower," she says through a full mouth. "Leave a little on my plate for later. It's thoughtful eating."

"Coffee? Or are we entering Can't Coffee the Bean month?"

She chews up the rest of the scone and nods her head.

"That's on hold. I needed all of my vices while Frankie was visiting. He's leaving tomorrow." She stares at the swirling mass of leaves painted by a local artist on the wall behind me. "At least I tried. That's pretty much what I say about his entire childhood."

"I'm sorry his visit was so stressful for you." Late at night I could hear her howling mournfully in her backyard. I couldn't decide if that was to further annoy her son, or if it was truly helping her stay calm. Either way, it's a relief he'll be away from her soon and I won't have to worry about keeping his secret.

"So you think Cedar killed Hawk? It's awful to imagine her being violent. I've seen what she can do with a steak—"

"Cedar is not guilty of anything. So many Townies have treated her poorly. In response, I've never heard her utter an unkind word." I realize I'm being defensive. "I do think there is someone here in town watching events unfold and using them to their own advantage. The fact that his death came right after their argument is suspicious. I'll get to the bottom of this for her, you can count on that."

She scoops the last piece of scone from her plate and puts it in her mouth, licking her fingers.

"You've become the resident detective. Everyone knows that. I've heard people talk about it at the grocery store. 'That Lanie lady, she got here just in time to solve all of our crime. Clean up this town.'"

I roll my eyes. "Isn't that the job of the police department? I'm here to market things."

November leans forward in her seat and lets out one of her trademark honks. "Lanie, if there's one thing you should've learned by now, it's that the Piney Falls Police Department is superb at issuing tickets for littering. They don't have experience in serious business like this."

"Why does everyone think I have unlimited time on my hands? The Sleepy Sounds people are coming soon. Without Cedar, I don't have enough hands to get everything done."

November raises ten sticky fingers. "Here are two right in front of you. Tell me what you need."

I've never thought of her as a resource, but she knows the history of the town. "You could give tours! We need extra help there. These brochures need to go to all the local businesses, and the Spruce Bark Motel needs a checklist for everything to be placed in their rooms, in case the investors are really excited and want to stay an extra day."

November's eyes widen. "Whoa. I said I'd help. Not become your Tulip Sloan clone's clone. Give me one thing at a time."

There is a harsh knock on my front door. In my old house in Chicago, no one ever knocked, it was too informal. Here, it is a personal trademark. When it's done this urgently, it's never good news.

"Are you expecting anyone?" November runs to the hall closet, where I keep a bat. "I'm trained in hand-to-hand combat, I can do that too."

"No, I'm sure it's just Cosmo." Ten-thirty is his busiest time. I'm secretly glad November is here. When I open the door, a tall, sour-faced woman with dark hair and sunken, brown eyes is standing on my porch.

"I've been told you're the person I need to speak with about my daughter's protection," she says tersely.

"What?"

"Olivene Moonlight. My daughter is Amaris. I was told to come here, that you were in charge of her protection." She speaks in a loud distinct voice as if my hearing was the problem before.

"Oh, you're Piper's mother. I'm Lanie Anders. Please come in." I open the door, taking care to give the OK signal to Vem.

"I'm sure you remember my friend, November Bean, from your Fallen Branch days."

Olivene nods but says nothing.

Vem crosses her arms. "Never cared for you. But your daughter is a different story. She's really growing on me."

Olivene ignores her comments and turns toward me. "Ms. Anders, I was assured my daughter would be safe here in town. She called me last week and said she was attacked. Can you account for this?"

I can sense her energy. Just like the no-nonsense people I encountered in the business world, she is powerful and without emotion. Her type left me with excruciating headaches at the end of each day.

November steps in between the two of us. She puts three long fingers in Olivene's face. "First of all, Lanie is a detective, not in charge of security. Second," she rolls one finger into her palm, "we've been doing a fine job of watching out for her. Cosmo moved Piper in next door so he could take care of her. She's got her own little apartment and likes it very well. And third," she moves this long finger stained with jelly, close to Olivene's nose. "Your daughter's attacker was apprehended. At least his head has been caught. Without the rest of him, there's nothing much to worry about. She's perfectly safe now."

Olivene moves closer to Vem, shooing her fingers away like an annoying insect. "I thought by taking my daughter in, YOU were ensuring her safety, November Bean. I should have known better. Did you flake out on that, just like you did your marriage?"

I know Vem's strength. When one of her beginner meditation students came to class drunk, she scooped this full-grown man up under one arm and carried him to his car and deposited him right on the hood. I step in between them quickly. "I'm not a detective, but that's flattering Vem. And I certainly never made the promise to keep your daughter safe. I haven't lived here long either. I think what she means to say is the whole town agreed to look out for her. The person who attacked her, Hawk Beechum, is now deceased. I think she's safe."

Olivene's face takes on a strange look. She scratches the back of her neck. Horrified? Relieved? "Hawk is dead? What good news. He's been chasing my poor daughter for years. We almost had him in Oklahoma."

I try to smile, to connect us, but she doesn't meet my gaze. "Piper said he was one of your friends you sent here to check on her. Now she's concerned you'll force her to leave again. Can you re-assure her she's safe?"

Olivene takes it upon herself to sit on my couch, uninvited. "An acquaintance from the old days is all. Friends close and enemies closer, as they say." She sighs. "Piney Falls is the perfect place for her. She can hone her craft and get to know the locals. I have no intention of making her leave. Could I trouble you for a glass of water?"

"Do you have anything toxic and clear? We'll make it look like an accident," Vem whispers in my ear. I frown at her before heading to the kitchen for a glass. "So, tell us, Olivene. Where are you living now?"

"We've been in Northern California for over three years – the longest our family has ever been in one place. I'm thinking we need a change of scenery though. With the current state of things here, I'm thinking we should be near Piper, in case there are more issues. Piney Falls might be a good move for the whole family."

November plops down beside Olivene as I bring a glass of water. "Where's Hal these days? Have you heard from him?"

Olivene clears her throat. "No, Hal ran off a few years ago. He just couldn't stand the life we had to live to maintain our daughter's safety. Men are always a disappointment."

"He always seemed nice to me. Smiled at everyone," November retorts.

I hand Olivene the glass and sit down opposite her.

She takes a drink and then stares hard at Vem. "Oh yes, you were the one. Always giving him those glances. I used to wonder if something was going on between the two of you?"

November lets out a huff in protest.

I lean forward in my chair. It's a good thing I'm well-versed in conflict resolution from my former job at *Work Ahead Office Supplies–The Most Profitable Office Supply Chain in the World.* "I'm sure Vem didn't have any interest in your husband. She was still a teenager, trying to find her way. We all absolutely adore your daughter. And Fallen Branch is fading more and more into history every day. We've got some interested buyers for the property. They have exciting plans for the place. I can show you if you want."

Olivene sets her glass on the table in front of her and stands abruptly. "That's a mistake. Those buildings, that soil; it's sacred ground. Many people toiled, gave everything they had to make it a success. It needs to be sold to someone who will treat it as a shrine."

My cheeks burn. "You're the first Fallen Branch member I've heard that from. Everyone else is very supportive of the idea."

"You can't possibly know everyone from Fallen Branch," she says dismissively, "nor can you understand what we created. Even if some have twisted those ideals to harm my daughter, what Zion began was truly magical. His plan would have worked."

Her eyes try to bore a hole through my head. It may be working.

"Would you like my business card? So you can get ahold of me quickly if there are more problems?" Without waiting for her reply, I push past Vem and open my large purse.

Olivene nods and I hand her a cream-colored card with the words, *Lanie Anders, Piney Falls Marketing and Publicity* written across the front in gold letters.

"I do need to go check on my daughter. Thank you for the water."

I see her out and then return to November, who is pacing in my living room.

"Why'd you do that? Open another avenue for her? Do you see that black cloud in here like the Asian Beetles we found on our hike, Lanie? It's her. She leaves behind a trail of darkness everywhere she goes. I can sense bad things are about to happen."

"Calm down. It's better if she contacts me by phone instead of ringing my doorbell every time there's a problem. Breathe with me."

We take in large, long breaths and let them out slowly until we are both feeling better.

"She's intense, that's for sure. Everyone came out of that cult with their own scars. She loves her daughter and that's evident. People can act like that and still love their children." *Can they? I'm not sure my mother excelled in either category.*

"One thing that concerns me though, is the lasting impression she made on Cosmo. He's a mess because of her. I need to find out why."

"I can do a ceremonial chant tonight and see what information makes itself visible. It would work better with some of her eyelashes." November stares out the front window as two squirrels scurry across the driveway carrying pine cones.

"For now, let's get you prepared for your tours. It will get both of our minds off Olivene Moonlight."

Vem shrugs. "You're probably right. As usual."

It is somewhat of a relief to know the tours are taken care of. Cedar tried to train two people who ultimately found it too challenging. One insisted he bring a tip bucket and his snare drum.

"Stay on script, please. We're trying to make everything look good. I don't want you to lie, but pretend like this a job interview for Piney Falls and the tourists are all your potential employers. Keep it light and interesting."

"You don't have to worry about me." She shakes her head enthusiastically. "November Bean is punctual and professional. I'll memorize this today and be the best tour guide this town has ever seen."

23

PRESENT DAY

Family Drama

When I knock on Cedar's door, she is slow to answer. I'm not prepared for the shocking sight that greets me. Unlike the professionally-dressed co-worker I see every day, she is wearing her grey, baggy sweats and no makeup. Her face is pale and its obvious she hasn't slept.

I reach over the threshold and hug her tightly. "You've been through so much."

"They thought I cut off his head — the only man I've ever loved," she whispers.

"I know. Why anyone would think you were capable of that kind of thing. There's no evidence against you, is there?"

She motions for me to sit on her uncharacteristically messy couch. I move her laundry to the side and sink into the soft foam.

"They took me to this cold, dark room. It reminded me of Zion's tortures. Deprive the offender of all senses so they had the opportunity to assess their wrongs. And then they brought in Boysie."

"Gladys's son-in-law? What did he say?"

"That he knew how we Fallen Branch acted. At night, when we were alone, we were still practicing our rituals. 'All a bunch of depraved nuts,' he said."

I will have to talk to Gladys about his treatment of Cedar. "Then he told you about the crime?"

She wipes her nose on a hankie and places it in her pocket. "Only that his head was sev-, sev—"

"Besides that," I'm trying not to be impatient. "What else did they find?" I reword things a bit. "Let's call it a mask. Refer to his head as a mask." I learned that in *Removing the Emotion from the Object,* a half-day seminar that left me underwhelmed and in the backseat of my car with Roald McPherson, seminar leader.

She takes short breaths in until her breathing returns to normal. "The 'mask' was found about two miles from town. On a road that leads to the back entrance of Fallen Branch. There were tire tracks. They looked at my tires, but the tracks didn't match my tread. That's when Boysie said I had an accomplice."

I roll my eyes. "Oh, that's ridiculous. Did Boysie tell you anything else?"

"Nothing. Just more name-calling. He's positive I've been receiving secret messages from Zion, who is instructing me to kill. I don't know if he knows Zion is my biological father."

"Gladys knows. So therefore I'm pretty sure everybody in town knows." I look at my watch. "I need to get out to Fallen Branch to make sure Vem does okay with her tour. There's repair work happening that needs to stay on schedule, too. Want to ride along? A change of scenery might be helpful."

"Okay," she shrugs. "Shouldn't I dress appropriately though?"

I smile. She is the only one in this town who cares about appearance. "Not today. You look radiant just the way you are."

When we arrive, there is a small group of about six people. November is dressed in her finest jumpsuit, fuchsia in color. Her bushy hair is pulled on top of her head, tied with a fuchsia ribbon. She is wearing sunglasses with fuchsia frames, even though the sun hasn't peeked through the clouds in days.

"Over to your left is the Eat the Wheat building. We only ate wheat products, using wheat we raised, ground and milled ourselves. Only breads and some berries we picked. Those days were filled with dread and sorrow."

"Is any of this true?" I whisper in Cedar's ear. "I've never heard any of you talk about food deprivation before."

"They forced us to eat foods of a certain letter of the alphabet. But I don't recall ever being confined to wheat."

I motion for Vem to join us.

"Spend some time reading the placards placed around the shelter. I'll be with you again momentarily." She's using her formal voice, the one she saves for meditation classes.

I fold my arms. "Vem, are you making this up?"

She cocks her head to the side. "I am. You distinctly told me to make things interesting. I can't make it interesting and be truthful without getting furious. You know what happens when I get angry."

"Howling? Mantras?" Cedar asks helpfully.

Vem shakes her head. "I lose control of my senses. There's no telling what bad words might come out of my mouth and there's nowhere for them to go but straight into the ears of the tourists. You don't want that, Lanie."

I look at Cedar. We discussed the reason to have tourists here was to prepare them for the idea of the rebirth of the land. Inviting them to enjoy the past and learn about the future. "I guess it doesn't really matter what you tell them about Fallen Branch. As long as they get the idea that it was a bad place and what we have coming will be exciting and much better."

November doesn't respond but looks behind me. "Cheese and mustard, are my eyes deceiving me?"

I turn around to see Frankie and Sy Romington, the realtor I met the other day, walking around the property. Without a word, I move quickly to where they are standing. "Frankie? What are you doing here?"

In a flash, Vem is by my side.

"Son? Is this what you meant by purchasing some property?" Her face twists in confusion. "March Franklin Bean, are you trying to undermine what we're doing here?"

Frankie smirks at his mother, but turns his body towards me. "I'm looking at properties. My father and I want a sound investment. This is perfectly good land. We might just leave it empty for a few years before deciding how to proceed."

I don't bother to smile. "But, we're doing something good for the community here. Don't you want your mother's traumatic childhood memories to lead to something positive?"

"No, he doesn't, Lanie. Now I get it. The reason he came here wasn't to upset his father, it was to do his father's bidding. They can buy this land and kick me in the gut one last time." November folds her hands around her compact body.

Tears begin to flow down my cheeks, taking makeup as they go. "Please don't purchase this, Frankie. I'm begging you." I'm sobbing an ugly sob like I did in sixth grade, when I was trying to emulate Tulip Sloan's great performance in

One Last Kiss. It's embarrassing, but somehow I can't stop. "All of this work, for nothing?"

"We're still in the process. Nothing is for sure yet." Sy says apologetically. "I thought you knew. Lance at the bank said he spoke with you."

I can hear Cedar in the background, finishing the tour. She is flawless in her presentation, excitedly telling the tourists about the luxury hotel and spa soon to be located on the property.

"I need to get back and call Dad. Let him know things are going smoothly." Frankie pats me on the shoulder. "Tough break for you, Lanie. Maybe you can find something else to do with your spare time. I hear the bakery is hiring."

TWENTY-FOUR YEARS AGO
FALLEN BRANCH COMMUNE

Hal Durning - Intake Form

I'm 23 now. I feel a lot older especially because that's what my wife, Olivene believes to be true. Been on my own since the age of 16 and by yourself you don't keep track of birthdays. I never got along with my parents. They were both drunks who cared more about the bottom of the bottle than about me. Dad supposedly worked at the feed store in Idaho Falls, but he usually forgot to show up. Mom worked as a teacher's aide at the grade school until they figured out it wasn't soup she was bringing for lunch every day.

I dropped out of high school when I couldn't take them anymore, not that they cared or noticed. I felt bad about leaving my younger sister behind, but she would find her own way one day. I packed up my things and took off. I'd already bought a car from my best friend. I didn't know where I was headed, just that I'd never be back. I moved to Portland, working the counter at an automobile parts store and then at the airport doing maintenance. The pay seemed good enough, I just needed something more from life. I took home the magazines from the auto parts store and read them at night, memorizing every detail about the places I wanted to visit someday.

I started working at the gas station across from my apartment on weekends and studying for my GED. When I passed that easily, I got one more job, two evenings a week at the dog shelter. The money piled up quickly. I wasn't one for socializing anyway. You guys will check all of this stuff out, right? Better tell you the truth then.

I worked these jobs, that's true. But all of that didn't leave me much time to sleep. There wasn't much of a choice for me, I had to take something to keep my eyes open. I slept about twice a week and when I crashed; I was out for ten hours. It was better than thinking about where I'd come from and wondering where I'd go.

By the time college started in the fall, I was on a racetrack and I couldn't get off. I needed something to help me sleep, but then I found I needed something to help me wake up when I did. I convinced myself it was necessary. I started selling extra pills as a way to add to my income without taking on another job. The money was good and I didn't have to find extra hours to do it.

After a few months, I decided to cut back on the "happy pills." Adderall. My airport buddy told me if you quit taking them too fast, you'd experience a crash. In my mind, I heard him say, "People other than you will have problems." You can twist anything in your head to make it sound right.

I decided on my next day off I'd take an extra sleeping pill and sleep through any effects of coming down from the medication. How hard could it be?

I woke up at three in the morning with the worst anxiety I'd ever experienced in my life. Felt like my heart might burst out of my chest. I clawed at it so hard I started bleeding. My insides needed to come out. I ran to the bathroom and spent the next two hours on the floor.

The next thing I remember is being in the hospital. My buddy from the airport came to check on me when I didn't show up for work two days in a row. Good thing he came, I wouldn't have made it much longer. That was when I realized I couldn't run from my past any more. I just didn't know where the future might be.

Olivene doesn't know any of this. I told her I traveled the world, meeting exotic people. I didn't want her to think I was some dumb kid making mistake after mistake when she was looking for someone her age who had it together. She fell for the Hal Durning I created.

Where was I? Oh yeah. I swore off the drugs after that. I knew it would take a lot of my savings to pay for my time in the hospital, but I signed up for a college class anyway, just to prove to myself I could do it.

I took World Economics, a Thursday night class. Quit working at the pet adoption place on Thursdays, so that seemed like a good concession. I continued working all three jobs, even though I knew it meant getting me back on the merry-go-round that circled hell.

When I came out after class one night, I saw this beautiful woman standing beside my car, tapping her foot. Much taller than me with shoulder-length, shiny, black hair and bright, brown eyes that jumped out at me from beneath her long bangs. She commanded my attention.

There was an order to Olivene that hadn't existed in my life before that night. She came from a preacher's family, where they knew exactly what was expected of them. I both admired and hated her for that. If only someone in my home would have cared. From the first day, she set my life on the right course. She made me quit two of my jobs. "You can't accomplish your goal if you're sending your mind in so many directions. One job, one class." We moved in together after a week, so she could help with the rent. She was right. For the first time in my life, there was someone waiting for me at the end of the day. I couldn't wait to hold her in my arms. I took another class and then another. It was peaceful and predictable. After six months, we were both bored by this life and what it was doing to minds that craved excitement and intellect. We both knew we were destined for something more.

Olivene encouraged me to look into alternative ways to live. A commune where we all worked towards a common good. I needed one assurance from her first: I wanted a family.

I dreamt about our beautiful children, a daughter who looked just like Ol, with dark hair and expressive eyes. Then maybe a son who looked like me but had twice the self-confidence. The four of us sitting around the dinner table, telling stories about our day. Like normal families. Olivene laughed when I told her that. She said there wasn't any such thing as a normal family, but I didn't really believe that.

I began reading everything I could find on how to raise children. I convinced Olivene we should marry as a first step. "Why would we need the confines of marriage, Hal?" she asked several times. "So our kids will be part of real family, Ol. This is what I want more than anything." She sighed. By the end of the month, we were Mr. and Mrs. Hal Durning.

I'd promised myself I would tell her who I really was – a high school dropout and former drug addict. I just couldn't find the courage. And now we would have a kid who needed a role model? What was I thinking? That day I found one of your brochures that you left on my windshield in the grocery store parking lot. It was a beautiful scenic place on the coast where people came from all over the world to put their labor into a community of like-minded people. People who wanted to change the world by first perfecting their own corner. It looked like the perfect place to teach us how to raise a child.

When I read the words of Zion, "Together we'll create a community that will serve as a model for the rest of the world!" I knew it was the place Olivene and Hal Durning were meant to be. More than that, I knew it would be a safe place to tell Olivene the truth about my past.

We stopped for coffee on the way here. Olivene's normally flawless skin was blotchy red. "What's wrong, babe? Are you having second thoughts?" If she backed out, I would support her. Olivene always knows if we've made a mistake.

"No mistake. You've got your wish, Hal."

I just sat and stared at her.

"We're having a baby, dummy!" she smiled. I couldn't believe it. On the way to fulfill one dream, another one came true. It's just like Zion said on the brochure, "We only need to visualize our truths and they appear. Just take care to think about what one considers truth."

So here we are, Hal, Olivene and Baby Durning. Ready to live our Fallen Branch truth.

25

PRESENT DAY

Cosmo's Dark Past

"Lance? What's going on? I thought we had a deal!"

"We had a tentative deal. Nothing was set in stone. I have to protect the interests of the bank and these other investors are prepared to offer us a much larger sum than what you proposed."

I can picture him in his grey, pinstripe suit, leaning back in his leather chair as his caramel socks are exposed to the world.

"This is illegal. I'll get a lawyer. I'll fight it."

He giggles. Like a young girl. "Where? In the courtroom of my golfing buddy, Judge Markley? Nothing illegal about a misunderstanding."

I hang up on him and throw the phone across the room. "I'm still going through with this," I say out loud. There has to be a way.

Drinking wine on my patio has become the best way to think. I may finish this bottle of Promptly Pinot from the Sassy Lasses Vineyard all by myself, without sharing with

Cosmo. One glass and then two. As smoothly as it's going down, no ideas are coming to me.

There is an abrupt knock on my door, like the urgent bad-news knocks of Cosmo, but I haven't heard from him today. As I walk to the door, it opens on its own and Vem and Frankie appear.

She shoves Frankie in my face. "Tell her," she commands.

He looks like if he could stab someone right now, it would be his mother. His lips squeeze together tightly. He takes one hand and runs it through his thick, wavy hair.

"Tell her, March. If you don't, I will and the story will change to fit my needs. And they are twisted." Vem's face is flushed; she is shifting her weight back and forth nervously. I've never seen her like this before without her using one of her calming methods.

Frankie sighs, loud and irritated. "She's making too much out of this, as usual. You realize my dad and I will put an offer in on the Fallen Branch property by the end of the week. Dad's always hated that place and when a friend told us we could buy it for private use, we jumped on it." He smiles and points his thumb at his mother. "It'll drive her crazy."

Vem lets out a howl. For once, I'm happy she's doing something completely inappropriate.

"Knock it off, November. No matter how many animal sounds you make, we're not changing our minds." Frankie shoves his mother, though not hard. Vem responds by putting her body uncomfortably close to his.

I press my palms together tightly, trying to think of a nice thing to say. "I already know you're trying to purchase the property. We went through this earlier. If your goal was to ruin my day, I'm afraid this was a wasted trip."

"What you didn't know was who cuddled up next to Franklin for this business venture." She thwaps Frankie on the back of the head. "Tell her," she commands.

"Who is this friend who told you about the property being up for sale? We didn't make our plans public outside of the community." Mentally I run through the list of potential big mouths.

"A former Fallen Branch member. They asked if we'd help them start another commune. Broken Branch, they're calling it. We're going to rebuild the place."

November nods vigorously. "You see? His father is pure evil. Got himself mixed up with Hawk."

I think about Hawk's plan to start his own version of Broken Branch, but say nothing. "You're working with Broken Branch? You are part of the group that has been harassing Piper and her family all these years?"

He snorts. "I've never harassed anyone in my life. And I don't know who this Hawk person is. We found out about a business deal and we're doing it." Frankie's eyes narrow into slits. "Thanks for all of the years you were checked out of my childhood, Mom. You can think about that the rest of your life, while my Broken Branch buddies are building a new society of freaks."

I move back, out of respect for November. If she punches him in the face now, I don't want to stand in her way. Son or not, he's an awful person. "You will not get away with this, Frankie. I can assure you of that. Your mother did her best to raise you. She didn't have the same basket of skills as most people do, but she did everything she could. Starting a cult won't change any of your childhood." I glance at Vem, who has sucked the inside of her cheeks so hard her face is hollow underneath her cheekbones. My insides are twisting.

"Just talk to your mom, Frankie," I plead. "Buy the property or not, but don't leave here without finishing things with her."

I scurry to my bedroom, not knowing how to usher them out without hurting November's feelings. I listen at my door, hoping to hear a reconciliation. Instead, my front door slams shut.

THE NEXT MORNING, I open my eyes with dread. So much has happened this month; so many bad things. It seems wrong to invite more misery. I wish there was another way, but there is only one person who has the answers.

I fight the little voice inside me that thinks maybe Piper did bring this evil to our community. Instead, I prepare mentally for the uncomfortable visit I must make. My phone buzzes as I'm walking out the door. *Movie night? I'd recommend a Tulip Sloan classic, but I'll snuggle up next to something better.*

Does he sense what I'm about to do? Stop it, Lanie. This is the loving person he's always been. I allow his kindness to seep in and my heart warms. At least there is something to look forward to at the end of this black day. *Sure. Can't wait to see your smiling face and the rest of you.*

The Aisley County Jail is on the second floor of the library building. When they city only had enough money for one state-of-the-art building, it was determined most city and county offices could co-exist in one space. Locals often joke about the librarians being trained in self-defense for a possible jail break. The elevator to the second floor is only accessed from the outside, keeping all patrons safe from possible criminal activity.

"I'm here to see Zion Scheddy."

The man at the desk stares blankly at me. "Relative?"

"No, um... I'm writing a book." At one point that may have been true. I came to Piney Falls to write a book about its history. Instead, I've solved mysteries and tried to save the town from financial ruin. Not exactly similar professions.

"I'll have to ask my sergeant about that. Hold on." He disappears into another room, where I overhear spirited discussion. An older, heavy-set man with small round glasses comes to the desk.

"Ma'am, we're not in the business of helping criminals become famous for their crimes."

I clear my throat. "The book I'm writing is more of a family history. I'm here on behalf of his daughter, Cedar Hill. To get some answers to personal questions. Dot the i's and cross the t's before he's transferred to a larger facility."

He folds his arms across each other and rocks back and forth on his heels. "Did you bring a notebook? A tape recorder?"

I unzip my purse and remove the Shanel wallet, Pale Primrose lipstick and three sticks of gum.

"That's all I have. My phone is in my pocket. I'm happy to leave that with you."

"You can have fifteen minutes. Don't want him converting you."

I suppress a smile. "That's not likely. Thank you, sir!"

He ushers me into a cold, sterile room, where I sit uncomfortably on a silver, metal chair. There are several long, black marks on the mint green wall. Scrapes from violent encounters? How many secrets have been told in this very space?

The heavy door swings open and a jovial face appears. He's gained weight since I saw him last. His long beard has been trimmed up to his neckline, making his unruly, dark eyebrows more prominent. His eyes are merry. If I didn't know better, I'd think he was enjoying his incarceration.

"Sister! What a pleasant surprise. Brother Kevin, this is my lovely friend, Leslie. She visited me at my home shortly before I came to stay with you." The guard nods in my direction before closing the door.

"What brings you here, Leslie? I sensed that day you were interested in learning more about my simple way of life."

It's somewhat of a relief he doesn't remember my name. "Your plan for living is intriguing. Not everyone with an idea to change the world actually attracts minds from all over to live in their self-made community. I studied your literature after we left the cabin." During all the seminars I used to attend, a common theme was that flattering clients was not only the easiest way to start a conversation, but produced the quickest results.

"What a joyous bit of news. With my trial coming up soon, I need a diversion from the dreary world of lawyers and constant spewing of details. Verbal garbage. Did you have questions?" He clasps his burly, handcuffed hands in front of him.

"I'd like to learn more about your ideas for the future, but first, I'd like to back up. Can you tell me about Hawk Beechum? What were your plans for him?"

He sits back in his chair, his handcuffs clunking on the table. "Hawk. Let's see. He was a lost little kitten. From the first day, he wanted nothing more than to please his Grand Elan. You know that's what they called me, Grand Elk? I didn't ask them to do that. They bestowed it upon me."

I know that isn't true, from Cosmo and Cedar's stories. He commanded everyone to call him that. "Yes, I heard about your many accolades. Hawk did whatever you asked of him? Were there things he did the others didn't witness?"

He leans forward, causing me to jump, and then smiles at my discomfort. "Sister, are you suggesting Hawk agreed to illegal activities on my account? Did you lie about your intent here?"

Removing the Cancerous Words from the Message, from the *Use Less to Mean More* seminar. I slept with the seminar organizer, Sherwood. "I'm interested in Hawk. Not necessarily any illegal activity. I'm sorry if that sounded wrong to you. Sometimes my words don't come out the way I'd planned."

He adjusts himself in the chair, causing it to squeak from his weight. He looks uncomfortable. Good.

"Hawk was an obedient soldier. He always offered to do more than I asked. That's why I was just as shocked as you when I discovered the extra funds."

"Yes – I was shocked. Not the Fallen Branch way." My palms are sweaty. I wish I had my phone to record this.

"Not in line with our principals at all. I didn't advise my people to steal from the Townies, but he showed up that day with thousands of dollars. 'Grand Elan, I've decided to honor you the best way I can. My skills from my previous life all lead to this service.' He opened the bag and showed me the cash. As you know, it had been going on for several months by that time. Before I left, I was planning on digging up those bags of cash to further my efforts, but I had to leave in a hurry. You're trying to find the location of the money, I assume? I can draw you a map. Will that make you happy, Sister?"

I gulp. "Most happy. You're so cooperative. And what a compliment, to have someone want to continue your work so badly."

He frowns. "Brother Hawk is continuing my message? Why didn't he tell me?"

"Yes, it's called Broken Branch. At least I think that's the group he's leading. Hawk came to see you?"

Zion crosses one massive leg over the other. "I've never heard of Broken Branch. I'm assuming by your information that this is another group fashioned after mine? What a ludicrous way to diminish my word. I should have sensed problems by his peculiar behavior. Who else is part of this farce?"

"Olivene and Hal Moonlight. And there are more." Those names fall out of my mouth, though I'm not entirely sure they're involved.

He laughs and shakes his head, before staring at me. "This is all making sense now. The woman was out to undermine me from the beginning. Always looking for a way to put herself in the spotlight. My biggest regret was announcing her daughter as my successor. The crescent birthmark, the joyous occasion. They overtook my better judgement. That gave Sister Olivene the power she needed. Between you and me, I thought this proclamation might make her more focused on her marriage than outranking me. But she was always intent on leading her own flock." He stops and looks up at me with concern. "Now, Sister, you're not planning to make your own mark on the world by stealing my teachings?"

"Oh, no, Zion. Your teachings are safe with me."

"In response to your question, yes, Hawk was here. He wanted to look me in the eye and make sure I was real. Apparently he's drifted in the harsh world too long. He seemed confused by my presence and his role in life. Now I understand why."

The officer opens the door. "Time's up, Elan."

I look at him with surprise. He's continuing to convert people from his cell?

"Thank you for your time, Zion. It's been enlightening." Without thinking, I stick out my hand, normal in business to shake. He engulfs mine in his fleshy palm and pulls me in closer. "Sister, please come visit me again. It's been such a wonderful week of visitors."

I step out into the hallway, wiping my hand on my shirt and ask to speak with the sergeant.

"Ma'am? Did he try to convert you? He does that with everyone. The lady bringing his supper last week asked where she could donate to his cause. He's a slick one."

"No, he confessed to a crime I'd like to tell you about. But first, can you tell me if he's had any other visitors?"

A short, round man with a bald head tries to squeeze by us. His nametag says Lumquest.

"Oh, sir, this woman wanted to see you."

He turns and eyes me suspiciously, "What about?"

"I'd like to see your visitor log for Zion Scheddy. Please."

Boysie walks into a nearby office and then sticks his head out, motioning for me to join him. He's holding a clipboard, thumbing through several papers. He runs a finger down each sheet. "A Henry Beech? And then last week, this one," he points to his paper and shakes his head. "Suddenly everyone wants to see the big guy. It really boosted his spirits."

I nod, feeling queasy.

Another officer knocks on the door. "This is the note he said you requested." He hands me a small square of paper, covered in squiggly lines.

I barely kick my shoes off at home when I hear Cosmo pulling up in my driveway. He is at the front door by the time I can get to it, looking more alluring than usual. We kiss as he runs his fingers through my hair.

"Where's the pizza?" I ask breathlessly.

"On the porch." He grins. "You might want to get it before the racoons realize there's a feast waiting."

I push past him and find a pizza box with a key on sitting on top. "What's this?"

"You said we needed to slow things down. I realized the first order of business should be a key to my place. At least the place that is temporarily mine. We'll be finding something together soon."

My throat tightens up as I hold it in my hand. "That's so thoughtful."

"I'll get some plates. We do need to talk about Olivene."

I set the pizza on the counter and put my hands on my hips. "Did you tell her to leave again? That woman was at my house this morning. She's not a happy soul. Can you be nice to her for a few days? At least let me get through the presentation to the potential buyers before fighting that battle?"

"That's part of the reason I'm here. Cedar said I should make this clear. She's such a mess with the interrogation, but she was adamant we get this out in the open, so we have no secrets."

This can't be good. I sit down on a wicker stool and fold my arms in front of me. "Go ahead."

"You remember I was a teen when Fallen Branch ended. Didn't know which end was up or down. It was easy for people to tell me what to do and they taught me to follow whoever gave the orders."

"And what DID you do?"

"Olivene was an older woman. Confident. She was funny

and smart. Several teen boys hung around her waiting to be given instructions. I was one of them."

"Olivene was your muse? That's a little disturbing."

"She wasn't my muse. She was my...girlfriend."

My feet hit the ground and the room starts to spin. "You can't be serious. You told me you hadn't been with anyone. Did you lie to me?"

"No, I didn't. Not exactly. She instructed me. We did things, just not the BIG thing. Every night she took a different guy into the private room we used for punishment. For me, she gave vague instruction. By the time we would have been — you know — the group disbanded and I was in jail."

"Cosmo, you're telling me she forced herself on you?"

The room is starting to spin.

"No, she didn't force me. She was barely older than me. I was taken in by her, just like everyone else. Like I said, we practiced. That's all. After I went away, I never heard from her again. I had a lot of time to think about those things in prison. I realized she used me, and everyone else around her. She was another version of Zion." He scratches his neck nervously. "Not a big deal, really."

The anger is welling up inside me. "This is a big deal, Cos. Something you should have told me before now. We're in a serious relationship. That means you tell the other person everything. Everything. Maybe the reason she upsets you so much is because you still have feelings for her."

"Lanie, you know I love you."

The hairs on the back of my neck stand up. "What else haven't you told me? Are there other things you're keeping? Other experiments?"

"What?"

His face twists and I feel sorry for his pain. At least I think I do. I can't gauge my emotions right now.

"No, of course not. Well, maybe. I've lived a lot of life. But I know for sure I don't want to be with Olivene. She's dark and creepy."

He was the one person in my life who never lied. After so many years of running from relationships, he made me feel secure. I changed my entire world because I'd finally found someone whose morals never faltered. I stand up and open the door. "I think you should go. We need some space for tonight."

He stares at me blankly.

Big strong Cosmo Hill reminds me of a lost puppy, wet from the rain and without hope for life. Part of me wants to scoop him up and make it all better. The other part is selfish and hurt.

"Please leave. I need to think about this. I don't do well with lies."

He passes by me, pausing as he gets to the door. "If that's how you feel, I'm not going to beg."

26

SIX YEARS AGO

Ferndale, California

"Dad, if you would just let her have her way, things would go so much better for us." Piper laid the car keys on the counter. She'd been driving for just under four months, without a license. Sawyer's mother said a driver's license was the surest way for the Firestarters to find them.

Hal clasped his hands together in front of him. "I know, honey. Your mom has always been very headstrong. It served us well for a time. Now that you're almost grown though, maybe we should think about a different way of life. We might stick around somewhere for a bit. Wouldn't that be nice?"

"I want to drive, too. I'm eighteen, way older than most kids when they learn," Sawyer insisted. If he told Hal his sister had been secretly planning a new life, to move away and get a culinary degree so the rest of the family could live in peace, maybe he'd appreciate it enough to let him get behind the wheel. "If you understand Mom is headstrong, then you should just give in. She always knows best, doesn't she?"

Piper and Hal ignored him, like always.

Ever since his unannounced return to the family, Hal had been vocal in his opposition to Olivene. No more whispering behind closed doors. "Piper, there are things you don't understand. Things we couldn't tell you. We always said we would sit down with you when you were old enough and explain–"

Piper rolled her eyes. "I already know enough. The Firestarters think I'm their goddess, or whatever. They won't stop until I'm in agreement with them and willing to lead the next generation of Broken Branch. I've studied their manuals so I know exactly what they think they will accomplish. Mom said I should learn everything about my enemy so I can defeat them. I know self-defense. I'm prepared for anything."

"What if I enrolled you in a cooking class? I know you want to learn how to be a chef. We would pretend you were still going to work with me."

Piper looked at her father with surprise. "How do you know that?"

He put a weathered hand on her shoulder. "I pay attention."

"Oh, yes! Thank you, Dad! I won't let you down, I promise!" She hugged his increasingly thin body tightly, hiding her tears in his shirt sleeve.

Sawyer shook his head and went to his room to play video games.

For three weeks, Piper attended a community college cooking class. She came home and whispered to Sawyer about the middle-aged women who showed up in their finest printed t-shirts to learn how to make gourmet meatloaf. How they often took their breaks in the high school cafeteria, which smelled like grease and tasted like salty freedom. All while Olivene thought she was picking produce with Hal.

The morning she forgot her *Beginner Pastries* book in her bedroom, Olivene was cleaning. She allowed nothing hidden and told the children it was the way she made sure the Firestarters left nothing behind.

Sawyer was in his darkened room, playing video games. He rarely spoke or showed his face in public. Olivene knocked on his door but didn't wait for a response. Sawyer was still wearing the same aromatic pajamas he'd had on for three days.

"Where's your sister?"

He ignored her.

"Where's your sister?" she asked again, more forcefully this time. "If I have to shut off the power, I will!"

"She's with Dad." His eyes didn't leave the screen. "Dammit! You made me crash. Can you shut the door?"

Olivene stormed in the room and slapped her son across the face. He grabbed his cheek but refused to look at her.

"Don't you ever speak to me that way! When I ask you a question, you answer. Now tell me where your sister is!"

Sawyer glared, but at the door, instead of his mother. "She's at school. Dad told her she could go. She wants to get away from you. One of these days, she's going to escape from your prison, Olivene. Then what will you do?"

His mother's eyes narrowed. "You don't need to worry about what I decide. Right now, your only concern is getting out of those filthy clothes and helping me clean. Or all of that," she made a swirling motion with her hand toward all of the video game equipment, "goes in the trash."

When Piper arrived home that day, her books and the

stuffed giraffe Hazel gave her were in a black plastic trash bag in the living room. Olivene was sitting on the couch, sipping a Bubble Fresh soft drink. Sawyer watched from the stairwell.

"How did things go today? How many pounds of plums did you get?" She looked coolly at her daughter, crossing her legs.

"You'll have to ask Dad. I need to get out of my clothes. They're terrible today. Lots of stains." Piper started walking toward the stairs.

"Why don't you take a seat down here? I'll cover a chair for you."

Sawyer recognized this calm tone. It was always followed by something ferocious.

Olivene rose and took a blueberry-colored towel from the unfolded clean clothes basket, the chore Piper has been meaning to get done when she finished her homework. She folded it gingerly into the creases of the recliner and pointed to the seat. "Have a rest, dear."

Sawyer looked at the door, wishing their father would enter. Even though it would certainly mean an argument would ensue, it would be better than this.

"We have provided you with a nice home, no matter where we live. We've made so many sacrifices to keep you safe. I would've killed to have all of the opportunities you've been given, the places you've seen."

He tensed. The wind up. Now for the swing.

Olivene took a deep breath. "At no time did I give my consent for you to be in public with other kids. You betrayed me. How many of them did you tell your real name?"

"Nobody! I swear! I just wanted to spend some time with people my age. They only think that we moved here from

Alaska. I haven't said anything more." Her shoulders tightened and she dropped her gaze to the floor.

Olivene sat in contemplation. Piper's shoulders heaved, the forced cry Sawyer recognized so well. The more time she spent creating a stir, the less time Olivene would have to lecture.

"You know better than to display emotion," she admonished. "You are getting older. We've talked about what your future will look like.

"We? You and Dad?"

"Of course! Who else would you think I'd be talking about?" Olivene snapped.

"I.... You and Dad should know something. I'm going to culinary school. When we lived in Nebraska, I discovered I really liked cooking."

Olivene seemed shocked. "Really?"

"I cook every day. I love to bake. I want to create. You've always told me I had a higher purpose. This is it."

Sawyer snickered. "Told you she would remove the chains."

Olivene ignored her son and studied her daughter's face. "Hmmm. I'll have to think about it."

"Mom, this was my idea. Can you not yell at Dad? Please?"

Olivene's face softened. "Do you think that's all I do? Yell at your father?"

"Can I go upstairs now?" She wiggled uneasily.

"Go. And take your brother. I've had enough of him for today."

Hal came through the front door with a bag of plums in his arms.

"Be nice?" Piper begged.

Olivene shot her a sharp look.

Hal's eyes darted from Olivene to Piper and then rested on Sawyer.

"She knows, Dad. The jig is up." Sawyer shrugged his shoulders and headed for the stairs.

"You two go up and I'll come talk to you later. We'll work it out."

Sawyer pushed past his sister and into this bedroom, slamming the door. The last thing he wanted was more emotion and she seemed to be an endless well of it these days.

She banged on his door with no response for a few minutes. "I'm coming in!"

Returning to his video game, he stared at the screen instead of his sister.

"You smell like a dead cat. Why can't you shower? You're so disgusting." Piper kicked his socked foot, the one resting on an upside-down packing box. "Talk to me, doofus!"

He sighed and threw his controller to the side. "What do you want? I'm three points away from Gold level!"

"Why did you tell Mom about school?"

He folded his arms over his chest. "Because they always focus on you. They've never done anything for my best interests. Nobody has ever chased me, or tried to cut my hair. And then Dad thinks you're the one who deserves special privileges?"

She sat down beside him on the couch. "I'm sorry. You deserve more."

"You're not the only one who's getting away from them. I can't stand Mom. Her temper is getting worse. You don't see through her like I do."

She looked at him with concern. "Where would you go? We don't know anyone."

"One day Mom accidentally left an email open. It was

from an old friend of hers from Fallen Branch. He's building a new commune. I wrote down his email address so I can contact him."

There was a loud bang downstairs. They looked at each other knowingly. "Bets on how long it lasts this time?"

Sawyer smiled, displaying yellow, unbrushed teeth. "She's really mad. At least an hour."

Piper squeezed his leg. "What was his name?"

"Hawk, I think."

27

———

PRESENT DAY

The Plot Thickens

"You didn't bring one for me?"

Urica Jolloby is standing at the counter when I go to drop off Gladys' scone. Her long, grey hair is braided into two plaits with butterfly-painted metal clasps holding them neatly in place. She is wearing a flowered tunic and black stretch pants. The complete opposite of the tight-lipped matron I pictured sharing her confidence.

"Sorry, Urica, I can run back and grab another one."

Urica makes a pushing motion with her hand. "Can't you tell when this old gal is joshing you? Sit down and visit with us for a bit." She pulls two folding chairs from the storage area over to Gladys' desk.

"Was just tellin' Urica 'bout the top secret work I've been doing for you." Gladys removes the scone from the white paper bag and begins to eat.

"You told Urica?" It's hard to hide my dismay. "I thought we were keeping this quiet."

"Don't worry about me, Lanie. I'm as quiet as a church mouse." Urica locks her mouth with an imaginary key and tosses it over her shoulder. "The things I've seen in my time – Fallen Branch days alone – would raise the hairs on your neck."

I never thought of her as a resource. "Since you brought that up, can you tell me a little about Piper and her parents?"

Urica leans back in her chair and stairs at the ceiling. "Olivene was pregnant when they arrived, but lost the baby not long after. Gossip was that's what made her unfriendly, but I have my doubts she was ever the kindly sort. Never cared for that one." She crosses one knee over the other, causing a noticeable creaking sound. "Sister Olivene didn't get the message we were all one unit. Thought it was more about how she could put herself in the spotlight, always trying to be Zion's favorite. When that didn't work she started in with the teens, trying to find any group willing to follow her. 'Spend your time with the adults, Sister,' Zion would say. Oh, did that make her mad." She moves her hands behind her head, lacing them together. "Hal was okay, I guess. When she got pregnant again, we were all happy for her. Piper – Amaris - was the cutest little thing. I had my days where I thought Zion's ideas were crazy. But then that little girl came with the perfect birthmark, born into the world at exactly the time Zion predicted she would be. Beautiful, blue-eyed baby."

"Olivene was pregnant twice?"

Urica nods. "Zion told her some mumbo jumbo about her destiny being tied to another child. I think just to keep her from being mad every day and causing disruption in the camp. He saw in the future she would be pregnant again and this time, the child would be our future leader. Sure enough, little Amaris arrived."

Gladys laughs. "Surprised he didn't help the process along himself."

My phone buzzes. *I can talk now if you have time. P*

"I have to go. Nice catching up with you ladies!"

"Slow down, Lanie! You're always running!" Gladys called after me. "She's running from something. You know I'm never wrong about those things," she says in a low but loud voice, not meant for my ears.

I don't want to go back to the bakery, but I need to talk to Piper, even if it means seeing Cosmo. I'm still reeling from the conversation we had last night. *Never had a girlfriend, Lanie. I waited for the right one.* How could I be so stupid? Everyone is capable of lies. I just didn't expect them from Cosmo.

I let myself fall in love with this man; be vulnerable. That was so hard for me, after a lifetime of downplaying the scars of my childhood. I came to terms with so much by letting myself have tender feelings.

Has he been thinking about this all along? Laughing with Cedar at night about how he has played a game with me, convincing me he knew nothing of relationships? And like a fool, I agreed to learn with him. Held myself back from the usual routine of sleeping with a man and then discarding him, so I could get to know someone for a change.

The way we left things wasn't good. I circle around the block to have a few more moments alone. In *Forgive Me Again,* Tulip Sloan had amnesia and could only remember that her husband lied about losing their fortune. She divorced him and a year later when the amnesia lifted, she remembered that she had stolen from his boss, causing him to lose his job and eventually everything else. The more I think about it, the more I realize how silly I've been. *I hadn't told Cosmo the most important thing about the old me. How could I be mad at him for the same transgression?*

Piper smiles and wipes her hands on her apron when she looks up and sees me standing at the counter. "Hi Lanie! We had a real run on baked goods today, but I've got some leftover Chicken Planet Pie from lunch. Should I heat a piece up for you?"

"No, thank you. I would like to talk to you though. Could we sit down for a minute?"

There are three empty tables, thankfully. It would be difficult to discuss these things with lots of eager ears.

"Cosmo is coming around to the lunch idea. He said next month we can try a panini press!" She says excitedly.

"That's great! You've brought in a whole new stream of business." She's so happy, I hate to bring her mood down. "Piper, I've been wondering: what do you know about Hawk Beechum? Did you have any contact with him, I mean, other than the times he tried to kidnap you?"

Her smile drops. "No. I didn't know him at all. My mom said he was an idiot. She could always tell when he was the one coming after me. Even though they were all in black, his figure was much more noticeable. Too many French fries." She laughs.

"Well, I worried, because–"

I feel a hand on my shoulder and a frothy cup of coffee appears in front of me. Cosmo's version of half-foam, with his newly gained ability to make a "C" in the frothy milk.

"I thought I heard you out here. I was hoping you'd stop in today."

He seems very upbeat, considering the way I treated him

last night. I smile, trying not to betray my twisted feelings in front of Piper.

"Cos, I was just asking Piper about Hawk." I avoid his gaze, though I can picture his rugged jaw line, full lips and those deep, blue eyes filled with hurt.

As he sits down beside me, the scent of his musky cologne drifts to my nostrils. He turns to Piper. "You know more about Hawk?"

"No, I don't." She blushes. Maybe she doesn't like the extra attention, or maybe she's hiding something. "He is – was - a part of that Broken Branch group. I'm glad he's gone. I'm safe now. Is that why you came, Lanie? Do you think I had something to do with his death?"

I have to tread carefully here. "I had a conversation at the jail. With Zion."

"What?" Cosmo pivots toward me. "And you didn't tell me? What's wrong with you? That guy is poison! Why would you subject yourself to that?" He leans in close. "Is this how you punish me for what I told you last night?"

The color is rising in my face. "No, Cos. I was planning this visit before." I refuse to meet his gaze. I love him so deeply it hurts to hear the pain in his voice. "I knew it would upset you, but I wanted to ask him about Hawk. To gain a little more insight on his behavior. He told me some interesting things. But as I was leaving, I found out something even more peculiar. Do you have any idea what that would be, Piper?" I learned that tactic in the *Open the Door to More* seminar. Clive Williams was the only seminar leader who never agreed to sleep with me. He said he had a "headache." I thought he was more attracted to the woman staying across the hall from me.

Piper pushes her thick, dark hair behind her ears. "I hate

games. You're going to tell Cosmo anyway. I went to see Zion, too."

He glances from my face to Piper's, like he's never met either of us before. "Do you know how dangerous that man is? Kid, I know this seems like fairytale stuff to you, but he killed several people. He's manipulative. You may think you know how to handle him, but there's no spider better at luring someone into his web. The toxin he spews will paralyze you where you stand."

She slumps backward in her chair. "I never believed my mom when she said he was dead."

"Everyone in Piney Falls thought that until recently." Usually someone else will chime in here and tell my story for me, adding amazing feats that aren't true, like I flipped him over my back or beat him senseless with one hand. It's my badge of honor in this town. "Zion faked his own death. I discovered he was living–"

"I know. I read all of that in the Broken Branch literature. But my mom has never believed that's actually Zion. She says Cosmo killed the real Zion; that the person in jail is someone who remade himself as a poor imitation. She says the real Grand Elan died because of his flawed principles, and she's adamant about that. I wanted to see him for myself and decide if that was true."

Cosmo stands up and paces back and forth before stopping in front of her, placing his hands on the table. "Why would you do that? Do you have to see everything to understand it's danger? Now that he knows you're out there, he won't leave you alone. Like the Firestarters!"

"That's legitimately Zion. They had to do DNA tests to prove it." I glance at Cosmo, not sure if he wants Piper to know Zion is his biological father. He shakes his head slightly. "He's not behind any of these attacks. He doesn't even know about them and he certainly knows nothing about Hawk's death."

Cosmo scoffs. "And you believed him? The master of deceit. If he told us the room was on fire and we saw the smoke, I'd have to double-check before I'd trust him."

"He didn't act like he knew me. I didn't tell him my name. Just Piper. It wasn't a name he recognized. It was disappointing, after all of these years of being told I'm the chosen one to succeed him and then...nothing."

I smile sympathetically. "He didn't know me, either. All of those years living in the woods might have left him without all of his faculties. There's something else you both should know," I continue. "Zion, the real Zion, said while Fallen Branch was still active, Hawk stole money for him. It was all buried at Fallen Branch. I wonder if that is how they've funded these moves across the country, chasing Piper and her family."

"Did he tell you where?" Piper asks.

"He drew me a map, but it doesn't make much sense. It's possible he doesn't remember. Just like not remembering my name, he's not quite all there."

Cosmo slaps his hands on the table. "We're going out there today. I have some ideas. I can round up three shovels."

"Cos, there are tours going on. We can't let the tourists think we're out there looking for buried treasure, because then everyone will be out there digging holes. How will that look when Mr. Walters and his team arrive next week?"

"We'll shut down the tours for today. Tell them we've got some maintenance to do. This is important. When the other Broken Branchers find out about Hawk's death, they'll no doubt want to send someone else to hurt Piper."

I don't have experience with break-ups because I've

never invested in a relationship. But it occurs to me that two people who have just agreed to a cooling-off period don't normally spend time together trying to solve a mystery. There isn't an easy way to approach the subject. "Are you sure we should be together? I don't want our issues to cloud what we're trying to accomplish."

He stares coldly at me. Usually I know the anger isn't directed at me. "Some things take priority over personal issues."

Piper covers her ears and hums. November must've taught her this coping skill. She looks one way at Cosmo and then the other at me. When she sees me glaring at her, she removes her hands. "This is how my parents lived my entire childhood. You two love each other so much more than they did. I saw it the first day I arrived. Knock it off. Please?"

"I'm willing to put everything aside for now. You both are very important to me." I glance adoringly at Piper, but can't bring myself to look into Cosmo's eyes.

We all wash dishes together, silently. When my hand accidentally grazes Cosmo's, I want to grab it tightly and pull him close to me. Instead, we finish our respective chores and then head to my car.

As I open the passenger door, Cosmo's leather jacket falls to the sidewalk. We went for a walk on the beach recently. He gently placed the coat around my shoulders and told me I looked like a fashion model preparing for her next runway show.

I throw it in the back seat, hoping Piper doesn't recognize it. "Sorry for the mess."

"Don't you want Cosmo to sit next to you?"

I gulp. "We're grown-ups. We can sit apart."

28

___

PRESENT DAY

A Hotel and a Hot tub

"Do you miss your dad?"

Piper leans on the car door and rests her head on her hand. "Yeah. Sometimes. He was gentle and funny. I thought he really cared about us, but Mom said he was a no-good liar. Maybe he did care, he just couldn't handle that life anymore. One day, when the Firestarters finally leave me alone, I'm going to find him. Maybe we can go out for drinks, like adults." Little twitches on either side of her mouth betray the emotions she's trying so desperately to hide.

"I bet he'd like that. It's hard to understand why people leave with no goodbyes. I never quite understood why my father left me. My mother, I could understand. He couldn't take living with her anymore. But she was more of the crazy sort." I chuckle, thinking back to the times my mother would want to reenact a love scene from one of Tulip Sloan's movies. I would become one of her paramours, telling my mother all the things she wished my father would have said. It seemed so normal at the time.

"Did the Firestarters want anything besides your hair?"

"Pieces of my clothing sometimes. As I got older, they started asking me to tell them Zion's rules. It was a game to see if I had them memorized or not."

"My research leads me to believe there is more than one group of them –"

Cosmo taps on the trunk lid and I pull the lever. He starts to get in the front seat, but turns abruptly and opens the back door. I don't look him in the eye.

"I think November is giving the tours this afternoon," I say after a long stretch of silence. "That ought to be entertaining."

"Did she have an accident?" Piper asks. "I'm just wondering. She's so..."

"Insane?" Cosmo asks. "Yes, she definitely must've had an accident."

"Cos!" I protest. "You know that's not true. Everyone dealt with Fallen Branch differently. I'm sure Piper's parents had their oddities from their experience."

"Oh, yes. My mom always had a plan. She told us that's how things worked in Fallen Branch; someone was thinking ahead in every situation. Dad hated that. He wanted to be impulsive. She said a family on the run couldn't afford to be impulsive. Just once, I wanted a surprise." Piper says wistfully.

I reach over and pat her leg. "That's hard."

"My mom says you have to train your mind for whatever you want in life. I should train my mind to deal with things in a matter-of-fact manner, not to react with emotion. It will serve me well as an adult."

We pull into Fallen Branch, on the fresh gravel I ordered especially for our upcoming visitors. The grass is neatly trimmed and all the buildings painted. Even though they'll be torn down, it needs to look appealing for our guests.

November, dressed in her finest navy-blue, one-piece jumpsuit with a tangerine belt, is showing the visitors each building. I can hear her booming voice the minute we get out of the car.

"Over here, you'll see the laundry quarters. Doing laundry was considered a gift. That meant you weren't working in the afternoon heat pulling weeds, or sewing in the winter rains. Some of us were happy to have the time to ourselves. Though we weren't supposed to think of anything that didn't improve our world, we'd sneak off and find friends and tell jokes. There is a joke about two naked men—"

I wave, trying to get her attention. She is once again embellishing the script I gave her. *Don't worry about me, Lanie. I know what to say. These people will beg to stay at our resort.*

She waves back and continues. "There's Lanie over there. She's the one who got the ball rolling on this project. You all must return once they build our spa. It will house the finest in body pampering and local cuisine. That is IF we can build our resort. My horrible, ungrateful son and his ten-days-over-the-expiration-date, coconut yogurt of a father have decided they want to resurrect this nightmare. Just to get back at me. Can you imagine?"

I rush to her side. "What a wonderful tour guide you've had today! Can we give her a big round of applause?"

Everyone claps.

"Wait! We've still got another building! I've got some

funny stories about sneaking out at night and playing 'what will you eat for an extra sleep ration?'"

I shake my head. "The rest of the grounds are unfortunately shutting down for some maintenance this afternoon, I do apologize for the inconvenience."

November frowns at me as if she will argue, but I pull gently on her arm and shake my head.

"We appreciate your patronage, please feel free to wander around this area and read the plaques. Stay in the grassy area only. When you're ready to go back to town, don't miss Cosmic Cakes and Antiquery on Main Street. The best square pastries you'll ever eat!"

Once the crowd has dispersed, I look around for Cosmo, but he and Piper have disappeared.

"What was the cause of all that, Naughty Neighbor? I was just getting into the groove!"

"I went to visit Zion in jail. He told me about money he hid out here. We're going to find it."

"Why didn't you say that in the first place?" Her demeanor doesn't change. "I know where Hawk buried money. I helped him once."

We walk behind the buildings, to a hidden area I've never seen before in my many trips to Fallen Branch. There is freshly overturned earth.

November puts one hand on a hip and uses the other to point at the disturbed ground. "Just where I remembered."

"Did Hawk tell you why he buried the money?"

"Because Zion told him to. Really, Lanie? There didn't have to be another reason."

"Do you know who he stole from?"

She shrugs. "Wealthy members of Fallen Branch. They didn't dare complain and admit they hadn't given up all of their worldly goods. Those kids went into town and sold fancy watches and nice jewelry on the street corner. Zion knew all about it."

We call for Cosmo and Piper to join us with their shovels. It doesn't take long before we've overturned all the moist ground in the area. There is only one thick, heavy bag, but evidence that there were once many more.

Cosmo opens the bag and counts. "At least $200,000. It was supposed to be invested in 'our future.'" He shakes his head. "If our future lived with the worms."

"What do we do now?" Piper asks worriedly.

"We don't tell Cedar, that's the most important thing." Everyone looks at me. "If the police think Hawk told her about this buried money, they would have a motive for her killing him."

"By golly. You're right, friend. We have to agree to keep this to ourselves. I can ceremoniously bury the rest of it in my yard for now. I'll get rid of the bad juju surrounding it, just to be sure won't befall terrible tragedy. Asian Beetles. Bugs are never wrong. Bad things were coming." November reaches for the bag.

"Putting her in charge?" Cosmo pulls the bag in close to his body. "I don't think so."

There isn't a right answer here. We can't take the money to the police until we have more information about the missing bags. I don't want it in my house, or somewhere it might cause harm to Cosmo or Piper.

"Okay, you take it for now. But this will have to be a quiet ceremony. No unnecessary sounds to attract strangers. Got it?"

She nods.

"Oh, and Frankie is... gone?" I hate to bring up such a sore subject.

"Yes, he's gone. Left this morning. Good riddance to the

shadows of his father." She makes large, sweeping gestures with her arms. "Until he becomes a man of strength and courage, he's blown away with my wind."

As we walk back to our respective cars, I pull on Cosmo's arm. "Wait," I whisper.

When the others are a safe distance ahead, I turn to him. "I didn't go see Zion as a sign of disrespect. I simply wanted to find out what he knew about Broken Branch."

He looks at the cloudy sky. "I know that."

"He does not understand what's happening here, so our theory that he is behind Broken Branch is wrong. Someone else is calling the shots."

He remains silent.

"Hawk went to see him also. If I'm not mistaken, to prove to himself that Zion was still alive. I think he made a break from Broken Branch. That may be why he's dead."

Cosmo nods. "You may be right about that."

A river of emotion runs through me. "Whenever we're done with all of this, we do need to talk. We need to lay everything out on the table. Both of us."

He looks at me with concern. "More bad news? I can't take anything else this week."

"Just know that you mean everything to me. Even if we have to take a break, my feelings haven't changed."

He grabs my hand and kisses it gently.

29

PRESENT DAY

Monday, Five Days before Sleepy Sounds Corporae Heads'
Arrival

"I t's okay to cry, hon. You've been through so much already." I hope Cedar can't feel my anxiety as I rub her back. We are just days away from the investors visiting and I need her focused on going over a checklist with each business owner. November offered to step in for Cedar, but I can't risk one of her loud honks or colorful descriptions of things that never happened when someone is considering investing millions of dollars in our community.

Last week I went door-to-door interviewing and selecting just the right places to take the Sleepy Sounds contingent.

"I just...can't...believe...he's gone," she sobs, again.

I hand her a tissue, the last one in the box. "You two had a great time together. I'm sorry you didn't have a chance to explore your relationship when you were kids."

Cedar sits down in her chair and smooths her hair. "Hawk was so exciting. He had these plans for expanding on Zion's little world. He said we'd create other branches – get it? - across the country. He said Zion told him to go forward with his plans."

It's very difficult to keep my mouth shut. Zion didn't know any of these things. I don't understand how she has been so blinded. "Did he mention any names? Maybe others who were involved with Broken Branch or his new creation?"

She looks up at the ceiling. "No. I don't think so. Did I tell you he was my first kiss? I thought I loved him."

Many, many times.

"Hawk was still clinging to the world of Fallen Branch. I've always wanted to feel like I belong in the regular world. I guess we were never meant to be."

I cross my arms and walk toward the window, not wanting her to see my face. "And what about Cos? Did he have a first kiss too?"

"Lanie, I know what you're asking. I saw Olivene and the hold she had on those boys. She was just as powerful as Zion in her own way. I don't think you should blame my brother for the things he did."

"What things did he do? Did they sleep together?" I hate the sound of my voice. Accusing, weak and pathetic. A person my mother would have found sadly amusing.

"He never told me that. Just that he kissed her. Maybe other kinds of experimenting, but he wasn't specific. He and his friends felt it was the right thing to do. She convinced them that was what normal people did."

I turn around and study her earnest face. "I'm sorry. I'm making this about me. Here you are hurting. Let's talk more about your last day together. Maybe we can figure out exactly what happened to him. What did you do with Hawk? Before he burnt dinner?"

"Well," she sniffs, "we were planning our future together. He would work odd jobs while I finished our projects here. He said he'd been in contact with others for years, people who would join us. We were going to start out in Ohio, where he had some friends. He decided he'd ask Cosmo if he could pick up some shifts, cleaning, or whatever until I was ready to go with him."

"Because he wanted to kidnap Piper?" It doesn't make any sense that he would ask Cosmo for a job after the things he said to him when we went to dinner with the happy couple.

She frowns. "In all of our talks, he was excited about his new version of Fallen Branch. Not like the crazies trying to kidnap the poor girl. He was going to be the leader of his new group, not Piper. He was checking up on her, for Olivene. That was all."

Hawk Beechum had many faces. I can't decide which one is real. It's a very good thing Cedar isn't one to read facial expressions. "What changed?"

"He did mention a falling out with the person who was leading Broken Branch. He would make a much better leader. I figured because he can be a little intense, the others in the group were jealous of his passion. But when—"

"What?"

"Well, you already know what happened at Cheese With Your Burger. He was another person that day. Agitated, now that I think about it. On the way to eat, he had me circle the block a few times. Almost as if he felt we were being followed."

"Did he mention anyone else? Maybe another former friend he visited?"

"No. He didn't trust anyone who stayed here. They weren't devout followers of Zion like he was. Other than me, he said they weren't worth his time."

My phone buzzes. I look down and see it's Gladys. "I'm going outside to take this. Back in a minute."

Cedar nods.

The door to the Welcome Center closes slowly behind me, the doorbell squawking. Luckily, there are only tiny sputters of rain. "Gladys? What did you find?"

"Well, dearie, I can tell you Hawk Beechum was in at least four locations with the Moonlights. He worked at the same landscaping place as Olivene. And hon, I did a little more researching 'cause I knew you'd be wanting more. You and me, we're snoopy like that."

I smile. "What else?"

"There were some big events around the time they lived in several places. In Kansas City, a karate instructor who taught Piper and her brother, Sawyer, was found dead in an alley on Bantam Street. And in Scottsbluff, Nebraska, a doctor's wife and son disappeared. Bodies never found. Blood in her kitchen was the woman's, but not any other clues. Next-door neighbors to the Moonlights. The husband has been in a psychiatric hospital, mute ever since. The most recent was Piper's classmate in culinary school. He and his girlfriend both disappeared."

"But why would Hawk kill these people? Wasn't he after Piper?"

"Maybe it wasn't Hawk doin' the killin'. Hawk's just a cog in the machine...but there could another person at the center of the coverup. I'm thinking, maybe a young girl who's angry about being chased around her whole life, lashes out at the wrong people?"

"Piper? That's insane, Gladys. She's a sweet girl. She

wouldn't hurt a soul. She's been so persecuted, I can't imagine her wanting to inflict–"

"Persecuted again and again. If people were chopping off my locks I'd be angry too. You told me the other day the attacks keep getting more violent as she gets older. She's had enough now. What if she killed these people she thought would harm her, and Hawk, being her mother's old friend, offered to help cover things up? And now, here she is finally ready to start her own life and he shows up, with all of her secrets ready to pop out of his portly belly?"

"Oh, Gladys." I'm at a loss for words. Her story seems too absurd to be true. "Keep researching. We might come across something a little more concrete."

I open the door, just far enough to stick my head back in. "I'm going to get coffee. Do you want anything?"

"No, I'm fine." She waves. "Thanks for listening. One of these days, you'll come in here and I'll be the old Cedar again. Happy, like you and Cos."

I can't keep putting this off. As I walk down the block, I still don't fully understand how it will happen, but I've never backed away from a challenge before. Dinner and candlelight? Wine on the patio? Whispered in his ear, as we drive down the highway on his motorcycle?

Entering the bakery, there is a heavy feel to the room.

"Doris, you know how to fold these boxes. I've told you a hundred times. Do you need me to make you a video?"

Poor Doris is standing, tight-lipped, behind the counter. She knows better than to reply to Cosmo when he's in one of his moods. It's better just to let them pass unchallenged.

"Cos? I need to talk to you for a minute."

Piper cheerfully smooths her apron, oblivious to the current situation, "Hi, Lanie! Do you want to try my new Earthbound Egg Panini? I made a secret sauce for the top!"

"Sure. Make me one to go. I want to talk to you for a few minutes when I'm done with Cosmo." We walk to his office where I motion for him to sit in his worn leather chair and close the door.

"I understand how your emotions are all over the place because of Cedar. She's doing better than you are." It's my second lie of the day.

"I know my sister. She didn't kill that nut. It has to be somebody else from Broken Branch. Have you made any headway with Olivene?"

"We're getting together this afternoon. She wants me to meet her at Fallen Branch for some reason. I was hoping you would go with me."

He looks a little shocked. "You want me for backup? Even though you don't trust us together?"

I do one of Vem's deep breathing exercises. I think of myself as a chicken and focus all of my energy on my chicken-sized brain. At least that's how I visualize her words. "I've been thinking about that. You were just a kid. Olivene took advantage of you. She assaulted you. I was manipulated as a kid too. I should have been more understanding."

He huffs. "She didn't assault me. I wanted to be there with her. It was powerful, and if Zion wouldn't have flaked out, we would've ended up in bed. Is that what you wanted to hear?"

"You're making this very hard, Cos. I'm trying to tell you I overreacted. What happened twenty years ago needs to stay there."

His face softens. "So you're taking me back?"

I bend over and kiss his silver hair. "I never wanted you gone in the first place. I was upset because that wasn't the Cosmo I know. But we missed a big chunk of each other's lives. We all grow and change." I avert my gaze to the space over his head, where last year's Piney Falls Pump-n-Go calendar hangs. "Which is why I need to tell you something, too. Can we meet for dinner tomorrow night and talk about it?"

Cosmo swivels his chair around and takes my hands in his. "There is nothing you could do, Lanie Anders, that would make me push you away. I'm sorry I didn't tell you about Olivene from the start. I didn't know if I could trust you, and then when I did, it never seemed like the right time."

Framing Your Mistakes in the Most Positive Light. Evan Morris. We met in the private bathroom in between the morning and afternoon sessions. I gulp. "Just promise you'll hear me out." This will crush him.

He pulls me down to kiss him. I feel guilty, pretending like everything is all right when I know it won't be soon enough.

Piper knocks on the door. "Your sandwich is ready. Don't want to interrupt anything disgusting so I won't open the door."

I turn the knob and she hands me a brown paper bag and my almond milk latte, half foam.

Cosmo touches my side as he gets up and leaves the room. "You two have a nice chat."

Piper nods and pulls the door shut and looks at me gleefully.

"Mom says I should stay here. She and Sawyer will move up soon. The Firestarters are gone. It's like my life is finally coming together. That Emma person from Cheese With Your Burger stopped in several times, asking me to hang out with her. She says we're, like, the only people under forty in town."

Her face displays a calmness I haven't seen before. If she killed Hawk, she is as cold-blooded as Zion. Maybe Gladys is right. They have conditioned her to detach from everyone, including those she kills.

"You should definitely spend time with someone your age." I tap my fingers on Cosmo's desk, absent-mindedly. "Did you see Hawk again, after he attacked you that day?"

She shakes her head. "I don't think so. Wait – he might have come here looking for Cedar. Come to think of it, I did see him."

"And you weren't panicked? He attacked you several times!"

She smiles a broad, sickly-sweet smile. "I called my mom that night after it happened. She reminded me I'm only as weak as I think I am. I looked him in the eye and he lost his power over me. Remember me telling you Mom says not to lead with emotion? I didn't that day."

None of this sits right. "Thanks for the sandwich and the coffee. You're an impressive addition to Cosmo's staff."

Her violet eyes are brimming with tears. "I'm lucky to have such a great friend, Lanie. Thanks for always having my back. Things are finally coming together."

I walk back down the street with a sense of unease. Piper has behaved as if she's a scared little mouse running from a cat for weeks now. She's always on edge, but now – after Hawk's death – she's completely calm. Could it be that she harmed the people in those towns, like Gladys said? Maybe they didn't move so much to get away from the Firestarters but to keep Piper from being arrested for horrendous crimes. That could be why Olivene is here. To protect her daughter.

Someone is thumping on my back. "Lanie? Glad I

caught you." It's Urica, out of breath and flustered. She thrusts a paper in my hand. "Gladys said you'd want to see this. 'Important doo-dads from Michigan', she said."

I look at the paper and then at Urica. "It can't be."

30

TWO YEARS AGO

Redondo Beach, California

On the first day of culinary school, Piper met Jordan, the twenty-four-year-old high school dropout with stringy blond hair longer than hers. He sat outside during breaks, smoking cigarettes with his yellowed fingers, and chugging blue energy drinks.

"Hey, hot stuff," he called when she came to join him after the third day. She should've been repulsed, but instead, she found herself intrigued. "I'm gonna open a restaurant in Kansas City when I'm done. Not barbecue like everyone else. Maybe Thai fusion. What about you?" He offered her a puff, but she shook her head.

"Haven't decided yet. Mom talks about Oregon all the time. I need to get some experience under my belt first. Then I'll think about my own place."

"You need your mommy's approval? Aren't we past that stage of life?" He took a long drag, then set the cigarette on the curb beside him.

Piper blushed. "No. We've moved around my whole life. I need to get my bearings somewhere. That's all I was saying."

"This isn't grade school where the teacher wipes your butt. This is real life. That's all I'm saying." He stood up and rubbed his foot on the cigarette butt.

It stung just a little. It was emotion, and Olivene had taught her to leave that at the door.

"Always lead with logic and not emotion," Piper recited. *"Be cheerful, no matter what. Whether I'm angry or happy, I have to use the same demeanor."*

Olivene smiled. "Perfect. I think you're ready for school. None of these kids have been through what you have. Don't let them in. They couldn't possibly understand."

"Wanna be my partner?" she asked brightly.

He chuckled. "I don't do partnerships. I'm a solo kind of guy. The last restaurant I worked in, me and this waiter dude agreed to split tips. He only split his once, when he thought I would give him weed. I was counting on that money to get a new phone. Bastard. You can't trust anyone these days."

"I didn't mean that kind of partnership. Just going up there together. Maybe renting an apartment or something."

"I'll consider it. We'd have to get more comfortable with each other first. My last roommate screwed me over. Told me he'd pay the gas and electric for six months so I could get a new game system. Never paid it."

She knew he wasn't someone she could trust. But there was a strong desire in her that overrode her common sense: a need for friendship. Some part of her that found pleasing him more important than remaining safe.

If she got the words just right, he laughed. She replayed

those scenes over in her mind before she went to sleep each night. Little by little, she told him things about their life. It began with small stories about Hal and Sawyer.

"My dad says the funniest things about coffee."

"Oh yeah?" He tapped his cigarette on the side of a silver Jeep, causing ashes to cascade to the ground. "My old man ran off before I started school. Don't think he wanted kids."

"Well, mine ran off too," She replied eagerly. "I try not to talk about it. We haven't seen him in three years."

"You want to smoke a joint with me?"

She shrugged. "Maybe."

He put the joint up to her mouth and then pulled it away. "First you have to tell me some deep dark secret about your life so that if we get in trouble for this, you'll never be able to blame me."

She was relaxed with him. He didn't care who she was or why she wasn't normal. All of the words began to fall out. "And they chased me again. Cut my hair. We had to move and I was never allowed to mention Cedar Rapids, Iowa - or the fact that we lived there - again."

He didn't turn to look at her but handed her the joint. "That's messed up, dude. No wonder your only conversation is with the burnout in class. I like twisted chicks, though. Tell me more."

Over the course of several months, Jordan was the only person she spoke to unless forced. He was a rebel who smelled like stale French fries, body odor, and marijuana and no one else would go near him. Whatever she said, he had nowhere to repeat her stories. He was her first real friend since Hazel.

On the day of graduation, Jordan told her to meet him in the alley where they'd had many deep discussions about life over a joint and sometimes a beer. She always took care to buy breath mints before going home. Olivene wouldn't tolerate that kind of behavior.

31

SIX MONTHS AGO

The Cold Shock of Reality

"I'm gonna miss you. I wish you would think about coming to Oregon with me. I won't know anyone." She thought about throwing her arms around him and kissing him. She'd seen other girls doing that with their boyfriends. The time never seemed right.

"I was thinking I might come up there for a few months. Maybe crash on your couch."

"Really?" she tried to hide her excitement, but it was too big to contain. "I'm staying with a friend for a while. But I'm sure she wouldn't mind one more person."

Jordan looked across the road to other members of their class arriving in their finest clothes for the ceremony. "I wouldn't be coming alone. My girlfriend, Jeana, wants to be a writer. She writes the best poems. I told her your story and she's really hyped. She wants to write a book about you. Your life on the run. We'd crash there until she got all of your story recorded."

"What?"

"I told her, but she won't tell anyone. She's awesome like that." He flicked his ashes in front of him, but the breeze blew them into Piper's face.

"You promised you wouldn't tell anyone! It was our secret!"

"I didn't promise. You decided that all on your own." He looked her in the eye for the first time in their entire relationship. "It's all cool."

Her years of training paid off. She got up, let out a deep breath, and opened the back door to the conference center. "Bye, Jordan," she said without any emotion.

Olivene was standing by the punch bowl, tapping her finger on the table and anxiously searching the room for her daughter.

"Mom," Piper said calmly.

Olivene snapped her head around. "Where have you been, young lady? Don't you know you're never to leave my side?"

Piper stood on her tiptoes and whispered in her mother's ear. Sawyer crossed his arms and stared at his sister.

"Where is this Jordan person?" Olivene asked.

Piper pointed to the back door. "Don't worry, Mom. I know how to take care of this."

32

PRESENT DAY

Dance Like There's No Tomorrow

"Polka, Polka, Polka. Is there anything better on a glorious Tuesday?"

I shut the radio off in frustration. A big detriment to living in such a remote area is that communication can be limited. Some days the Internet is out in the entire town. The Sleepy Sounds Corporation can improve that. The large luxury hotel, complete with four-star dining and a lobby fountain will be the crown jewel of Piney Falls. We'll offer day trips to Astoria and Tillamook, and even historical tours of the area. Maybe they'll ask me to take charge of their marketing. I have already mapped out a five-year plan, just in case.

"Hello?" There is a knock at my window.

"Cedar? What's wrong?" I reach over and open the car door. It's starting to rain and her perfect hair and makeup shouldn't be deconstructed. She is a work of art. I notice she's carrying a large, blush-colored bag I've never seen before.

She opts to sit in the back seat where I've stored all the extra promotional material for the investors. Cedar straightens her hair and wipes the few raindrops from her violet, silk top. "Cos told me you are going to meet Olivene. I need to talk to her about Hawk."

"Are you sure? You're pretty emotional. I don't want her to make this harder for you." Or for me. Olivene asked me to meet her on "sacred ground" so she could show me how important it is to her. She'll already be annoyed I'm bringing Cosmo.

"Yes, I'm sure. You taught me that words need to be said and not kept hidden in the dark. Besides, the way things are going between you and Cos, I need to make sure he won't have a meltdown. It would devastate him if Olivene caused you two to break up."

I'm glad I'm sitting in the front seat so she can't see the color rise in my cheeks. "He told you about that?"

"We talk about everything, Lanie. Maybe someday the two of you will share that kind of intimacy."

"I've been meaning to talk to you about that. It's not normal conversation for a brother and sister –"

The passenger door opens and Cosmo slides in, wearing his black leather coat. "What am I missing? Something deep and disturbing, I hope." He kisses me gently on the cheek. He causes electricity to flow through my body every single time he's nearby.

"Nothing at all. Cedar was telling me we're all prepared for Sleepy Sounds."

"Hawk and I were going to open coffee shops in each group we started," Cedar begins as we head out of town. " A way for everyone to make money and learn service. In such a short time we made so much progress. Hawk Beechum was the one true love of my life. Just like the two of you; once your find your other half you just know it."

Neither one of us in the front seat responds as she drones on and on. More than anything I'd like to stop the car and tell her this nauseating conversation has to stop. When this is all over with, she needs to take a long vacation away from here.

When she pauses to takes a breath, I change the subject. "I wanted to run something by both of you. I've been researching the Moonlight family. They may be involved in some very serious events."

"Oh? Like what?" Cosmo cracks the window, letting in the wind's swirl inside and tiny droplets of rain that pepper my car door. Something that drives me mad.

"Gladys scoured the dark web. She found deaths or disappearances in places where the Moonlights were living. All around the same time. Piper's karate teacher in Kansas City, their next-door neighbor in Nebraska, and someone Piper went to culinary school with; those are just a few."

Cedar leans up between the seats. "Do you think Piper killed Hawk? Is she evil and we missed the signs?"

"I admit the thought has crossed my mind. We need to be careful in the way we question Olivene about this. She's here to protect her daughter. And Cos, no shovels." I giggle as I think about him hitting Zion over the head when we found him, just to shut him up.

"Fair enough. Don't think you're right about Piper though. You badgered me until I let her under my skin. She's harmless, as far as I can tell."

We pull into Fallen Branch and a sense of pride bursts in my chest. It's not the same neglected space I saw when I moved to town. The buildings formerly covered in peeling paint all sport a fresh pale-yellow coat. There are wooden signs, directing visitors to different sections of the camp. The grass is mowed and the sandy pit in the center has been raked nicely, ready for a welcoming fire when our guests arrive.

There are no other cars in the parking lot. "Should we walk around, or just sit here and wait for her?" Cedar asks.

"We should walk around. This makes me nervous, especially knowing that woman hated being late for anything. You sure she didn't say she was coming in the back way?" Cosmo's knee bounces.

"What back way? I've never heard of a back way."

"C'mon, I'll show you. Want my coat, Cedar?" The rain is now coming down steadily.

"I've got an umbrella in the back. Hold on." I get out and run to the trunk, pulling the hood of my robin's-egg-blue coat over my hair.

This place feels eerie. The air is always heavy and the old memories seem to hang around like a melancholy fog, no matter how much new paint is on the buildings. I shake those feelings aside and hand Cedar the umbrella.

We walk about a half-mile to the back of the camp, through tall hemlock trees to an area I've never seen before. A large, red barn, paint peeling, sits in a clearing. "Maybe this part of the camp should be included in the tours. Did anything significant take place here?"

"Nothing worth the memories," Cosmo says under his breath.

From seemingly out of nowhere, a figure appears in front of the barn. She is walking with purpose but when she sees us in the distance, she stops, puts her hands on her hips, and stares. Her demeanor is just as unfriendly as it was the first time I met her. When we reach her, the rain has increased from a drizzle to a full-on downpour. She motions for all of us to enter the barn in front of her.

"You're a little early. I thought we were meeting in the parking lot. I wanted to take a trip down memory lane first."

"I'm surprised. You don't seem like the sentimental type." It just falls out of my mouth before I can catch myself. "Sorry. I didn't mean that. We all process in our own way."

She moves uncomfortably close to my fiancé. "You brought Cosmo and his ever-present sister? Did you think you'd need muscle? Or maybe he couldn't wait to see me again?"

She is baiting him. I hope he doesn't take it.

"Olivene. I told Lanie everything, I have to say it felt good to get rid of all of that black tar clouding my insides. We don't keep secrets." Cosmo shifts his weight uncomfortably from one foot to the other. "What about you? Does Hal know about all of your conquests?"

She guffaws. "Men can be useless. Hal was no exception. You'd know about that don't you, Cedar? Hawk Beecham was just another idiot."

"I loved him. And he loved me!" she protests.

"Why did you want to meet me here?" I step between Cosmo and Olivene. "In the rain? We could've just talked over coffee. And what are you doing in the barn?"

"I want to show you something." She motions for us to follow her to the other side of the barn and I trail behind her.

Cosmo catches my arm. "Don't turn your back on her," he warns quietly.

Olivene leads us to a far corner where there is a hole in the ground similar to the one where we found the buried cash a few days ago.

"What is so exciting about this?" Cedar asks.

"This was how we lived all those years on the run, constantly moving, working minimum wage jobs. Thanks to the gracious donations of Fallen Branch members, money buried here at the request of Zion, may he rest in peace." She smiles and folds her long arms across her chest as if she's waiting for a gasp.

When none of us responds, she continues. "Well, most of the money, anyway. I've been told you found the rest. Stupid Hawk. I told him to move it to another location, now that you've been trying to sell the place."

"That wasn't your money, Olivene. That should have been returned to everyone who thought it would start a new colony." Cosmo bends down and peers into the hole, making sure nothing is left.

"Zion chose our family. He knew it would be difficult to protect our daughter. He spoke to me in my dreams and said this was the right thing to do."

"There's a lot of that going around." Hawk had the same delusions. "I talked to him in jail, where he is very much still alive. He never mentioned that once." I glare at her, trying to make myself appear bigger as Vem always tells me to do if we're approached by wild animals.

Cosmo stands up and brushes off his pants. "Don't bother, Lanie. For her convenience, he'll never be the real Zion."

"What about Hawk? How is – was – he involved in all of this? He was a good, decent man and you tortured him. You and your daughter killed him!" A tear slides down Cedar's exquisite cheek. So much for me preserving her makeup.

Olivene rolls her eyes. " I didn't kill Hawk. He contacted me years ago when we began putting together a new Fallen Branch group."

"Broken Branch?" I ask.

She ignores my question and continues. "From the beginning, he went on about making improvements to the plan. Some book he read told him how to create a better version of our commune. I told him if he wanted to join us, he'd need to follow our rules. Recently he decided he couldn't do that anymore. Poor fool probably spouted off his tenets of Gorman to the wrong person and they didn't have the patience to deal with him." She sighs. "He did this to himself."

"Gaummond! And if he wasn't here working for you, why did he show up when Piper did?" I half-yell, already exasperated with her. I tried to get through the book, but half of the words were misspelled and he totally lost me when he insisted his followers drink twelve, perfectly-colored raw eggs before every meditation.

Cosmo rubs his chin. "Wait, a minute. YOU are the leader of Broken Branch? Then why are these people chasing after your daughter?"

33

PRESENT DAY

Fallen Branch Barn

"Cos, one thing at a time." I touch his arm.

"Hawk was here to retrieve more cash for us. I didn't realize he was serious about starting another group . I'm not sure why the sudden change–"

"He saw Zion. The real, live Zion. That and spending time with Cedar changed him." I know the last part isn't true, but I want her to feel he truly loved her.

"He was playing you, Olivene! He started his own group, away from the likes of you!" Cedar cries. "He would have made a great leader!"

Olivene rolls her eyes. "Yes, Cosmo, to answer your question, I'm the leader of Broken Branch, for now. I kept in contact with the young men I knew from Fallen Branch. They all encouraged me to keep working toward Zion's master plan, so that when Amaris was ready, she could take over. I needed her under my complete control to groom her for the role. They came and scared her a little, to keep her off- balance, to teach her how to control her emotions."

"For her entire life, you've told people to follow you from town to town just to scare Piper? To force her to be on guard at all times? Cutting her hair and making her think she'll be kidnapped, all for your amusement? That's sick!" *Poor Piper.* I want to hold her in my arms right now and tell her I'm sorry I misjudged her.

Cosmo sighs. "It's one of Zion's tactics. Keep them off-balance and unsure of themselves. Makes them putty in your hands."

"This has nothing to do with Zion!" Olivene screeches. "My daughter needed to learn to respond quickly without emotion; skills others don't possess. It was all part of her training."

"Taking pieces of her clothing and locks of her hair were a part of Zion's original proclamation. The child born during the eclipse would have special powers in all of her being. Including her hair." Cedar interjects.

Olivene balls up her fist. "I DIDN'T tell them to take her hair. That was all Hawk's idea – he and his friends. When I found out who was behind it, I tried to stop them."

"You've driven your daughter crazy with this plan. You've got her killing people, like my poor Hawk." Cedar moans.

Olivene looks puzzled. "You think she killed him? I am the one who orders killings. Whenever someone makes too many mistakes or refuses to obey. It was always Zion's plan. Jez Dillon is at the bottom of a lake in Missouri. Found out he was a mole and I sent Hawk to clean up the mess. There were always different circumstances, but always justified."

"The karate teacher in Kansas City?" I ask.

"He was concerned that my daughter was too aggressive. Threatened to turn us in to social services. Same with the nosy woman in Nebraska. She said Sawyer needed help and she'd get it for him if I couldn't. I didn't count on her son being there."

"What did Hal have to say about all of this? He was an even-tempered guy. I can't imagine him being okay with you murdering everyone you meet." Cosmo inches closer to her, putting space between her and the women he loves.

"Can you believe he lied to me from the first day of our relationship? I didn't even know his real age until we'd been at Fallen Branch for a few months." She huffs. "He knew the plan from day one. I should have known he would fail. Several times he betrayed me; trying desperately to remove Amaris from my control. He left and tried to live on his own a few times, but every time he came crawling back. He was worthless without me and he knew it. And then he forgot his place in Gran Elan's plan. That was his biggest downfall."

Incredibly, she looks proud of herself.

"You make it sound like he was disposable. Like he wasn't your husband! This is sick, even for you, Olivene," Cosmo's eyes shift around the barn.

I wonder what she planned for me today? Did she invite me out here to kill me too? I, too, look around, trying to discover any traps she may have set. I wonder what kind of tools might be in the barn to protect us? Cosmo should have brought his shovel after all.

"Does Piper know? She's said nothing about her father being dead. Either she's an excellent liar or you've kept the truth from her all of these years." I already know Piper didn't inherit her mother's cold heart.

Olivene shakes her head. "It served no purpose to tell her. Once she's been installed as the leader of our organization, she'll learn about everything being done in her honor."

"Someone will figure this out eventually. The bodies will start turning up. You got lazy and left Hawk's head," Cedar says defiantly.

"I told you before, I didn't kill Hawk." Olivene shakes her head at Cedar. "Leaving mementos behind is not my style. When I get rid of someone who no longer has purpose, I make sure they're completely disposed of." She smiles like she just swallowed something delicious. "I learned this little trick from a mortician in Iowa. If you put a dead body on wood chips with alfalfa and a bit of moisture, the body heats up so hot it becomes compost. That's how I got rid of most of the troublemakers. Hal is fertilizing a garden somewhere in California by now."

"And what if your daughter doesn't want to go along with this? What will you do then?" I ask, ignoring the gruesome description she seems to enjoy.

"That won't happen. I've orchestrated things so carefully for over twenty years. Hawk and a few others became lost, but everything else, including Piper moving here, was for the good of Broken Branch. She'll be ready soon enough to learn what's required. If you're interested, I could show you a detailed chart of every move, every single little thing I did to prepare my daughter for her role."

"We don't need to know," Cosmo begins.

"She took self-defense lessons to prepare her for the people who would want to harm her. She learned to watch her back and escape from those who looked to take her out. She learned how to live with little outside resources. Everything I did had a purpose. Few parents prepare their children for life as I have.'"

I think back to my days at *Work Ahead Office Supplies - The Most Profitable Office Supply Chain in the World*. I planned every bit of the road to my success, including all the men I slept with at the seminars. Olivene has done the same thing.

"Miss Anders, you've been very thorough in your investigation. I'm impressed, though it's a little sad this is your last day, and you'll have no one to share your findings with."

Those words hit me hard, though when I asked Cosmo to come with me, that's what went through my mind. "That's it? I've done nothing to make you want to get rid of me."

"Didn't you listen? I said I know about your investigation. I've received word from my contacts you've been asking about our family under a fake name. We can't have outsiders like you questioning our motives."

I cock my head to the side. "I admire you. We're not so different, Olivene."

She raises her brow. "Don't think you can work me. I'm much too smart."

"I was once as driven as you," I continue. "Always met my goals, no matter who I stepped on." I move to her side. "The problem with that life is that it's not really living. And the people you crush during your journey to the top will inevitably come back to haunt you." I nod to Cosmo.

He moves in quickly and grabs one arm and I grab the other while he pulls her off balance, forcing her to the ground. Even as she struggles, we hold tightly. Cosmo puts his knee in the center of her back.

"Cedar? Do you have anything in that suitcase of a purse we could use to restrain her until the police get here? And my next question is, can you call the police?"

She drops her bag and umbrella and begins pulling out tissues and cosmetics.

"Call the police first," I huff, trying to keep Olivene still. "What was your plan, Olivene? How were you going to kill me?"

I can sense someone standing behind me, but I can't turn around without letting go of Olivene. Suddenly I feel something around my neck.

"Her plan was to invite me to the party," he hisses in my ear, as everything goes dark.

34

———

PRESENT DAY

It's Now or Never

My head is spinning but the incidents of the past five minutes are clear. Someone brought me to the ground and thinking quickly, Cosmo leapt on top of them. There is movement around me.

"Leave her alone! I've been in prison and I know a hundred quick ways to kill someone!"

When I'm done coughing and the tears clear from my eyes, I can see Cosmo has Vem's son, Frankie, on the ground. He has his knee in the middle of Frankie's back and his arms pulled up behind him, just like he had with Olivene a few minutes ago.

"My little man. Always thinking you were stronger and braver than you really are," Olivene remarks snarkily. She stands and brushes the dirt off her pants. "You'd be wise to get off my investor. I wouldn't have invited Lanie out here without a very detailed plan for her demise."

Horribly, I admire that in her. "Why is Frankie here? Is he in Broken Branch?"

Cosmo, seeing the danger in the situation, brings Frankie up to a sitting position without letting go of his arms. "Talk to her, punk!" he commands.

Frankie coughs and then spits on the ground in front of him. "My dad always hated Zion. He thinks that freak made my mom weird. We decided, once Mom left, that we'd buy this land and turn it into our own cult. For kicks." He smirks.

I sit up and try to catch my breath. "He came to my house and admitted that the other day. I just don't know why you would go to all of this trouble. You could start your own cult in California, away from your mother."

He shrugs. "We wanted November to be humiliated. When they sent the first Broken Branch brochure to our house, a lightbulb went off in Dad's head. He realized this was our chance. He contacted Olivene and we've been planning this ever since."

"What about Lance from the bank? Was he a friend of your father's too?"

"He's former Fallen Branch," Cosmo offers. "Dirtbag, as I remember. I went to talk to him about getting a loan to open my bakery. He said as a general rule, they didn't give loans to Fallen Branch people. Even though he was one himself."

"Dad found out he's been running a side game at the bank for years. Skimming a little from this account, a little from that. He's ours now." Frankie smiles. "You'd be surprised how easily all of this came together."

"Why did he let me go through with the tours and the painting? With Sleepy Sounds coming in a few days? It seems like a pointless waste of time for him."

"We couldn't have it looking like we were going to restart the cult without getting the town in an uproar. Can you let me go? I can barely breathe!" Frankie gags dramatically.

A sick picture forms in my head. "Now that you take your orders from Olivene, what other projects have you done for her, Frankie?"

"Don't say a word!" Olivene commands.

"I get it." As hard as I stare, Olivene refuses to make eye contact with me. "I used to be a very successful business-woman. I know how you have to discard some people you feel are dead weight. But how have you killed these people without being caught? Didn't the police ever question you?"

Cosmo looks at me quizzically.

"I studied death for years. The karate teacher was an accident in the alley. No cameras, no witnesses. He thought I was there for help with Amaris. She was defiant. We already went over this." Olivene paces, her hands moving nervously up and down.

"How did you kill Hal?" Cosmo persists.

Olivene purses her lips. "Like all men, he wasn't capable of following orders. The final straw was his idea that Amaris should live with his parents because he thought Hawk would cause her real harm. His death was my favorite." She looks off in the distance, as if recalling a joyous occasion, not the death of her husband.

"I tracked him down to a motel in Redondo Beach. We had a tryst, a trip down memory lane. He knew what was coming so he didn't resist. I even let him take sleeping pills before I shot him. You know the rest; he made nice compost for a farmer."

"What about Jordan from Piper's culinary class?" The longer I stall her, the more time Cosmo has to formulate a plan. At least that's what I hope is going on.

"Piper, the poor child, thought she could buy him off. I

had to step in." She sighs. "They would've gotten hit crossing the street eventually. I did the world a favor."

"And Hawk? I don't believe you didn't kill him." There are lots of tools in the barn, but none that look like weapons she's ready to use.

Olivene belly laughs. "After all of this, my confessing to these delicious murders, why wouldn't I claim the one that would delight me the most?"

"Stop it!" Cedar yells. "I can't take any more of this. You didn't shoot a deer. This was a person. A wonderful person."

"I wouldn't go that far," Cosmo whispers.

I clear my throat. It's time show my cards. "I do understand getting rid of underperforming adults, Olivene. The only question left for me is why you felt a child had to die. Your child."

35

PRESENT DAY

A Shocker

"Why would you suggest something so horrible?"

Olivene's teeth are yellow and very crooked. I can see that now that I'm studying every inch of her tanned face. Maybe it's her personality that gives her appearance an evil glow.

"You're more twisted than I thought, Miss Anders."

I could be imagining this, but I think she winked at me. I suppress a feeling of satisfaction. "Not insinuating. I know for a fact. Urica Jolloby remembers changing the diapers of a little blue-eyed beauty, with the crescent-moon-shaped birthmark. When Fallen Branch ended, you moved to Michigan along with your friends, Birdie and Christian Finch. Your daughter, Amaris was quite sickly. She made many trips to the emergency room; every one of them recorded her eye color, unusual birthmark and the fact that she had a life-threatening disease."

Her eyes soften for a minute. "My daughter was sick. All babies get sick."

"Five months later, Birdie and Christian also had a child. A daughter."

She returns to her hardened state, after some kind of memory flashes across her face. One that left her temporarily human.

"What is your point, simpleton?" She scoffs.

"That sick little girl died in Michigan. Hazel Finch's death certificate notes her unusual birth mark, her blue eyes, and the date of her birth, the day Piper was allegedly born." There is no sound in the barn. "Birdie and Christian Finch moved to Texas four years later, without a child. You and Hal moved all over the country with your son, Sawyer, and your green-eyed daughter, who is as healthy as a horse."

"None of this proves anything."

"Piper came over to my house last month and tried on some dresses. Sleeveless designer dresses. She looked stunning, by the way. I noticed she had no birthmarks of any kind."

"She's had it removed. Along with her contacts, she wanted to conceal her identity." Olivene snaps. "You're getting tiresome."

"You switched babies; gave up your child so you could fulfill Zion's prophecy. Don't you want everyone to know how much you've sacrificed?"

Cedar gasps audibly. "You gave up your own baby? Abandoned the real Piper?"

"That's cold, even for you, Olivene," Cosmo adds. "You're telling me the girl back at my shop is an imposter?"

Olivene paces around the barn before arriving back in front of us. "Not an imposter. Do you know how hard this has been for me? For us? Only someone with my kind of inner strength would be capable of giving up so much for the movement. We needed a healthy child to carry on. The four of us made the decision early on. It was the only way."

"The child you gave birth to during the eclipse needed her mother. She needed both of you. Instead, you just handed her off to someone else."

"The doctors told us she wouldn't live to see adulthood. A genetic disease. We had to make other plans. Birdie and Christian knew sacrifices would have to be made. It's exactly what he — the real Zion — foresaw. The leader of the next generation of Fallen Branch would have many struggles on the way to the top."

"How will she become the leader if you're calling all the shots, Olivene? She sounds more like a puppet," I snap.

"You don't have any idea what you're talking about!" she harps. "I've groomed her for over twenty years. She'll be exactly what I want her to be. She may not have been born during the eclipse, but I constructed everything else in her life to make her Amaris Moonlight. The child I gave birth to became someone else's for the good of the cause. Because I'm strong, I succeeded. Hal wasn't. He cried for months. Zion would be so proud of us."

"You realize that is the real Zion sitting in jail? The police did DNA tests on his medallion and Cosmo and me. He's our father." Cedar blurts.

Olivene looks at Cedar sharply. "That imposter is your father? No wonder he got caught. A weak version of the strong man who was going to lead us into the future."

Two men appear in the doorway. One is very large and muscular with a big nose and a bushy mustache. His face twists in a snarl. The other is lanky and grey-haired, stooped over and looks defeated. They are both holding large guns.

"Finally! You were supposed to be here an hour ago!" Olivene yells in exasperation.

The older man comes over to Cosmo and motions for him to get off Frankie. Cosmo pauses. The man pushes on him with his gun and Cosmo stands, reluctantly. "Brother Donovan? Why would you get involved in this? You were a decent guy!"

The man stares blankly at Cosmo. "Olivene has guided me since I was a teenager. After Zion died, I was lost. Thankfully, she stepped in and showed us all how to function in the outside world. She found me my first job in the cemetery." He rubs the back of his neck with his free hand. "At first I was skeptical about starting Broken Branch, but over the years, she's developed a real plan for our future. This place will come back better than before. You could join us, too."

Cosmo shakes his head furiously. "Not ever going to happen, man."

"Where she will take us is to a grave. She's going to kill us, Donovan. There's no future!" Cedar hisses.

"The investment group will be here in a few days. This place will be crawling with people. They'll find our bodies," I add helplessly.

Olivene straightens her mint-green blouse, plucking out straw from between the buttons. "We have many resources. I think all of you will be placed ornately throughout the town. That will keep any potential tourism away, don't you think?"

I've got to think of something quick. I try to catch Cosmo's eye, but his hatred is his focus, and that rests squarely on Olivene.

"Mom? What are you doing?" An unexpected but not unwelcome visitor appears in the doorway. "Do you have to hurt them? They've been so good to me!"

She seems oddly calm.

"Baby!" Olivene's voice softens. "What are you doing out

here?" We were meeting later. This isn't a good time for you to be at Broken Branch." She rushes to her daughter's side, but Piper holds her hand out, keeping her mother at a distance.

" I came out here to tell you that Sawyer surprised us. He's back at the motel. I've been standing outside listening to your disgusting conversation. About me and who I really am. All these years, you made me think I was born during the eclipse? And Daddy? He was in on it, too?"

Olivene tries again to move closer, but Piper continues to resist. "Sawyer is...here?" She seems thrown for a minute. "You ARE the chosen one," she insists. "Zion said he saw us as your parents. Not Christian or Birdie. He got the celestial vessels mixed up, that's all."

I can't contain myself. "Piper, honey, I know this all a big shock. You're better than this. They are trying to turn this community into a place where people can't think for them-selves. You've seen how destructive that was for Cosmo and Cedar, and even Vem."

One of the men hands Olivene a gun. She moves to my side and pushes it in my ribs. "Don't try to confuse my daughter. She's about to enter an important phase of her life, one where she doesn't need distractions like you or the other Townies."

"Deep down, I've always known something was wrong." Piper cocks her head to the side and one tear rolls down her cheek. "The love in your voice, every time you spoke about Hazel. It wasn't the same with me."

"Oh, baby," Olivene tries to return to her daughter's side, thankfully giving my ribs a break.

Piper pushes her mother away. She is sobbing now, though trying to suck her anger in as it releases. The two sides of her – the controlled version Olivene created and the sweet, emotional young woman we've come to love – are fighting for dominance.

"I liked it when you and Dad fought over me. At least then I could pretend you really loved me. The rest of the time, I was a robot. 'Do this, act that way, be strong.' Chiara showed me how a real mother loved her child. Ever since, I've known our family had cracks. Dad wanted more for me but his presence made everything harder. I was relieved when he left for good."

Olivene furrows her brow. "You were right to feel relief without that man in our lives. He was nothing but trouble."

Piper shakes her head. "This isn't about Dad. He was smart to leave us."

"What are you going to do with us now, Olivene? Kill us in front of your daughter?" Cosmo goads. "Your mom was about to have us snuffed out, kid. You'll wake up tomorrow and we'll be gone and Mommy will tell you it was an accident like all the rest."

Seeing Piper made Olivene lose her focus and she appears flustered. "We're not going to – we're just having a conversation. You can go back into town and wait for me, okay baby?"

"I'm not going anywhere." Piper widens her stance and wipes her tears with her shirt. "You're going to let my friends go. Whatever you have planned for me, I'll go along with it. As long as you leave my friends out of it. Let them go back to their normal lives and we'll pretend like they were never here."

"Yeah, Mommy. Let us go." Cosmo mocks. "You don't want your daughter seeing you at your real job. Killing anyone who gets in your way."

Olivene contemplates for a moment, her eyes darting from her daughter to each of her hostages. The barn has become uncomfortably quiet. "Jake, can you take Cosmo outside and have a conversation with him? He's disruptive and I want to talk to my daughter."

"NO!" I yell as I try to lurch forward.

"It's okay. I can handle myself, Lanie." Cosmo puts his hand on my shoulder as he walks by. I grab it and kiss it, trying unsuccessfully to keep him close.

"I don't want anything to happen to him! Promise me, Mom!"

Olivene smiles. I've come to know this expression for the evil that it belies. "He'll be just fine. You'll see him tomorrow at work."

The gunman shoves his gun in Cosmo's back. "C'mon, bud. We'll discuss the weather out where we can see it."

Cosmo forcefully shoves his elbow into the gunman's crotch. Instinctively, I reach back and hit Olivene in the throat. I don't know what comes next, that's all I've seen Vem do.

Frankie tries to tackle me, but his lack of physical prowess makes him easy to take to the ground. I put my foot on his chest, the way I saw in the *Self Defense for the Working Woman* seminar. It was co-taught by Lorice and Laurie McNab. I wasn't experimental enough to sleep with them both, so instead I slept with the man who sat next to me.

From out of nowhere, November's welcome voice whispers in my ear, "I waited exactly five minutes, as instructed by Piper. That was four minutes and twenty seconds too long." She grabs Frankie by the back of the head and yanks him to her side. She holds his neck like a mother cat does to paralyze her kittens and fortunately, it seems to work; he doesn't struggle. "What am I going to do with you, son?"

"Let him go." Olivene is pointing the gun directly at me, her voice raspy. She is holding me tightly to her side once more. She turns to face her daughter, forcing me to turn as well. "I'm sorry, baby. You're going to learn a hard lesson about life today. Sometimes you have to let go of the people you like for the greater good. This is one of those days."

A shot rings out. I look around the room, fearful something has happened to Cosmo. Instead, its Olivene on the ground, clutching her stomach. Vem lets go of Frankie in her shock and he runs from the barn, without concern for his mother. Cosmo still has the other man in his grasp, confining him easily. I survey the barn, trying to understand the origin of the gunshot. My eyes come to rest on Cedar who is frozen in place as the other lanky henchman runs by her and out of the barn. There is a gun in her well-manicured, shaking hands.

"Mom!" Piper screams as she runs to her side.

"The police are already on their way. I'll call to make sure they bring an ambulance," November pulls her phone out of her pocket and dials as she kneels down beside Olivene, feeling for a pulse.

"Get something to tie him up with!" Cosmo yells, snapping me out of the frozen state of panic I'm in.

November takes the elastic purple scrunchie from her head and hands it to him. "This will work for now."

There are several old ropes in the barn and I find one and bring it to him. Quickly, he whips the rope around Donovan's arms and legs, trussing him in much the same way he did Zion when we prepared him to be carried down the mountain. He slumps forward and doesn't resist. If I didn't know any better, I'd think this was a relief to him.

"Put your hand firmly on the wound," I say quietly to Piper. The only dead person I've ever seen was my grandmother. My mother insisted we watch her take her last breaths, so I would have a dramatic base in which to give my performance as Tulip Sloan in *Love's Last Gasp*. I watched her take her last breaths and then the spirit of the one woman who cared about me left her body. I can see the same thing happening with Olivene.

"Now is the time to tell her whatever you need to say." I rub Piper's shoulders.

"Mom, I tried to love you. You made it so hard," she says between sobs.

Cedar is still standing with the gun in her hand. I want to comfort her, too, but this situation seems more pressing. "Cos!" I gesture wildly with my head to bring his attention to his sister.

"Cedar, give me the gun," he says calmly. "We will tell the police I did this."

"No, Cos! You just got your pardon! You can't go back to prison!" she protests.

The awfulness of the situation sinks in. Someone will have to be held accountable for this crime. Earlier I wondered if I would lose Cosmo forever. Now I'm sure of it.

"It's self-defense. We all saw what happened. No one is going to prison." November says matter-of-factly. "I need to find my son. If anyone needs to pay for this, it's him."

I wonder how much of this story she heard; If she knows her son has been working with Olivene all along.

"Where did you get the gun, Cedar?" Cosmo is holding her firmly, stroking her head.

"It was Hawk's. He was talking crazy. When he disappeared, I went over to his place looking for him and found it. I didn't want him hurting anyone. I've had it in my purse ever since."

Piper looks up suddenly, her hands covered in blood. "Did my mom say what happened to my dad?"

36

TUESDAY BEFORE SLEEPY SOUNDS INVESTORS ARRIVE

There is a lot to work out. The police took Cedar into custody, even as Cosmo threatened to take them down. I'm glad they come into his bakery for coffee every day and understand his love for his sister trumps all rational behavior.

Piper knelt beside her mother until the ambulance took her away. In Piney Falls, there is no hearse so all bodies are transported via ambulance. It was a strange sight, the natural urgency of the paramedics in caring for a body whose soul had already gone. Maybe long before her death.

Only a few policemen remained of the impressive group that initially arrived. Including the cars assisting from neighboring Telllum, there were six cars and ten officers, all taking pictures and collecting evidence. Piper wrapped her arms around her middle and stood, looking small and alone. After I completed my interview, I went to her side and she turned and hugged me tightly, her hands still covered in her mother's blood.

"Lanie, I know she was awful. I've known it my whole life. So why does it hurt so bad?"

I pull her dark head into my chest. "Because she was always there, good or bad."

She gulps. "I don't think she loved Dad. She never acted like it. I want to tell him how sorry I am for being such a brat. Do you know where he is?"

I kiss the top of her head gently. "You've been through enough. Give yourself some time to process today's events, and then we'll discuss your dad."

"What do I do now, Lanie? Who am I?" Stored up her entire life, there are still endless tears to run down her cheeks.

I put my hands on her shoulders and turn her to face me. "You're Piper Moonlight. A brave young woman who has endured more in her life than anyone I know. Only second to Cosmo Hill in baking abilities. She's independent and smart. She could make a good life for herself in Piney Falls." There is one person who hasn't been addressed. "What about your brother? He'll need you now. He's never been on his own, either."

"I have to go back to the motel and talk to him. "Her voice quivers. "What will he do without Mom?"

"Not to worry. I'll go with you to talk to him." I guide her out of the barn. "If you'll wait for me in my car, we can pick him up. I'll make dinner and you both can stay as long as you like."

When she leaves, I go find Vem. After several pauses to honk and meditate, she's finished her interview with the police. It's a good thing they know her, too. We stand together outside, where the sky has cleared and the sun is shining brightly. "The police said Frankie was responsible for Hawk's death. How long have you known? Why didn't you tell me?"

"I didn't know. This is all on his father, Vem. Not you."

"I should have figured that out. All along, I should have known he was only here to hurt me. And now he's disappeared. With his father's resources, he'll be hard to find." She looks at me hopefully. "At least now he won't be messing up your land deal."

Sleepy Sounds. "I've got until Friday to pull everything together and make it look like nothing ever happened. The bank will have to sort out their issues with Lance and I'll need assurances we're moving forward. Cedar's being questioned by the police, again. She'll be in no shape to help me if they even let her go."

"November Bean, at your service!" She salutes me. I've always marveled at her ability to make me laugh regardless of the severity of the situation. A policeman navigates around us, putting up yellow tape across the entrance to the barn.

"We'll have to work all night. I'll make sure Piper and Sawyer are comfortable and then–" I forgot all about Cosmo. I almost lost him today. He's down at the police station without me. "Vem, can you take Piper to pick up her brother and the drop them at my house? Let her whip up something to eat that suits her and make her comfortable?"

November pushes her glasses up on her face. Without her purple headband, her hair is wild and untamed. She looks almost feral. "Anything you want. You know, she could come to my house too. I've got a great leftover corn chip and hummus casserole. Also, there's another bottle of Sassy Lasses wine in my chiller. For later."

"I've got something to do to first. It might take a while."

37

———

PRESENT DAY

Some Words Are Harder Than Others

I've been sitting in my car for almost two hours outside the police station. Cosmo isn't answering my texts. I went inside right off and asked to speak to him or Cedar and I was told to go home. Gladys' son-in-law, Boysie Lumquest, said I wasn't family and I couldn't be in the interrogation room. It makes little sense to me, since I witnessed everything too.

The rain begins again; drops are gently dancing down the windshield and my car windows are steaming up. I don't know how long to sit here, waiting. We've put this off long enough and after the events of today, I realize we aren't promised tomorrow. After the day we've had, it's obvious secrets destroy relationships and I want ours to prosper if it can.

I lean the seat back and close my eyes. Visions of the events that unfolded are unavoidable. Olivene's hateful voice, her strange way of showing affection for her daughter. Not unlike my mother. We were both used by adults for some higher purpose we couldn't understand.

I drift off, dreaming of lying in Cosmo's arms, safe. We talk about our future together and giggle about our day. There is a knock on my window as the door abruptly opens.

Cosmo moves to the passenger side of the car, his hair damp from the now constant rain pelting him. "You've waited out here this whole time? I didn't expect you to, since we're – whatever we are."

I put my seat upright and wipe the drool from my chin. I pull him in close and kiss him, hard. When I let him go, he looks down at his shoes, unable to meet my eyes. Gently, I lift his chin.

"You matter to me. I told you that before. I'm more upset with myself than you. I shouldn't have treated you like that over a teenage crush."

Cosmo stares at my cloudy windshield. "Why did that upset you so much? It was so long ago."

I take a deep breath. "Because I did things far worse. And it wasn't in high school. It was before I moved here. My entire adult life really."

He frowns. "What are you talking about?"

There is another knock on the window. Cedar is bent over looking in the window, soaked to the bone. "Can you take me home?"

I nod and she gets in, shaking the drops from her hair. "Thanks for waiting, Lanie. The police don't think they'll press charges, but they'll continue investigating."

"What a day, sis. Didn't know you had that in you." Cosmo smiles and pats my leg absently. It is the reassuring touch I missed.

"You don't have to meet with the investment group,

Cedar. Vem offered to help. After what you've been through, it's understandable if you want to stay home for a while."

She leans forward from the back seat. "Thank you, Lanie. I think I need to see this through. Before Hawk, it was the reason I got up every morning." She leans back and runs her fingers through her soggy hair. "I need to immerse myself in something and not relive her face or her ugly words. I have to find some way to get past all of this."

For so long I thought Cosmo was a murderer. I didn't know how to act around him. Now his sister has killed someone and it feels equally awkward. Our sweet Cedar.

"That must've been so awful for you."

"It was awful for all of us," Cosmo interjects. "Today shouldn't have happened. Thanks to Cedar, we all survived. Piper can finally live a normal life. There were people I knew in prison who wouldn't have had the guts to do what you did today, sis. Superhero kind of brave."

When we arrive at her apartment, she reaches up and rubs my cheek. "I don't know what I'd do without you, Lanie. You've given me confidence. Hawk did that, too. Neither of you liked him, but he was the other part of my soul. Just like the two of you, some pieces are just meant to fit together."

I glance at Cosmo. His beautiful eyes are misty.

"I've been telling her that for months now, sis."

"I'll check on you in the morning, Cedar. Could I have a few minutes with your brother?"

"Okay. But you're both old enough to do that stuff inside." She chuckles as she steps out. "It feels good to laugh. We need to do that more."

We both watch her walk slowly up the stairs to her apartment and I brace myself for what comes next. "Today taught me a good lesson about time, or the lack of it. Maybe I was worried about losing you, or admitting I wasn't who you thought I was. Either way, it's time this comes out. Cos, I had lots of experiences before I moved here. More than I can count. I never intended to have relationships with them or cared who they were. I just wanted to feel a certain way for a few minutes, and then I wanted them to leave. It didn't matter if they were good people or bad people. I was a horrible, destructive person."

I take his hand and stare down at my shifter. "That's why it's been so slow with us. At least I think it is. I was afraid of hurting you. I've never allowed myself to care about someone before and I didn't want to break your heart. After all the events of today, I realized it had to be said before more time passed; before something else crazy happened and I risked losing you again. Does that make sense?"

He pulls his hand away and rubs his chin. "Oh boy. Lanie, I don't know what to say." His knee bounces up and down, faster and faster. "I never thought of you that way. To be honest, I figured you were just as inexperienced as me, in all ways. This was the last thing I expected."

"Lots of people have these kinds of relationships, but I did it without concern for the other person. That Lanie, who seems like she lived in a different time, was reprehensible. I didn't care who they were or what feelings they might have. That's the ugly truth right there."

"I'm glad you told me. We don't need secrets." He looks at me earnestly. "I'm gonna have to think about this. Too many things have happened today, and my mind isn't prepared to handle much more. Can we talk again tomorrow? When we've been able to get ourselves past all the events of today?"

I nod. Tears of relief are running down my face. It's out in the open now. The best man I've ever known gets out of the car without kissing me or squeezing my hand.

38

DAY OF INVESTOR'S VISIT

A Change of Plans

"I realize Hawk's killer is still out there somewhere. But today, we have to focus on the future of Piney Falls. We are expecting three people. Derrick Walters, the president of Sleepy Sounds, two members of his staff, and someone new representing Piney People Savings and Trust. I spoke to the bank president and he's decided he'll send Marsha Danforth instead of Lance, now that it's clear he was working with Broken Branch." I hand a sheet of paper to Vem, who is dressed in her most proper solid black jumpsuit, unusually demure black-rimmed glasses, and black canvas shoes. Her hair is pulled up dramatically high on her head, frizzy fluff draping over a black band.

"When they looked into all of the land sales Lance had done, they found he'd been skimming money from each sale, just as Frankie said."

"That snake has been embezzling from the bank for

years. Never liked him. Smelled like stale pizza and turnips," Vem sniffs.

There is no way to emphasize this enough without upsetting her. "Your job will be to give them the history of Fallen Branch. No editorializing. Just the facts. We especially don't want them to hear what happened, so keep them to the main part of the camp. Tell them the rest of the property is a wild, uncleared path or something. Got it?"

"You're sure you don't want me to give them an exciting recap? I meditated over this last night and it came to me that March Franklin's misdeeds should be brought out in the light. Keeping things quiet never helps. That was the whole reason you came to Piney Falls, remember? To bring stories into the light?"

"I came to town intending to create a fictional story for a class. Since then, I've become a completely different version of myself. Let's not force the investors to relive the past when they're trying to create a blazing future." I can see she is disappointed. It's good she has something to think about besides her missing son. "For today, stick to the outline on your paper. Maybe once they've broken ground, we can get into the specifics of a tour. You could do a 'tall tales' tour or something."

I turn to Cedar, who is exquisitely dressed in a tweed jacket and skirt with an olive shirt underneath. "And you will tell them about the financial impact on the community, how you've researched the businesses it will bring in. This is your moment to shine, Cedar Hill. Show them around town a bit and introduce them to the business owners."

"The ones you carefully selected who learned how to speak in complete sentences," November adds. "I was there when you told her. You should stay away from Burt

Comings. Three words at a time and at least one is a curse I've never heard of."

I smile. This day will be a challenge if I don't. "He's not on the list."

"Cedar, you're bringing them to Cosmo's at noon for lunch. Is Piper still okay with fixing them something?"

Cedar nods. "She's already at the bakery. Cos told me she's adamant she will not let what happened stop her from putting on the best luncheon of her career today."

I wonder if Cosmo will be as friendly and open with me. Olivene's misdeeds cut him deeply, but mine are worse. I look at my watch. "We've got exactly one hour before we meet them at Fallen Branch. We should get out there and make sure nothing interesting is happening. Any questions?"

Both women shake their heads.

"I'm so incredibly proud of both of you. Vem, your son hurt you to the core. And yet, you're still here, helping when you're needed." I squeeze her shoulder. "And Cedar," I take her trembling hand in mine. "You saved our lives. After the tremendous loss you suffered, then what transpired with Olivene... There aren't words enough to express my gratitude. This is a strong female tribe. No one can break us."

"That's what besties do for each other." Vem wraps her arms around our shoulders. "It's better for me to be working on something instead of sitting at home, wondering where March Franklin is hiding. I can't bear the thought of him stuck in a cave and wiping himself with leaves, even though It would mortify his father." She sniffs again.

"Thank you, Lanie. It's only because of you that I knew I could save us." Cedar pulls away. "And Cosmo knows how amazing you are as well. He loves you, no matter what happened in your past."

I purse my lips. "I wish he wouldn't tell you about our private talks. But if I expect him to accept me for all of my issues, I have to accept him, too."

It's already fifteen minutes past when I wanted to arrive, so we all scurry to my car for the short drive. "Vem, do you remember when you found that Asian Lady Beetle? You said it was bad luck, that it represented someone who would try and worm their way into our hearts. It wasn't Piper. It was Olivene. She did that to Hawk, and to her husband. She tried to do it to Cosmo, but he was too smart. Sometimes you actually make sense. I just wanted you to know that."

She rolls down the window and lets out a howl.

When we reach the gravel parking area, I leave the car running. "Would you two set things up in the picnic shelter? I want to drive around to the barn and make sure the police have finished their investigation. Just in case."

"Shouldn't we go with you? In case another Broken Branch member is lurking around?" Vem asks.

"No, I can handle myself." Last night I placed a knife under my seat for that very reason. "You two go and I'll be there soon."

When I reach the back of the camp, I turn off the car and sit. Last month, the biggest concern I had was telling Cosmo about my past. So many other serious issues have come up since.

The big red barn – where I thought I was going to lose my life, where Cosmo almost lost his and Olivene breathed her last breath – is standing majestic amongst the weeds. Someday this will make a great location for social gatherings. Happy events.

As I wander through the tall grass to the barn, my heart is heavy. Without concern that I might be contaminating a crime scene, I duck under the yellow caution tape and walk inside. Over to the right, I was on the ground, knocked out by Frankie. To my left, my dear sweet Cosmo stood, ready to defend me. And in the center, the soiled space where Olivene died. I drop to my knees and begin to cry. *So much for this being a good makeup day.*

"Why would you come back?"

The voice raises the hairs on the back of my neck.

"Frankie? You know the police are looking for you. There will be lots of people on the property today and they're expecting me back. You won't be able to get away with anything."

I turn around to see him, dirty and disheveled, wearing the same clothes as the day of the incident. "I thought you'd be long gone; that your father would've sent someone for you."

"Do you have something to eat?" His voice is shaky and I can smell him from some distance. I watch him for a moment. There's nothing left of the swagger he displayed every other time I've met him. He's a sad, pathetic, shell of a person.

I remember there's a Pantheon Powerberry Scone in my Shanel bag, one of Piper's new creations. I've been keeping in my freezer since last week, and had been looking forward to eating it today. "Here," I hand it to him. "That's all I have."

He unwraps it and eats ravenously for all of thirty seconds. I look away, trying to avoid the further demise of this boy who is so loved by November.

"Broken Branch is dead. Olivene is dead. Whoever is left should scatter if they know what's good for them. The police know all about it. "

"I wanted my mom to suffer."

"Why? What did she do that was so horrible? She loved you so much, Frankie."

He wipes the crumbs from his chin. "Do you know what it was like, growing up with a mother who barked at the moon and howled when she didn't like someone? It was a constant humiliation. Even the kids in my private school who didn't know their parents laughed at me. She could've worked harder to be normal. She just chose not to."

"Oh, Frankie. She didn't have anything to draw from. Her parents didn't raise her, so her well of knowledge was limited. Can't you see that?"

He laughs brusquely. "So she's pulled you into her web as well. Do you find her charming? Quirky? You don't have any understanding of what it's like growing up with a mom who isn't all there. You haven't suffered the way I have."

Dance like Tulip Sloan, Lanie. Practice while I'm with my boyfriend. If you're lonely, watch her movies. You don't need friends.

"The only thing you're suffering from is ignorance. You have a mother who loves you so much she let you go."

"Abandoned me, you mean. I came home from school on spring break and she was gone. Just a note. You don't do that to a kid. Dad said he always knew she was too selfish to be a good parent."

I look at my watch and realize I'm late. "I don't have time to take you back to town. But if you wait here in the barn I'll send someone later. They'll have to take you to the police. Your father will get you a good lawyer. At least you'll be warm and fed."

He sits down on the ground, fiddling with his expensive tie.

"This is your father's hate. If you would stop and think about it, you'd realize he's the one bringing your life into the dumpster."

He nods and looks at the ground. "Why do you like her so much? You're not from the cult. You're normal."

"Nobody is normal, son. We're all a bit off. I used to be closed off like you and it was a lonely life. Maybe prison will give you time to think about that."

There is a blanket in my trunk that I hand to Frankie. Cosmo and I used it when we went down the hill above my house and watched the stars. I push away those feelings. They can't be here today.

"Good luck, Frankie," I say before getting into my car. Luckily, I have some powder for my face and Blushfully Berry lipstick.

When I return to the camp, the visitors have arrived. I recognize Derrick before I get out of my car. The $2500 suit, the closed-off demeanor; he's every large client I ever had at *Work Ahead Office Supplies - The Most Profitable Office Supply Chain in the World.* Marsha Danforth from the bank is smiling and nodding behind November. By his side are two people: another man who is standing a few steps behind them wearing an equally impressive grey, pin-stripe suit, holding an umbrella over Derrick's head on this partially sunny day and a woman with imposing black sunglasses.

November, loud and confident, is explaining the history of the camp. "On this date over thirty years ago, a young man came here with a vision. To create the perfect community, where the only goal was to be sustainable and live without the constraints of modern society."

So far, she's not straying too far from the script.

"People came from all over the world to experience the peace and calm of our world. They gave up their fortunes to hoe the fields and wear rags. That was the best part of Fallen Branch. The worst part..." her voice falters. "The worst part was that so many of us lost our childhoods, our connections with the things that mattered most. We didn't develop the ability to function in the real world. So when Zion destroyed it all so violently – the world as we knew it came crashing–"

"What November means is that Zion left the camp and unbeknownst to everyone, he was living up in the hills," I point to the looming, tree-covered hills behind us. "He left all the people who spent their adult lives becoming dependent on him without a way to function in the real world. I'm Lanie Anders. I've spoken with you on the phone." I extend my hand to Derrick, who shakes it firmly.

"Ms. Anders, these are my associates, Laura McNern and –"

"Tyler Feckler. *Changing the Feckless Mind to Fertile in Fifty Minutes.*" If I had any reaction left in my body, it would collapse right here and now.

39

PRESENT DAY

An Unexpected Turn of Events

"You've heard of my seminars? I'm flattered. I gave those up last year when Mr. Walters offered me a deal I couldn't refuse."

His brown eyes bore through me to the other side of the camp. I can't tell if he's just that motivated to impress his boss, or he's trying to make sure I remember. During the very first marketing seminar I attended in Portland, fifteen years ago, I noticed a brown-haired Adonis who was all-too-eager to please.

"Can you give me some pointers?" he asked. For the first time in my professional career, I felt powerful. I invited him back to my room and pretended to be an expert on marketing instead of brand new in my field, too. After promising we'd share more trade secrets over eggs and coffee, I snuck out under the cover of darkness, planning never to see him again.

"Yes, I've heard of them."

He reaches out and grabs my hand firmly, taking care of the niceties I can't make my body perform. "So nice to meet with you, Ms. Anders. I've heard so much about you, I feel like we've already met."

I nod weakly. *Focus, Lanie. Don't screw this up.* "November has been giving you some of the history of Fallen Branch. What do you think of the property so far?"

"It's just as you described, Ms. Anders. I can see this space filled with vacationers," Derrick gestures broadly, "relaxing after a day exploring the Oregon Coast."

"Much of the property is undeveloped, so you won't have to spend time removing existing buildings," I offer, taking care to look directly at Derrick and no one else.

"There's more to see if you'll follow me," Cedar chimes in. "Any questions you might have, I'll be happy to answer along the way. We'll continue the tour in town and then stop for lunch at a delightful bakery."

Bless you, Cedar.

"Are you ok. Lanie?" Vem whispers. "You're as white as a gosh-darned ghost."

"I...um...I haven't worked with people in my field for a long time. Just not quite at the top of my game."

"Cedar's got this down. I heard her going over her schedule. Cheese With Your Burger for a small sample shake; Urica's Art Gallery for a postcard with a picture of her most recent painting, the Flanagan Family; and then we all meet at the bakery. It's all handled. We even have time for meditation if you want."

There are no words that come out of my mouth, only a gesture to the car where I know she will talk all the way back to town. Thankfully.

"I'm going to sit in the car and do my Meditation for Sons Lost in the Woods," Vem announces as we pull up in front of the bakery.

I've completely forgotten about Frankie. I'll call someone when we're finished here and then explain it all to Vem. "You come in when you're ready. We'll save you a seat."

Cosmo has moved several tables together with a reserved sign on them, forcing some of the regular crowd to leave. I asked him to make sure the more vocal members of the community, who would be sure and spill the story of Olivene, would not be present.

Piper is stirring a steaming pot of soup, telling Doris stories of her days on the run. "Do you know that the wind blew so hard in Nebraska, our door blew off its hinges?" Her face is pale and there are dark circles under her eyes. She is sad but there is also a lightness around her. She is free.

I tap on the counter, trying to get her attention before Cosmo sees I'm here.

"Lanie! We're just about ready. So good to see you today!"

The last time I saw her, she was eating tuna from a can in my living room. Sawyer, without a hint of emotion, laid on my floor watching videos on my phone. Piper and I sat up and cried – we cried – until three a.m.

I lean over the counter, speaking softly. "How are you doing?"

She half-smiles. "This sounds dumb, I know. I feel happy. I'm relieved that all of this is in the open. No more Broken Branch. No more Firstarters. I can get on with my life. I might find my birth mother, Birdie Finch. I know she did some horrible things, but I'd like to see what she looks like. I need to figure out who I am, you know?"

My mouth twists in a way I know will eventually produce wrinkles. I still haven't told her about her father. "It's only been a few days. Give yourself time to grieve. What about Sawyer? He doesn't seem like he's much for conversation."

She sighs. "Yes. Just like me, he's been taught to keep his emotions inside. He told me he's met some people on the internet that he wants to visit. I think he should have a chance to spread his wings, too. That girl, Emma, from Cheese With Your Burger, called again. I think I might hang out with her after work. Like friends, you know?"

I forgot to talk to her about the immaturity of this girl. "No, I don't think that's a good–"

The door jingles and Cedar walks in with the group, nodding to me. She is calm and professional like her entire world didn't just turn upside down. If she can do it, so can I.

I motion to the table Cosmo especially set up for them, the only one in the entire bakery with matching chairs. As they sit, Piper comes around the counter sporting a brand-new, solar-system-themed apron that says, "Cosmic Cakes and Antiquery, A Baked Goods and Historical Experience," boldly emblazoned across the front. I'm pleased he took my advice and ordered these for this event.

"Good morning, ladies and gentlemen. I'd like to offer you our soup of the day, Cauliflower Cosmos Puree, to start while you look over our daily lunch specials. May I get you something to drink?"

I marvel at her calm outward appearance.

Placing myself strategically between Laura and Derrick, I take a deep breath, assaulted by the familiarity of his cologne, *Power Musk*. I can't remember if Tyler wore it as well? Without a suit and their pretenses, they were all the same. One smell, one personality. The bile rises in my throat. "What do you think of our little hamlet so far?"

His face breaks into a professional smile. "Very ch–"

There is a large bang in front of the store. My eyes move to the window just as Vem falls to the ground.

40

PRESENT DAY

Awkward Endings

In front of the building, my best friend is lying motionless on the sidewalk. There is no blood, but her normally pale face is the color of chalk. She's obviously not conscious.

There is no doubt in my mind who did this without even looking at him. He doesn't have the decency to run like the common criminal he is.

"Frankie! What have you done? This changes nothing." I bend down and check her pulse, hoping others will follow me soon and restrain Frankie. In a matter of moments, Cosmo rushes past me and tackles Frankie to the ground.

"You think this is fun, punk? I didn't get the chance to finish what I started the other day." He pushes himself on top of Frankie, yanking his arms back so tight I'm afraid he'll dislocate them. He pulls a weapon from Frankie's hand, a small gun of some kind.

"Don't hurt him, Cos. We want him in picture-perfect health when the cops arrive."

Cosmo eases up a little and lifts the gun toward the light. "Looks like a riot gun. Not meant to kill."

"It's some theatre for your little group. She's not dead, just performing in her own way." Frankie snickers in a muffled voice.

"Why are you here, Frankie? How does this benefit you at all? The whole thing with Olivene is over."

"My dad and I want this deal. We funded Broken Branch and everything was going fine. Then Olivene called Dad and told him Hawk was going to kidnap her kid and ruin all of our planning. Dad sent me up here to scare him away. I followed him around for a couple of days and when he left the burger place, I offered him a ride. Cult members are so gullible." He laughs. "You watch enough horror movies and it's almost too easy." Frankie smiles a broad smile, reminiscent of Vem's. If only he were like her in ways that counted.

"Dad will be really proud of me. Taking down ole' Hawk and putting November in her place. Now he'll see I'm a real man."

"Killing Hawk didn't make you a man. Hurting your mother most certainly doesn't make you a man. From my vantage point, the only man here has you pinned to the ground."

Vem begins to stir and Derrek pokes his head out of the door. "Is there anything I can do?"

"Get this freak off me! This whole town is full of cult members and freaks!" Frankie's voice instantly changes into that of a wounded animal. "That lady wanted to kill you! She was coming in the building to take you out and I tackled her and took her weapon. Get this monster off me and find help!"

I can hear an emergency siren, the only police car on duty. They rarely turn on the siren, especially when the police station is four blocks away. Cedar asked them to stand by in case the man with the Fishin' Fool hat from the city meeting, or someone else tried anything funny.

Derrick glances from Cosmo astride a squirming Frankie, to me holding Vem's hand. "It looks like you've got this situation well in hand. My team and I will help inside until you're finished here. I started my career in a coffee house similar to this one."

He closes the door and walks back inside. I catch Cosmo's eye and we share a smile.

"What happened?" Vem is trying to sit up.

"No, sweetie. Stay down there and rest. We'll get you checked out." Gently but firmly, I force her shoulders back to the ground. There is a rattle, something out of the ordinary that makes me panic. "Cos, this could be serious!"

"Ohhh, my chest." She grabs her ribs.

"Franklin shot you with something. I'm sure they can remove it without issue. Don't worry."

"No, it's not in me. It's in my beads." She unzips her jumper to display a chest full of colorful beads weaved into a vest. In the middle of a deep purple bead, dead center in her chest, is a bullet.

I'm almost afraid to ask. "What is this?"

"With March Franklin still on the loose, I worried he might cause trouble. We needed all the help we could get, so I made a vest of healing beads. Enough good juju for the entire town." She blinks rapidly and puts her hand to her face. "I'm going to be fine. Just take me home."

"The best juju, Vem." I hug her gingerly and kiss the top of her head. "Rest now. We're still taking you to the hospital to get checked out. For my peace of mind."

I'm grateful Cedar and Piper have remained inside. With all the trauma they've experienced in the past few days, they don't need to see any of this.

"Lanie, is there anything I can do for you?" Tyler's hand is on my shoulder. "I've got some emergency care training!"

I gulp. "We've got everything under control, thanks." I glance over at Cosmo, who is glaring at us both.

Officer Briggs arrives and takes Frankie into custody. "Is there anything you want to tell your mother before you leave?" he asks.

"Dad will get me out of this," he hisses. "We'll be back here, making your pathetic life even more miserable. Don't get too comfortable, November."

"March, my poor boy," she moans, as the ambulance driver, a recent addition to her Saturday Morning Moan class helps her into the back of his vehicle.

After a stiff hug from Cosmo and a few words of encouragement for Cedar, I follow them in my car and sit in the waiting room while they check Vem over. Staring at my phone, I start a text, but then change my mind and put it away. Cedar is perfectly capable of handling Derrick Walters. She'll make this work.

"Care for some company?"

Tyler Feckler, his grey suit jacket folded neatly over one arm, is standing beside my chair. His face is kind and open.

"You remember me. Do I deserve company? I didn't treat you very well." I pull the sweater one of the nurses lent me tightly around my middle.

"The first time, I was devasted. New to the business world, I thought I'd made a love connection we could tell our grandkids about. 'That one fateful meeting at a convention.'"

"First time? I don't remember there being more than

one. That sounds even worse." There is no emotion left in me today or I'd feel embarrassed.

"The second time was at the Tape and Stapling Convention. Five years later, to be exact. I was giving the seminar, '*Find your Tape, Connecting Employees with Powerful Bonds.*"

I put my hands on my head, right in the spot where a terrible headache has developed. "Now I remember. We had drinks and then dinner. I didn't think you'd remember me."

"How could I forget the beautiful woman who stole my heart? That time, you instructed me. Out by three a.m., you said. No attachment, just an evening of fun, scripted and directed by you. I was too lovestruck to say no. I sent flowers and cards for months. No response. "

"Tyler, I'm so sorry. I treated everyone like they were disposable. It wasn't just the people I met at seminars, it was also my employees."

He raises his eyebrows. "Your employees?"

"No, I didn't sleep with them. I just kicked them to the curb when things got too complicated. Emotions didn't work for me, so I disposed of them. They were instructed to intercept any deliveries like that or I'd fire them." It feels good to get this off my chest.

He chuckles. "Yes, I learned that lesson. So many people in our field don't like the uncertainty of relationships. We like our lives to be mapped out for success without all the messy potholes."

"Well," I stand and begin to pace, "moving to Piney Falls definitely changed me. I have someone in my life, better than I deserve, really, and I'm doing my best to move forward."

"The handsome goon who wanted to tear my face off? Good match for you. He's the brawn, and you're the brains. Of course you deserve to be happy. Don't let yourself believe you don't. I've moved on too. Married, with a child due next month. We don't have to be defined by our past."

We pause, awkwardly, not knowing what comes next.

"What you've put together here is quite something. Derrick has been complimenting you all morning. We could use someone with your passion and drive. There's no one who could better represent our brand."

November walks gingerly to the waiting room, standing uncomfortably close to my chair. "Only some bruised ribs. He laughed when I told him about my diet. 'I'm more concerned with your insides than what's happened on your chest.' Was he referring to my lack of bosoms?"

"Your bosoms are fine, Vem. Let's get you home." I wrap my arm around her shoulder. "Your bosoms, and just about everything else, are perfect."

"What about your investors? Did March ruin that for you? Oh, Lanie. I feel terrible."

"Not to worry. Cedar has it all taken care of."

"You came to check on me! Golly, that's kind." She reaches her hand out to Tyler and as he reaches out, she hugs him.

"I'll be in touch, Lanie."

"Thank you, Tyler. I'm glad we had a chance to talk." I ignore the desire to hug him goodbye.

We walk carefully to my car and I settle Vem in the front seat. "You know, Lanie, my son wasn't the only follower of Olivene's. She had that whole troupe of people just waiting for her commands. Hawk's murderer is probably one of them."

As in Piper's case, I don't want to break the bad news that Frankie is a murderer when she's still raw. "You're right. There are lots of people involved. We can feel good that they've lost their source of funding for now, and if the property sells, there's not much they can do here."

"In the most recent Fallen Leaves newsletter, they listed the names of everyone in Broken Branch. Just came right out and listed them. Now it's there for everyone to see. I'll have to make sure there's no one else on the list who might want to hurt Piper."

I hadn't thought about it, but Piper may still be in danger. The resistance group who wanted to harm her wasn't concerned with Olivene's leadership. Now that she's gone, they may be empowered.

The tension on Vem's face eases as we pull into her driveway. She is grateful for the help but insists I go home and drink some wine, celebrating our victory.

I pour myself a glass of Sassy Lasses Rebel Riesling and stand on the back porch; my thinking area of late. Things don't seem settled. Frankie was just the noisy part of this fringe group; the others are still out there watching, waiting. The list of former Fallen Branch members who still live in Piney Falls is sitting in a box in my closet.

Vem, please text me the names of known Broken Branch members from your newsletter.

A few minutes later, I receive a text back from her. I go down the list, checking it against the one Gladys gave me. My finger stops on one listed twice.

I dial the number for Cosmic Cakes and Antiquery and no one answers. I text Cosmo, Cedar, and then Piper. No response. Now it's time to panic.

41

ONE HOUR LATER

Concessions Must Be Made

Sawyer is sitting on the front step of the Spruce Bark Motel waiting when I stop to pick him up. He waves and half-smiles. His long hair, face and vacant eyes are strikingly similar to that of his horrid mother's, making it hard to remove memories of her from my mind.

The shop is dark when we arrive. It's not unusual for them to close early on days they sell out of baked goods. In this town, no one has a coffee without a scone. What is peculiar is the fact that I can't get ahold of anyone.

I message Cedar, hoping for something. No answer. Out of ideas, I walk to public records to see Gladys as Sawyer lumbers back to the car. She and Urica are in deep discussion while sharing a large, turkey sandwich.

"You had quite the day, Lanie Anders!" Gladys remarks. "Glad it's over?"

"It's not quite over. I need to find a few people: Cosmo,

Cedar, and most of all, Piper. Have you seen them?" I stand with my hands on my hips, as close to the two women as I dare get when they are eating.

"Cedar brought that group into my gallery. I followed the script, just like you said, Lanie. My, that secretary gal was sharp. She did her homework on this place. And Cedar knew the answers to all of her questions. She's quite the business lady." Urica leans back in her chair and folds her arms to match mine. "Why's it so important to find them?"

"Piper might be in trouble. Thanks to the information Gladys gave me, I've come to believe we've had Broken Branch members right under our noses for quite some time."

Both women gasp dramatically.

"Should I call Boysie?" Gladys asks. "He can put out an alert!"

Cosmo will hate me for doing that if he's not in trouble. "Not yet. But I have an idea." I explain the whole plan I came up with on the silent drive into town. It all hinges on my hunch being correct. "Tell Boysie to have a patrolman meet me at Piper's apartment."

She nods vigorously. "I'm all over it, Lanie."

I knock on Piper's door, wondering how I'll handle it if things are as bad as anticipated. Hoping and at the same time dreading she'll answer, I knock again. After a few minutes, the door opens a crack.

"It's me, hon. Let me in."

"No, Lanie. You can't see."

I stick my foot in the door so she can't slam it shut. "I'm not leaving. I know what's going on here. Please let me in so I can help you."

Reluctantly she opens the door enough for me to come in. "Where is she?"

She hesitates. "Bathroom."

"Did you–kill her?"

"I thought about it." Piper's bottom lip trembles. "Just like my mom. Well, the person who pretended to be my mom. I found out someone betrayed me and that was my first instinct – to get rid of them."

She stares at me as if waiting for a response. I give her none.

"Instead, I took her down, just like I learned in my karate class. I taped her hands and feet together and covered her mouth with tape. And when she wouldn't stop trying to scream, I hit her over the head with my lamp."

"Let me see." I push past her and into the bathroom where Emma Williams is lying on the floor. I crouch beside her, trying to judge how and if she is injured. There is a small amount of blood by her head but when I lift her up, I can see it's a small flesh wound. She opens her eyes and tries to scream.

"I know you're Broken Branch. I found your name on a list of known Broken Branch members. You came here today to kidnap Piper yourself, only she outsmarted you. Olivene is dead, the land deal is dead, and your whole group is about to go up in flames."

"Their group, but not ours."

We both turn around to see Sawyer, towering over us in the doorway.

"What are you talking about, Brother? What group are you in?"

"I started corresponding with Hawk after Mom left her email open one day."

Piper's eyes grow wide. "I remember! That's how I knew his name!"

"He started this group and I agreed to help him. We don't need Zion or Mom. We're calling it, 'Better Branch.'"

"That's why you're here, Sawyer? To kidnap me for your cult?" Piper's voice wavers. "They'll never stop chasing me. I can't have a normal life." Piper still has the lamp in her hand. For a brief moment, I wonder if she'll hit Sawyer with it too.

I look over at his dirty pant legs and impulsively throw my arms around them. "You're not taking your sister anywhere, son. Unless you plan on including a middle-aged, slightly robust woman on your journey."

Sawyer sighs loudly. "Take it easy, both of you. I'm not here to kidnap anyone. I wanted to see my sister before I joined the others. You can let go, Lanie. It's not like I could drag you down the stairs without anyone noticing."

For a brief moment I wonder if he is playing us as his mother would. Emma makes grunting noises. She is a product of fear and misinformation; another generation of Fallen Branch about to sprout. This has to end.

"We're going to fix this once and for all." I release his legs and stand up, brushing my pants off. "And our friend, Emma, will help us."

Emma shakes her head furiously.

"Go get her phone, Piper."

She returns quickly and hands me a ruby-studded case.

"My friend, Gladys, called the police and they will be here soon. We can tell them about your kidnapping plot, but then we'd have no real proof. That's the thing about Gladys." I grin. "She has access to everything. Once we get those damning emails that I know are in here, she'll find out who they belong to. I can't wait to see Boysie's face when we tell him we've cracked a decades-long kidnapping plot and you're the reason it failed."

Emma attempts to scream again, but Piper has done a good job taping her mouth.

"Shouldn't we do that anyway?" Piper asks.

"Yes. But I want to give this girl a chance to redeem herself. If she were to cooperate, we might not send a group email to all of her Broken Branch friends, telling them how she screwed up and got them all arrested. We could pin the whole thing on someone else."

"Who?"

The police car pulls up out front. "Let me handle this. Take the tape off her mouth." I redirect my gaze at Emma. "But if you say anything at all before I tell you, the deal is off and this all falls on your shoulders. Understood?"

Emma nods.

"And Piper, you hold on to that phone for now."

Thankfully, Officer Briggs has been briefed and is fully aware of the situation. He takes Emma into custody and the three of us follow him to the police station. Piper listens intently as I explain what will happen next. While we're in the waiting area, I quickly type up a script on my phone and as soon as I'm done, send off a discreet text to Gladys, hoping she isn't napping.

Boysie Lumquest looks grim as he walks down the hall to greet us. "This seems crazy to me. But I don't cross my mother-in-law. Learned that the hard way. Are you gals ready?"

We both nod and follow him to the interrogation room, where Emma is waiting. She tries to stand when we enter, but a policeman forces her to sit back down. "I'm sorry, Piper. It was so stupid. I shouldn't..."

I put my finger to my lips, reminding her to be quiet. After a few minutes, they bring Zion into the room.

"I haven't been surrounded by such beauty since the first

gathering of my followers." He sticks a burly hand out but none of us are interested in shaking it.

"We're not here for compliments. You know Olivene was pretending you were dead. I'm giving you this chance to prove to your followers that the one and only Grand Elan still exists. With the permission of the police department, we're going to make a video. You must read exactly what I wrote or we'll turn it off and you'll never get this chance again. Understand?"

He looks from one of us to the next. His eyes rest on Piper. "This is the girl? The imposter who was offered as my replacement?" He scoffs. " She came to see me before. I don't understand how anyone could be fooled."

"It's now or never." I hand him my phone and he reads it carefully. "I suppose this is sufficient."

Boysie enters with his own phone, ready to record.

"Emma, you squeeze in tight next to Zion. We don't want any confusion." Emma moves to his side, clearly upset by her proximity to the person she still thinks is an imposter.

Boysie points his phone at them. "Go ahead, Zion. Any time."

Zion's face changes in an instant, from sober inmate to animated leader. "Greetings, followers! Oh, how I've missed addressing you these many years. I learned so many lessons from my time in the woods."

I motion for him to read what's on the phone.

"But for now, I must tell you of a grave misdeed. There are always those who want to steal our spotlight. Some more successfully than others. Our own Olivene Moonlight destroyed our mission. She murdered former members, including Jez Dillon. He made a list of those who were lost and if it weren't for him, we wouldn't know today which members who took the dark path." He extends his thick arm and places it on Emma's shoulder.

"Young Sister Emma came to me with her concerns. She worried that people thought I was dead and no longer able to lead. She told me of this plot and of the young woman, the daughter of Birdie and Christian Finch, who was forced to play the starring role."

Piper moves reluctantly into the frame and waves before ducking out again.

"Sadly, the child born 'Amaris' has perished. We need to leave Hazel Finch alone and let her live her life. It's time for us to be at peace with ourselves, to do good things for our communities, and say goodbye to Fallen Branch." Zion chokes up a little. He pats Emma's hand and she pulls it back. "Emma assures me you will all follow my orders. Under my direction, she has given the police all the information about the imposters. You can contact her with questions, and please don't hesitate to send your cards and letters to comfort me in my confinement. Grand Elan's blessing on you all."

He leans back, his pleasant face instantly transforming into a scowl. "Disgraceful."

"That was perfect. Thanks for cooperating." I smile at Zion, for once, truly happy we are in the same room.

As Zion and Emma are taken away, Boysie pats me on the back. "That was a brilliant idea, miss."

"Oh, Piper, can you give him Emma's phone?" Once this goes out on the group message, I'd assume you'll be receiving quite a few angry messages in return. Maybe even more confessions to various crimes."

We still have the matter of Sawyer to deal with. Piper and I sit down on either side of him.

"I'm not going to lead your group. I'm going to stay here

and work in the bakery," Piper reiterates. "And maybe ask Lanie to teach me about fashion." She smiles shyly at me.

"We don't need you, Sis. Hawk had some great ideas, but we're going to see if we can't make a group without one specific leader. We're going with a counsel for Golden Branch. I leave tomorrow for Ohio; that's where we're all meeting. The plans changed a bit when Hawk died, but we're moving forward." He smiles the trademark family smile.

Piper rubs his shoulders. "But why do you need a group at all? Don't you want to be independent? We've waited our whole lives for this."

"I want to be a part of something. We've never been allowed to connect with anyone, and these people really like me. It's not going to be like Fallen Branch. Something better."

Piper hugs her brother tightly. "I'll miss you. But you'll always know where to find me."

We all rise to leave, but Boysie has received instructions from his mother-in-law and moves in front of Sawyer. "You and me are going to have a long chat about Hawk Beechum first, son."

42

THREE DAYS AFTER INVESTOR MEETING

Some Shelves and Some Heart

"I brought your shelves."

I know this isn't the real reason he's here, but I'm glad either way. He sets down the two stained, hemlock-wood shelves. Both are decorated with ornately carved clusters of verbena flowers, my favorite.

I haven't been out of the house in two days; changing from the leopard-print pajamas to the lavender silk set I used to wear on Sundays just to treat myself. Too much has transpired and there's no other way to handle it. I tried texting Cosmo over and over and he didn't respond. After one very important call, my phone sat untouched for almost twenty-four hours until this morning when the constant buzzing became too powerful for me to ignore.

"You wanted them by the front door?" He brought the tools to hang them, even though there are more pressing issues lurking in the air between us.

"Yes, that would be great. Right where we talked about putting them. I'll pour you some wine." The location of some shelving doesn't seem as important as it did two months ago. My world was Cosmo, Derrick's investment company, and nature.

I sit down with two glasses of Sassy Lassies wine and wait for him; wondering what he'll say, and if I should beg him to stay in my life.

When I hear the drill stop, I turn my body around to view his masterpiece. It does look lovely. A great place to put things that used to have meaning.

He wipes his hands on his pants and sits down beside me, placing a bag of pastries on the table. "Wouldn't be the first time we had pastries and wine."

I take a sip and lean my head back. I'd rather not look him in the eye if he's about to crush my soul. "Mmm-hmm."

"It's time. We need to get through this, once and for all." He takes a gulp of wine, turns his body to face mine, and sets his glass on the table without using the coaster I specifically placed there for him. "What you said the other day knocked my legs out from under me. I think I'm fine with it, and then I'm not. I spent time in prison and you were on the outside; this perfect woman who was so devoted to her work she didn't get involved with anyone. It can make a guy crazy. Then I saw that investor dude talking to you and I went to bad places."

I gulp. "I understand. What I did all of those years was so wrong. When I came here, I didn't realize how broken I was. How much in me needed to change. I just set it to the side and decided I would deal with it when the right time came. But there you were, so eager to be with me. So much more than I deserved. There was never a right time to tell you that I wasn't the person who deserved all of your love." I am determined to get through this without crying. "I don't think I could continue living here if there's no us."

Cosmo grabs my hands and squeezes them in between his. "Look at me, Lanie Anders!" he commands.

I turn my head to face him and bite the inside of my cheeks.

"That stuff you told me was shocking, I'll give you that. I think – no, I know – the woman sitting in front of me is kind and loving and has only one man in her heart. There isn't room for more. You want to hear how I know that?"

I nod my head.

"Because you worried about my feelings. Because every time we touch, I can feel it. There's only you for me and me for you. Leave if you want, but there will never be another woman for me. Ever."

I lean forward and kiss him with such passion that I know this time I won't be able to stop. He leans back on the couch and I fall on top of him, ripping at his shirt and exposing his muscular frame. I bury my face in the thick, silver hair of his chest.

"There's something you have to see first," he whispers.

I sit up. "What?"

He pulls me to the picture window in my living room. "This is why I didn't answer your texts. I've – well, November and I – have been busy putting things together."

I look in my driveway, where an enormous painting sits. In the center is a large, A-frame home with picture windows and tall trees on either side. A man and a woman embrace on the lawn. Urica stands beside it, pointing to the painting and then herself.

"What is this all about?"

"You weren't excited about having a key to my place. I can't say I'm thrilled about spending the rest of my life next to November Bean." He gestures toward Vem's house, where we can hear enthusiastic students learning to howl.

"November called together an emergency online meeting of those receiving the Fallen Leaf newsletter. She explained all that you've done for us and what you're trying to do to remove the curse on the old Fallen Branch property. It was unanimous."

"What was unanimous?"

"They all decided the best use of the money we found would be to purchase the Flanagan Hospital property. For you; for us to build our own place."

"I...don't know..."

"The first time I asked you, it was impulsive. We barely knew each other. Now, we've bared most everything. I feel like this time, it's for real." He bends down on one knee and kisses my hand. "Lanie Anders, knowing each other's darkest secrets, at least I hope, and still being madly in love, will you marry me? Before something even crazier happens?"

I take his head in my hands and guide him up to my mouth. We kiss, slowly.

"Last time I didn't say anything. But today, with all of my heart, I say yes, Cosmo Hill. I want to marry you."

I wave to Urica and close the curtains so that our tender first moments together are only between us. After touching each other gently and sliding into bed, we can finally release everything pent up for these months. Every emotion we've felt, or hidden, together. We cry and then we laugh and then we hold each other in serene peace.

After I lie blissfully in his arms for an hour, I feel ready to tackle the constant buzzing from my phone: seven messages from Cedar. I'm glad I didn't know that ahead of time. It would have felt like she was there, in the room with us.

"What's going on?"

"You sound out of breath, are you on an adventure?"

I look over at Cosmo, who is sleeping soundly. "You could say that."

"I never got to talk to you after Derrick and his group left. I know you've been busy and I didn't want to bother you." Her voice falters. She must've heard about Piper. "Things went great. They loved the town and the Fallen Branch property. I told them about all the work you put in."

"As did you, Cedar," I climb out of bed quietly and grab my robe. "Have you heard anything more from them?"

"Yes, just this afternoon. Mr. Walter's secretary called. He said he's been trying to call you but you didn't answer. I explained that you had a series of unexpected events. Lanie, they want to go ahead with the deal and purchase the land!"

"That's wonderful! We're going to celebrate!" I'm waiting for what I already know will come next.

"They were so impressed with all that you did to put this together. It's one of the best presentations they've ever seen."

"It's not just me. It was us. You know that, Cedar."

"There's more," she whispers as if there's someone else in her empty apartment. "I haven't told Cos yet. The Sleepy Sounds Corporation wants to hire me to work in their corporate headquarters. They want me to move to San Diego! Isn't this unbelievable, Lanie?"

I peek my head inside the room one more time, glancing at Cosmo sleeping soundly. "Not unbelievable at all. You – we – deserve this. Everything is working out exactly as it should."

The End

PIPER'S SCORPIO Scones
  2 cups flour
  3 Tablespoons sugar
  4 teaspoons baking powder
  ¾ tsp. salt
  6 Tablespoons butter
  1 cup berries
  2 eggs
  ½ cup of heavy whipping cream
  ½ cup dark chocolate chips
  <u>Directions</u>

  1. Preheat oven to 425 degrees.
  2. Beat eggs and cream for about 1-2 minutes
  3. Mix in dry ingredients and whisk until combined
  4. Cut butter into cubes and break into batter (I use my hands to combine everything!)
  5. Add eggs and knead dough until its one ball
  6. Add fruit into dough (carefully)
  7. Spread dough into a disk on a floured surface and cut into 6-8 pieces (depending how big or small you want them)
  8. Top with chocolate chips
  9. Bake for 15 minutes on a greased baking sheet, rotating halfway through
  10. Enjoy!

ENJOY AN EXCERPT FROM BOOK THREE IN THE PINEY FALLS MYSTERIES SERIES!

TALES OF NAYBOR WAY

"What will his name be this time, Daddy?" Pookie loved the feeling of the wind gently lifting her long, brown braids as they bumped down the dirt road.

"Will we leave the top down, or should we put it up so he doesn't think we're being boastful. Most people don't have a convertible car and we don't want them to feel bad. Isn't that right?" She turned her large brown eyes to her father, Welcome, who smiled broadly.

"You're absolutely right, Pookie. We don't want our new help to feel uncomfortable about his unfortunate circumstances. We'll put the top up when we get to town. It's not right to be prideful because we have more. You must also remember that young girls who chatter on and on may also be considered prideful to someone who doesn't have much to say."

Pookie lowered her eyes. "Sorry, Daddy. I get excited when we have new hired hands. They have such interesting stories!"

She folded her thin tanned arms across each other and sat silently for ten minutes, the rest of the ride into the center of Flanagan, Oregon. When she saw a familiar site, she forgot her sorrow and began bouncing in her seat. "There it is, Daddy! The movie theatre!"

Welcome laughed. "Pookie, my darling. You are always the brightest sunlight in every day. Any father should be so lucky. What is on the marquee today?"

"Oh, Daddy!" Pookie squealed. "Tulip Sloan! She's my favorite actress! So beautiful and glamourous!"

"Well don't keep me wondering, which picture is it?"

"*Hasty Engagement.* It's her newest one! Oh Daddy!" They pulled up in front of the Flanagan Majestic, Welcome taking care to put the roof up on their cherry-apple red Packard Darrin. He pulled three quarters from his pocket and held them in his palm.

"This one is for you." He pointed to the first, silver circle. "This one is for Fred. And this one is for sour chews. But only a few. I don't want you up all night with a bad stomach."

Pookie reached across the seat and kissed her father's pale cheek. "Thank you, Daddy. You're the kindest most wonderful, most perfect –"

"Mornin', Welcome."

A man wearing a white fedora and brown pants with suspenders, who resembled every other man in Flanagan as far as Pookie was concerned, tipped his hat. "Mornin' Pookie. Looks like you're off to the picture show. Good to stretch a girl's imagination before she's grown and lookin' for a proper husband."

Welcome straightened his jacket. "Nice to see you, Rogers. What's brought you out on this glorious August day?"

The man stepped aside, revealing a thin, blond-haired man with hollow cheeks and a long, pointed nose. His shirt was torn and dirty and he smelled like he'd slept more than once in someone's barn.

"Welcome, this here's Raymond. Found him sleeping in my barn night before last. I can tell he's a decent sort of fella. Just down on his luck. I know you can always use the help on your farm. Raymond, please meet Welcome Naybor, a man of great in-te-gri-ty."

Raymond put grubby hands to his mouth, concealing a girlish giggle. "Never heard of a man with that sort of name."

Welcome got out of the car and straightened the jacket on his small, round body. He straightened his round glasses and walked around and shook Raymond's hand, just like he was an important person. "The last name is Nah BOR. Welcome Nah BOR. Pleased to meet you Raymond. What did you say your last name was? We can always use the help at our estate."

"Raymond Dockly." He put his hand in Welcome's, standing back so as not to get his fancy suit dirty. "Come here four years ago from Oklahoma. Worked on the ships for a time, hauling things to Canada. The pay was good but my feet need dry land for a while. Now that my belly's been empty a bit, I need to work."

"Have you done farm labor?"

Pookie got out her door and went to stand beside her father, almost his height. "I'm Pookie Welcome. It's not my real name, but my Daddy says it's better than the one my mother gave me. She left me on the doorstep."

"This isn't appropriate now, Pookie," Welcome shook his head. "You can conversate with Raymond on our way home. Run along and find your friend now."

Pookie kissed her father on the cheek. "Ok, Daddy. We

shall discuss all glorious things on the way home. Nice to meet you, Raymond!"

"And you too, Miss!" He called after her, as she skipped down the street.

When she reached the ornate, gold swirls that outlined Flanagan Majestic, she stood patiently.

"Thought you'd never come," her dark-haired pal slugged her in the arm, his usual greeting. He squinted, the late-morning sun bouncing off the deep, red scar across his cheek. "What took you so long?" He held his hand out expectantly.

Pookie reached into the pocket of her jean overalls and pulled out a shiny quarter. "Another man in need. Daddy liked him well enough. He'll be coming home with us today."

They settled into their plush, red velvet seats with one box of Tart Chewies and one box of popcorn. "You dumping today?" Pookie asked, offering her extra-large box of Tart Chewies to her friend.

"Sure." Freddy took the box from her hand and dumped it into their popcorn, shaking gently to mix their favorite concoction.

"Why do you think your Daddy likes those bums? Is it cause he don't want them to make fun of his name? Cause everybody does, you know."

Pookie turned to face her friend. "Freddie Chandler, no one makes fun of my Daddy. He's the most charitable man in the entire county. He gives work to people who need it. He even shares our crops with those who need them. In the trunk, we brought two baskets of vegetables today."

"Welcome Naybor chops up his workers when he's tired of 'em. That's what my mom says and she don't lie."

"Nah BOR. You say that every week. Nobody is chopped

up. Don't be thick. Be quiet now, the movie is about to start and I won't miss a Tulip Sloan production to listen to your silly babbling."

"Why don't you go to school with the rest of us? You're smart enough for a girl."

Pookie sighed loud. The man in the seat beside her put his fingers to his lips.

"I told you. Daddy says I'm much too bright for local school. He'd miss me terribly if I went to boarding school. It's better for him to teach me; he and Miss Dandridge. Besides, I'm so far beyond everyone my age, I'd be bored. Now hush."

The newsreel began. Stories of happy living after the end of the war and new industry growing every day played on the screen, but all Pookie could think about was Tulip Sloan. Her silky, blonde hair, curving gently around her face and large, weepy eyes. A velvety, rich voice using words like "daahling" and "duhuty." Just like she imagined her mother would speak.

She knew she wasn't supposed to think of her mother like that. She had abandoned Pookie on her father's doorstep because she couldn't be bothered to raise her. He took one look at this brown-eyed beauty and knew he couldn't allow anyone else to raise her.

From the time she could speak, he was teaching her. She could read and write before her fifth birthday and when she was seven she began reading portions of "Tales of Willoughby Manor," her father's favorite, 957 page book, to him before bed each night.

As always, Tulip, the heroine, saved herself from peril. At the end of each movie, she turned to movie goers and told them to hug and kiss the ones they loved dearly, because the world was about to get much too dark.

The lights came up and the everyone in the theatre stood and cheered. Pookie looked over at Fred, who stubbornly sat in his seat. She kicked him, but he shook his head firmly, staying seated.

"Get up!" she hissed. "People will think you don't understand theatre."

"Well maybe I don't much. How is it Miss Sloan is always outsmarting the men? Everybody knows a woman ain't near as smart as a man."

Pookie sighed and yanked on his arm, hard. "You're backwards, Freddie. In just about every way. Girls can do anything boys can do. Let's get outta here before we get in trouble."

Reluctantly, he stood and followed her outside. "Your daddy give you enough for a Grommy's Grape Soda today? I'm parched."

A man with a large scar over one eye appeared in front of them as they tried to exit the theater. "You Welcome's girl?" He yelled more than asked. "I've been watching you for some time now."

Pookie nodded, too afraid to speak. She looked for a way to move around him but there was none. She nodded toward Freddie, but he took that as a sign to run instead of coming to her aid.

"What do you want, mister? My Daddy can give you a job if you want. He's always hiring the less –"

"Bad things goin' on at that farm. Rumor has it, you're in danger. Best watch your back, girlie."

Luckily, Pookie's arms were pliable enough to wriggle her free from his grip. She began to run, but her curiosity got the better of her. She stopped, halfway down the block. He wasn't following her. Instead, he stood in place, his wide-brimmed hat tipped back exposing his scar. His gaze never wavered. Was he sad? Or was that anger? He was well dressed, like Daddy. He held no resemblance to the men they'd hired to work the farm – no hollow eyes or clenched mouth.

Something compelled her to wave at him. Maybe he was just a lonely man who needed a friend. "I'll be fine, Mister!" she called.

He raised his hand slowly to the brim of his hat, tipping it in response.

She continued walking until she reached her father's car, looking around at Saturday shoppers walking up and down Flanagan Avenue. Were they staring at her? Did they know? It was silly to think anyone would be concerned with a twelve-year-old girl, especially one who didn't attend public school or having more than one friend in the entire world.

Welcome came out of the bakery with his arms full of breads. He laughed at a joke the door closed behind him. His face opened into a wide grin when he saw her standing there. "Anything exciting from your afternoon, Pookie?" He patted her on the head and placed the bread in the back seat before standing with his hands on his hips, waiting for her reply.

She looked at her father's round face. His brown eyes danced behind his wire spectacles. His bushy mustache looked like those men sported in the Hollywood magazines she read to see Tulip Sloan's latest stories. She always thought he was the most handsome man she'd ever seen. "Nothing at all, Daddy."

Buy Your Copy Now!

www.ingramcontent.com/pod-product-compliance
Lightning Source LLC
Chambersburg PA
CBHW051250210726
48287CB00002B/430

9 781953 270184